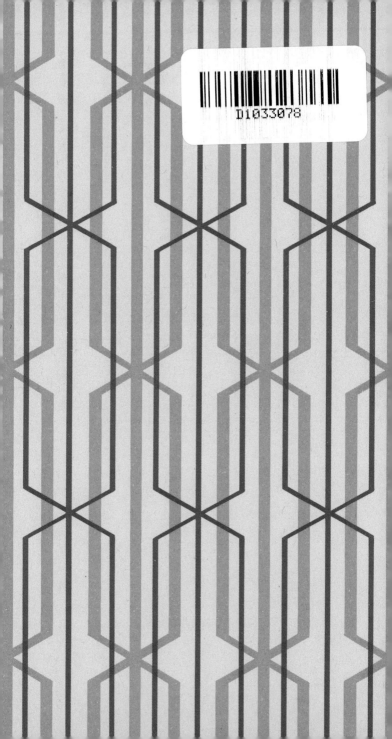

THE STOLEN WHITE ELEPHANT

THE

Stolen White Elephant

ETC.

BY

SAMUEL LANGHORNE CLEMENS
(MARK TWAIN)

Short Story Index Reprint Series

BOOKS FOR LIBRARIES PRESS
FREEPORT, NEW YORK

First Published 1882
Reprinted 1970

STANDARD BOOK NUMBER:
8369-3486-5

LIBRARY OF CONGRESS CATALOG CARD NUMBER:
70-121530

PRINTED IN THE UNITED STATES OF AMERICA

CONTENTS.

———◆———

THE STOLEN WHITE ELEPHANT.[1]

———◆———

I.

THE following curious history was related to me by a chance railway acquaintance. He was a gentleman more than seventy years of age, and his thoroughly good and gentle face and earnest and sincere manner imprinted the unmistakable stamp of truth upon every statement which fell from his lips. He said : —

You know in what reverence the royal white elephant of Siam is held by the people of that country. You know it is sacred to kings, only kings may possess it, and that it is indeed in a measure even superior to kings, since it receives not merely honor but worship. Very well; five years ago, when the troubles concerning the frontier line arose between Great Britain and Siam, it was presently manifest that Siam had been in the wrong. Therefore every reparation was quickly

[1] Left out of " A Tramp Abroad," because it was feared that some of the particulars had been exaggerated, and that others were not true. Before these suspicions had been proven groundless, the book had gone to press. — M. T.

made, and the British representative stated that he was satisfied and the past should be forgotten. This greatly relieved the King of Siam, and partly as a token of gratitude, but partly also, perhaps, to wipe out any little remaining vestige of unpleasantness which England might feel toward him, he wished to send the Queen a present, — the sole sure way of propitiating an enemy, according to Oriental ideas. This present ought not only to be a royal one, but transcendently royal. Wherefore, what offering could be so meet as that of a white elephant? My position in the Indian civil service was such that I was deemed peculiarly worthy of the honor of conveying the present to her Majesty. A ship was fitted out for me and my servants and the officers and attendants of the elephant, and in due time I arrived in New York harbor and placed my royal charge in admirable quarters in Jersey City. It was necessary to remain awhile in order to recruit the animal's health before resuming the voyage.

All went well during a fortnight, — then my calamities began. The white elephant was stolen! I was called up at dead of night and informed of this fearful misfortune. For some moments I was beside myself with terror and anxiety; I was helpless. Then I grew calmer and collected my faculties. I soon saw my course, — for indeed there was but the one course for an intelligent man to pursue. Late as it was, I flew to New York and got a policeman to conduct me to the headquarters of the detective force. Fortunately I arrived in time, though the chief of the force, the celebrated Inspector Blunt, was just on the point of leaving for his home. He was a man of middle size and compact frame, and when he was thinking deeply he had a way of knitting his brows and tapping his forehead reflectively with his finger, which impressed you at once with the conviction that you stood in the presence of a person of no common order. The very sight of him gave me confidence and made me hopeful. I stated my errand. It did not flurry him in the least; it had no more visible effect upon his iron self-possession than if I had told him somebody had stolen my dog. He motioned me to a seat, and said calmly, —

"Allow me to think a moment, please."

So saying, he sat down at his office table and leaned his head upon his hand. Several clerks were at work at the other end of the room; the scratching of their pens was all the sound I heard during the next six or seven minutes. Meantime the inspector sat there, buried in thought. Finally he raised his head, and there was that in the firm lines of his face which showed me that his brain had done its work and his plan was made. Said he, — and his voice was low and impressive, —

"This is no ordinary case. Every step must be warily taken; each step must be made sure before the next is ventured. And secrecy must be observed, — secrecy profound and absolute. Speak to no one about the matter, not even the reporters. I will take care of *them;* I will see that they get only what it may suit my ends to let them know." He touched a bell;

a youth appeared. "Alaric, tell the reporters to remain for the present." The boy retired. "Now let us proceed to business, — and systematically. Nothing can be accomplished in this trade of mine without strict and minute method."

He took a pen and some paper. "Now — name of the elephant?"

"Hassan Ben Ali Ben Selim Abdallah Mohammed Moisé Alhammal Jamsetjejeebhoy Dhuleep Sultan Ebu Bhudpoor."

"Very well. Given name?"

"Jumbo."

"Very well. Place of birth?"

"The capital city of Siam."

"Parents living?"

"No, — dead."

"Had they any other issue besides this one?"

"None. He was an only child."

"Very well. These matters are sufficient under that head. Now please describe the elephant, and leave out no particular, however insignificant, — that is, insignificant from *your* point of view. To men in my profession there *are* no insignificant particulars; they do not exist."

I described, — he wrote. When I was done, he said, —

"Now listen. If I have made any mistakes, correct me."

He read as follows: —

"Height, 19 feet; length from apex of forehead to insertion of tail, 26 feet; length of trunk, 16 feet;

length of tail, 6 feet; total length, including trunk and tail, 48 feet; length of tusks, $9\frac{1}{2}$ feet; ears in keeping with these dimensions; footprint resembles the mark left when one up-ends a barrel in the snow; color of the elephant, a dull white; has a hole the size of a plate in each ear for the insertion of jewelry, and possesses the habit in a remarkable degree of squirting water upon spectators and of maltreating with his trunk not only such persons as he is acquainted with, but even entire strangers; limps slightly with his right hind leg, and has a small scar in his left armpit caused by a former boil; had on, when stolen, a castle containing seats for fifteen persons, and a gold-cloth saddle-blanket the size of an ordinary carpet."

There were no mistakes. The inspector touched the bell, handed the description to Alaric, and said, —

" Have fifty thousand copies of this printed at once and mailed to every detective office and pawnbroker's shop on the continent." Alaric retired. " There, — so far, so good. Next, I must have a photograph of the property."

I gave him one. He examined it critically, and said, —

" It must do, since we can do no better; but he has his trunk curled up and tucked into his mouth. That is unfortunate, and is calculated to mislead, for of course he does not usually have it in that position." He touched his bell.

" Alaric, have fifty thousand copies of this photograph made, the first thing in the morning, and mail them with the descriptive circulars."

Alaric retired to execute his orders.   The inspector said, —

"It will be necessary to offer a reward, of course. Now as to the amount?"

"What sum would you suggest?"

"To *begin* with, I should say, — well, twenty-five thousand dollars.   It is an intricate and difficult business; there are a thousand avenues of escape and opportunities of concealment.   These thieves have friends and pals everywhere —"

"Bless me, do you know who they are?"

The wary face, practised in concealing the thoughts and feelings within, gave me no token, nor yet the replying words, so quietly uttered : —

"Never mind about that.   I may, and I may not. We generally gather a pretty shrewd inkling of who our man is by the manner of his work and the size of the game he goes after.   We are not dealing with a pickpocket or a hall thief, now, make up your mind to that.   This property was not 'lifted' by a novice. But, as I was saying, considering the amount of travel which will have to be done, and the diligence with which the thieves will cover up their traces as they move along, twenty-five thousand may be too small a sum to offer, yet I think it worth while to start with that."

So we determined upon that figure, as a beginning. Then this man, whom nothing escaped which could by any possibility be made to serve as a clew, said : —

"There are cases in detective history to show that criminals have been detected through peculiarities in their appetites. Now, what does this elephant eat, and how much ?"

"Well, as to *what* he eats, — he will eat *anything*. He will eat a man, he will eat a Bible, — he will eat anything *between* a man and a Bible."

"Good, — very good indeed, but too general. Details are necessary, — details are the only valuable things in our trade. Very well, — as to men. At one meal, — or, if you prefer, during one day, — how many men will he eat, if fresh ?"

"He would not care whether they were fresh or not ; at a single meal he would eat five ordinary men."

"Very good ; five men ; we will put that down. What nationalities would he prefer ?"

"He is indifferent about nationalities. He prefers acquaintances, but is not prejudiced against strangers."

"Very good. Now, as to Bibles. How many Bibles would he eat at a meal ?"

"He would eat an entire edition."

"It is hardly succinct enough. Do you mean the ordinary octavo, or the family illustrated ?"

"I think he would be indifferent to illustrations ; that is, I think he would not value illustrations above simple letter-press."

"No, you do not get my idea. I refer to bulk. The ordinary octavo Bible weighs about two pounds and a half, while the great quarto with the illustrations weighs ten or twelve. How many Doré Bibles would he eat at a meal ?"

"If you knew this elephant, you could not ask. He would take what they had."

"Well, put it in dollars and cents, then. We must get at it somehow. The Doré costs a hundred dollars a copy, Russia leather, bevelled."

"He would require about fifty thousand dollars' worth, — say an edition of five hundred copies."

"Now that is more exact. I will put that down. Very well; he likes men and Bibles; so far, so good. What else will he eat? I want particulars."

"He will leave Bibles to eat bricks, he will leave bricks to eat bottles, he will leave bottles to eat clothing, he will leave clothing to eat cats, he will leave cats to eat oysters, he will leave oysters to eat ham, he will leave ham to eat sugar, he will leave sugar to eat pie, he will leave pie to eat potatoes, he will leave potatoes to eat bran, he will leave bran to eat hay, he will leave hay to eat oats, he will leave oats to eat rice, for he was mainly raised on it. There is nothing whatever that he will not eat but European butter, and he would eat that if he could taste it."

"Very good. General quantity at a meal, — say about — "

"Well, anywhere from a quarter to half a ton."

"And he drinks — "

"Everything that is fluid. Milk, water, whiskey, molasses, castor oil, camphene, carbolic acid, — it is no use to go into particulars; whatever fluid occurs to you set it down. He will drink anything that is fluid, except European coffee."

"Very good. As to quantity?"

"Put it down five to fifteen barrels, — his thirst varies; his other appetites do not."

"These things are unusual. They ought to furnish quite good clews toward tracing him."

He touched the bell.

"Alaric, summon Captain Burns."

Burns appeared. Inspector Blunt unfolded the whole matter to him, detail by detail. Then he said in the clear, decisive tones of a man whose plans are clearly defined in his head, and who is accustomed to command, —

"Captain Burns, detail Detectives Jones, Davis, Halsey, Bates, and Hackett to shadow the elephant."

"Yes, sir."

"Detail Detectives Moses, Dakin, Murphy, Rogers, Tupper, Higgins, and Bartholomew to shadow the thieves."

"Yes, sir."

"Place a strong guard — a guard of thirty picked men, with a relief of thirty — over the place from whence the elephant was stolen, to keep strict watch there night and day, and allow none to approach — except reporters — without written authority from me."

"Yes, sir."

"Place detectives in plain clothes in the railway, steamship, and ferry depots, and upon all roadways leading out of Jersey City, with orders to search all suspicious persons."

"Yes, sir."

"Furnish all these men with photograph and accompanying description of the elephant, and instruct them to search all trains and outgoing ferry-boats and other vessels."

"Yes, sir."

"If the elephant should be found, let him be seized, and the information forwarded to me by telegraph."

"Yes, sir."

"Let me be informed at once if any clews should be found, — footprints of the animal, or anything of that kind."

"Yes, sir."

"Get an order commanding the harbor police to patrol the frontages vigilantly."

"Yes, sir."

"Despatch detectives in plain clothes over all the railways, north as far as Canada, west as far as Ohio, south as far as Washington."

"Yes, sir."

"Place experts in all the telegraph offices to listen to all messages; and let them require that all cipher despatches be interpreted to them."

"Yes, sir."

"Let all these things be done with the utmost secrecy, — mind, the most impenetrable secrecy."

"Yes, sir."

"Report to me promptly at the usual hour."

"Yes, sir."

"Go !"

"Yes, sir."

He was gone.

Inspector Blunt was silent and thoughtful a moment, while the fire in his eye cooled down and faded out. Then he turned to me and said in a placid voice, —

"I am not given to boasting, it is not my habit; but — we shall find the elephant."

I shook him warmly by the hand and thanked him; and I *felt* my thanks, too. The more I had seen of the man the more I liked him, and the more I admired him and marvelled over the mysterious wonders of his profession. Then we parted for the night, and I went home with a far happier heart than I had carried with me to his office.

II.

NEXT morning it was all in the newspapers, in the minutest detail. It even had additions, — consisting of Detective This, Detective That, and Detective The Other's "Theory" as to how the robbery was done, who the robbers were, and whither they had flown with their booty. There were eleven of these theories, and they covered all the possibilities; and this single fact shows what independent thinkers detectives are. No two theories were alike, or even much resembled each other, save in one striking particular, and in that one all the eleven theories were absolutely agreed. That was, that although the rear of my building was torn out and the only door remained locked, the elephant had not been removed through the rent, but by some other (undiscovered) outlet. All agreed that the robbers had made that rent only to mislead the detectives. That never would have occurred to me or to any other layman, perhaps, but it had not deceived the detectives for a moment.

Thus, what I had supposed was the only thing that had no mystery about it was in fact the very thing I had gone furthest astray in. The eleven theories all named the supposed robbers, but no two named the same robbers; the total number of suspected persons was thirty-seven. The various newspaper accounts all closed with the most important opinion of all, — that of Chief Inspector Blunt. A portion of this statement read as follows : —

"The chief knows who the two principals are, namely, 'Brick' Duffy and 'Red' McFadden. Ten days before the robbery was achieved he was already aware that it was to be attempted, and had quietly proceeded to shadow these two noted villains; but unfortunately on the night in question their track was lost, and before it could be found again the bird was flown, — that is, the elephant.

"Duffy and McFadden are the boldest scoundrels in the profession ; the chief has reasons for believing that they are the men who stole the stove out of the detective head-quarters on a bitter night last winter, — in consequence of which the chief and every detective present were in the hands of the physicians before morning, some with frozen feet, others with frozen fingers, ears, and other members."

When I read the first half of that I was more astonished than ever at the wonderful sagacity of this strange man. He not only saw everything in the present with a clear eye, but even the future could not be hidden from him. I was soon at his office, and said I could not help wishing he had had those men arrested, and so prevented the trouble and loss ; but his reply was simple and unanswerable : —

"It is not our province to prevent crime, but to punish it. We cannot punish it until it is committed."

I remarked that the secrecy with which we had begun had been marred by the newspapers; not only all our facts but all our plans and purposes had been revealed; even all the suspected persons had been named; these would doubtless disguise themselves now, or go into hiding.

"Let them. They will find that when I am ready for them my hand will descend upon them, in their secret places, as unerringly as the hand of fate. As to the newspapers, we *must* keep in with them. Fame, reputation, constant public mention,—these are the detective's bread and butter. He must publish his facts, else he will be supposed to have none; he must publish his theory, for nothing is so strange or striking as a detective's theory, or brings him so much wondering respect; we must publish our plans, for these the journals insist upon having, and we could not deny them without offending. We must constantly show the public what we are doing, or they will believe we are doing nothing. It is much pleasanter to have a newspaper say, 'Inspector Blunt's ingenious and extraordinary theory is as follows,' than to have it say some harsh thing, or, worse still, some sarcastic one."

"I see the force of what you say. But I noticed that in one part of your remarks in the papers this morning you refused to reveal your opinion upon a certain minor point."

"Yes, we always do that; it has a good effect. Besides, I had not formed any opinion on that point, any way."

I deposited a considerable sum of money with the inspector, to meet current expenses, and sat down to wait for news. We were expecting the telegrams to begin to arrive at any moment now. Meantime I re-read the newspapers and also our descriptive circular, and observed that our $25,000 reward seemed to be offered only to detectives. I said I thought it ought to be offered to anybody who would catch the elephant. The inspector said : —

"It is the detectives who will find the elephant, hence the reward will go to the right place. If other people found the animal, it would only be by watching the detectives and taking advantage of clews and indications stolen from them, and that would entitle the detectives to the reward, after all. The proper office of a reward is to stimulate the men who deliver up their time and their trained sagacities to this sort of work, and not to confer benefits upon chance citizens who stumble upon a capture without having earned the benefits by their own merits and labors."

This was reasonable enough, certainly. Now the telegraphic machine in the corner began to click, and the following despatch was the result : —

FLOWER STATION, N. Y., 7.30 A. M.

Have got a clew. Found a succession of deep tracks across a farm near here. Followed them two miles east without result ; think elephant went west. Shall now shadow him in that direction.

DARLEY, *Detective.*

"Darley's one of the best men on the force," said the inspector. "We shall hear from him again before long."

Telegram No. 2 came : —

BARKER'S, N. J., 7.40 A. M.

Just arrived. Glass factory broken open here during night, and eight hundred bottles taken. Only water in large quantity near here is five miles distant. Shall strike for there. Elephant will be thirsty. Bottles were empty.

BAKER, *Detective.*

"That promises well, too," said the inspector. "I told you the creature's appetites would not be bad clews."

Telegram No. 3 : —

TAYLORVILLE, L. I., 8.15 A. M.

A haystack near here disappeared during night. Probably eaten. Have got a clew, and am off.

HUBBARD, *Detective.*

"How he does move around!" said the inspector. "I knew we had a difficult job on hand, but we shall catch him yet."

FLOWER STATION, N. Y., 9 A. M.

Shadowed the tracks three miles westward. Large, deep, and ragged. Have just met a farmer who says they are not elephant tracks. Says they are holes where he dug up saplings for shade-trees when ground was frozen last winter. Give me orders how to proceed.

DARLEY, *Detective.*

"Aha! a confederate of the thieves! The thing grows warm," said the inspector.

He dictated the following telegram to Darley : —

Arrest the man and force him to name his pals. Continue to follow the tracks, — to the Pacific, if necessary.

Chief BLUNT.

Next telegram : —

CONEY POINT, PA., 8.45 A. M.

Gas office broken open here during night and three months' unpaid gas bills taken. Have got a clew and am away.

MURPHY, *Detective.*

"Heavens ! " said the inspector ; " would he eat gas bills ? "

"Through ignorance, — yes ; but they cannot support life. At least, unassisted."

Now came this exciting telegram : —

IRONVILLE, N. Y., 9.30 A. M.

Just arrived. This village in consternation. Elephant passed through here at five this morning. Some say he went east, some say west, some north, some south, — but all say they did not wait to notice particularly. He killed a horse ; have secured a piece of it for a clew. Killed it with his trunk ; from style of blow, think he struck it left-handed. From position in which horse lies, think elephant travelled northward along line of Berkley railway. Has four and a half hours' start, but I move on his track at once.

HAWES, *Detective.*

I uttered exclamations of joy. The inspector was as self-contained as a graven image. He calmly touched his bell.

"Alaric, send Captain Burns here."

Burns appeared.

" How many men are ready for instant orders ? "

" Ninety-six, sir."

" Send them north at once. Let them concentrate along the line of the Berkley road north of Ironville."

" Yes, sir."

" Let them conduct their movements with the utmost secrecy. As fast as others are at liberty, hold them for orders."

" Yes, sir."

" Go ! "

" Yes, sir."

Presently came another telegram : —

> SAGE CORNERS, N. Y., 10.30.
>
> Just arrived. Elephant passed through here at 8.15. All escaped from the town but a policeman. Apparently elephant did not strike at policeman, but at the lamp-post, Got both. I have secured a portion of the policeman as clew.
>
> STUMM, *Detective.*

" So the elephant has turned westward," said the inspector. " However, he will not escape, for my men are scattered all over that region."

The next telegram said : —

> GLOVER'S, 11.15.
>
> Just arrived. Village deserted, except sick and aged. Elephant passed through three quarters of an hour ago. The anti-temperance mass meeting was in session; he put his trunk in at a window and washed it out with water from cistern. Some swallowed it — since dead; several drowned. Detectives Cross and O'Shaughnessy were passing through town, but going south, — so missed elephant. Whole re-

gion for many miles around in terror, — people flying from their homes. Wherever they turn they meet elephant, and many are killed.

> BRANT, *Detective.*

I could have shed tears, this havoc so distressed me. But the inspector only said, —

"You see, — we are closing in on him.   He feels our presence; he has turned eastward again."

Yet further troublous news was in store for us. The telegraph brought this : —

> HOGANPORT, 12.19.

Just arrived.   Elephant passed through half an hour ago, creating wildest fright and excitement.   Elephant raged around streets; two plumbers going by, killed one — other escaped. Regret general.

> O'FLAHERTY, *Detective.*

"Now he is right in the midst of my men," said the inspector.   "Nothing can save him."

A succession of telegrams came from detectives who were scattered through New Jersey and Pennsylvania, and who were following clews consisting of ravaged barns, factories, and Sunday school libraries, with high hopes, — hopes amounting to certainties, indeed.   The inspector said, —

"I wish I could communicate with them and order them north, but that is impossible.   A detective only visits a telegraph office to send his report; then he is off again, and you don't know where to put your hand on him."

Now came this despatch : —

BRIDGEPORT, CT., 12.15.

Barnum offers rate of $4,000 a year for exclusive privilege of using elephant as travelling advertising medium from now till detectives find him. Wants to paste circus-posters on him. Desires immediate answer.

BOGGS, *Detective.*

" That is perfectly absurd ! " I exclaimed.

" Of course it is," said the inspector.   " Evidently Mr. Barnum, who thinks he is so sharp, does not know me, — but I know him."

Then he dictated this answer to the despatch : —

Mr. Barnum's offer declined.   Make it $7,000 or nothing.
Chief BLUNT.

" There.   We shall not have to wait long for an answer.   Mr. Barnum is not at home ; he is in the telegraph office, — it is his way when he has business on hand.   Inside of three — "

DONE. — P. T. BARNUM.

So interrupted the clicking telegraphic instrument. Before I could make a comment upon this extraordinary episode, the following despatch carried my thoughts into another and very distressing channel : —

BOLIVIA, N. Y., 12.50.

Elephant arrived here from the south and passed through toward the forest at 11.50, dispersing a funeral on the way, and diminishing the mourners by two.   Citizens fired some small cannon-balls into him, and then fled.   Detective Burke and I arrived ten minutes later, from the north, but mistook some excavations for footprints, and so lost a good deal of time ; but at last we struck the right trail and followed it to the woods. We then got down on our hands and knees and continued to keep a sharp eye on the track, and so shadowed it into the brush. Burke was in advance. Unfortunately the animal had stopped to rest; therefore, Burke having his head down, intent upon the track, butted up against the elephant's hind legs before he was aware of his vicinity. Burke instantly rose to his feet, seized the tail, and exclaimed joyfully, "I claim the re——" but got no further, for a single blow of the huge trunk laid the brave fellow's fragments low in death. I fled rearward, and the elephant turned and shadowed me to the edge of the wood, making tremendous speed, and I should inevitably have been lost, but that the remains of the funeral providentially intervened again and diverted his attention. I have just learned that nothing of that funeral is now left; but this is no loss, for there is an abundance of material for another. Meantime, the elephant has disappeared again.

MULROONEY, *Detective.*

We heard no news except from the diligent and confident detectives scattered about New Jersey, Pennsylvania, Delaware, and Virginia, — who were all following fresh and encouraging clews, — until shortly after 2 P.M., when this telegram came: —

BAXTER CENTRE, 2.15.

Elephant been here, plastered over with circus-bills, and broke up a revival, striking down and damaging many who were on the point of entering upon a better life. Citizens penned him up, and established a guard. When Detective Brown and I arrived, some time after, we entered enclosure and proceeded to identify elephant by photograph and description. All marks tallied exactly except one, which we could not see, — the boil-scar under armpit. To make sure, Brown crept under to look, and was immediately brained,

—that is, head crushed and destroyed, though nothing issued from debris. All fled; so did elephant, striking right and left with much effect. Has escaped, but left bold blood-track from cannon-wounds. Rediscovery certain. He broke southward, through a dense forest.

BRENT, *Detective.*

That was the last telegram. At nightfall a fog shut down which was so dense that objects but three feet away could not be discerned. This lasted all night. The ferry-boats and even the omnibuses had to stop running.

———◆———

III.

NEXT morning the papers were as full of detective theories as before; they had all our tragic facts in detail also, and a great many more which they had received from their telegraphic correspondents. Column after column was occupied, a third of its way down, with glaring head-lines, which it made my heart sick to read. Their general tone was like this:—

"THE WHITE ELEPHANT AT LARGE! HE MOVES UPON HIS FATAL MARCH! WHOLE VILLAGES DESERTED BY THEIR FRIGHT-STRICKEN OCCUPANTS! PALE TERROR GOES BEFORE HIM, DEATH AND DEVASTATION FOLLOW AFTER! AFTER THESE, THE DETECTIVES. BARNS DESTROYED, FACTORIES GUTTED, HARVESTS DEVOURED, PUBLIC ASSEMBLAGES DISPERSED, ACCOMPANIED BY SCENES OF CARNAGE IMPOSSIBLE TO DESCRIBE! THEORIES OF THIRTY-FOUR OF THE MOST DISTINGUISHED DETECTIVES ON THE FORCE! THEORY OF CHIEF BLUNT!"

"There!" said Inspector Blunt, almost betrayed into excitement, "this is magnificent! This is the greatest windfall that any detective organization ever had. The fame of it will travel to the ends of the earth, and endure to the end of time, and my name with it."

But there was no joy for me. I felt as if I had committed all those red crimes, and that the elephant was only my irresponsible agent. And how the list had grown! In one place he had "interfered with an election and killed five repeaters." He had followed this act with the destruction of two poor fellows, named O'Donohue and McFlannigan, who had "found a refuge in the home of the oppressed of all lands only the day before, and were in the act of exercising for the first time the noble right of American citizens at the polls, when stricken down by the relentless hand of the Scourge of Siam." In another, he had "found a crazy sensation-preacher preparing his next season's heroic attacks on the dance, the theatre, and other things which can't strike back, and had stepped on him." And in still another place he had "killed a lightning-rod agent." And so the list went on, growing redder and redder, and more and more heart-breaking. Sixty persons had been killed, and two hundred and forty wounded. All the accounts bore just testimony to the activity and devotion of the detectives, and all closed with the remark that "three hundred thousand citizens and four detectives saw the dread creature, and two of the latter he destroyed."

I dreaded to hear the telegraphic instrument begin

to click again. By and by the messages began to pour in, but I was happily disappointed in their nature. It was soon apparent that all trace of the elephant was lost. The fog had enabled him to search out a good hiding-place unobserved. Telegrams from the most absurdly distant points reported that a dim vast mass had been glimpsed there through the fog at such and such an hour, and was "undoubtedly the elephant." This dim vast mass had been glimpsed in New Haven, in New Jersey, in Pennsylvania, in interior New York, in Brooklyn, and even in the city of New York itself! But in all cases the dim vast mass had vanished quickly and left no trace. Every detective of the large force scattered over this huge extent of country sent his hourly report, and each and every one of them had a clew, and was shadowing something, and was hot upon the heels of it.

But the day passed without other result.

The next day the same.

The next just the same.

The newspaper reports began to grow monotonous with facts that amounted to nothing, clews which led to nothing, and theories which had nearly exhausted the elements which surprise and delight and dazzle.

By advice of the inspector I doubled the reward.

Four more dull days followed. Then came a bitter blow to the poor, hard-working detectives, — the journalists declined to print their theories, and coldly said, "Give us a rest."

Two weeks after the elephant's disappearance I raised the reward to $75,000 by the inspector's advice.

It was a great sum, but I felt that I would rather sacrifice my whole private fortune than lose my credit
with my government. Now that the detectives were
in adversity, the newspapers turned upon them, and
began to fling the most stinging sarcasms at them.
This gave the minstrels an idea, and they dressed
themselves as detectives and hunted the elephant on
the stage in the most extravagant way. The carica-
turists made pictures of detectives scanning the country
with spy-glasses, while the elephant, at their backs,
stole apples out of their pockets. And they made all
sorts of ridiculous pictures of the detective badge, —
you have seen that badge printed in gold on the back
of detective novels, no doubt, — it is a wide-staring
eye, with the legend, "WE NEVER SLEEP." When
detectives called for a drink, the would-be facetious
bar-keeper resurrected an obsolete form of expression
and said, "Will you have an eye-opener?" All the
air was thick with sarcasms.

But there was one man who moved calm, untouched,
unaffected, through it all. It was that heart of oak,
the Chief Inspector. His brave eye never drooped, his
serene confidence never wavered. He always said, —

"Let them rail on; he laughs best who laughs
last."

My admiration for the man grew into a species of worship. I was at his side always. His office had become
an unpleasant place to me, and now became daily more
and more so. Yet if he could endure it I meant to do
so also ; at least, as long as I could. So I came regu-
larly, and stayed, — the only outsider who seemed to be

capable of it. Everybody wondered how I could ; and often it seemed to me that I must desert, but at such times I looked into that calm and apparently unconscious face, and held my ground.

About three weeks after the elephant's disappearance I was about to say, one morning, that I should *have* to strike my colors and retire, when the great detective arrested the thought by proposing one more superb and masterly move.

This was to compromise with the robbers. The fertility of this man's invention exceeded anything I have ever seen, and I have had a wide intercourse with the world's finest minds. He said he was confident he could compromise for $100,000 and recover the elephant. I said I believed I could scrape the amount together, but what would become of the poor detectives who had worked so faithfully ? He said, —

"In compromises they always get half."

This removed my only objection. So the inspector wrote two notes, in this form : —

DEAR MADAM, — Your husband can make a large sum of money (and be entirely protected from the law) by making an immediate appointment with me.

Chief BLUNT.

He sent one of these by his confidential messenger to the "reputed wife" of Brick Duffy, and the other to the reputed wife of Red McFadden.

Within the hour these offensive answers came : —

YE OWLD FOOL : brick McDuffys bin ded 2 yere.

BRIDGET MAHONEY.

CHIEF BAT, — Red McFadden is hung and in heving 18 month. Any Ass but a detective knose that.

MARY O'HOOLIGAN.

"I had long suspected these facts," said the inspector; "this testimony proves the unerring accuracy of my instinct."

The moment one resource failed him he was ready with another. He immediately wrote an advertisement for the morning papers, and I kept a copy of it : —

A. — xwblv. 242 N. Tjnd — fz328wmlg. ⚓Ozpo,—; 2 m ! ogw. Mum.

He said that if the thief was alive this would bring him to the usual rendezvous. He further explained that the usual rendezvous was a place where all business affairs between detectives and criminals were conducted. This meeting would take place at twelve the next night.

We could do nothing till then, and I lost no time in getting out of the office, and was grateful indeed for the privilege.

At 11 the next night I brought $100,000 in bank-notes and put them into the chief's hands, and shortly afterward he took his leave, with the brave old un-dimmed confidence in his eye. An almost intolerable hour dragged to a close; then I heard his welcome tread, and rose gasping and tottered to meet him. How his fine eyes flamed with triumph ! He said, —

"We've compromised ! The jokers will sing a different tune to-morrow ! Follow me !"

He took a lighted candle and strode down into the vast vaulted basement where sixty detectives always slept, and where a score were now playing cards to while the time. I followed close after him. He walked swiftly down to the dim remote end of the place, and just as I succumbed to the pangs of suffocation and was swooning away he stumbled and fell over the outlying members of a mighty object, and I heard him exclaim as he went down, —

"Our noble profession is vindicated. Here is your elephant!"

I was carried to the office above and restored with carbolic acid. The whole detective force swarmed in, and such another season of triumphant rejoicing ensued as I had never witnessed before. The reporters were called, baskets of champagne were opened, toasts were drunk, the handshakings and congratulations were continuous and enthusiastic. Naturally the chief was the hero of the hour, and his happiness was so complete and had been so patiently and worthily and bravely won that it made me happy to see it, though I stood there a homeless beggar, my priceless charge dead, and my position in my country's service lost to me through what would always seem my fatally careless execution of a great trust. Many an eloquent eye testified its deep admiration for the chief, and many a detective's voice murmured, "Look at him, — just the king of the profession, — only give him a clew, it's all he wants, and there ain't anything hid that he can't find." The dividing of the $50,000 made great pleasure; when it was finished the chief made a little.

3

speech while he put his share in his pocket, in which he said, "Enjoy it, boys, for you've earned it; and more than that you've earned for the detective profession undying fame."

A telegram arrived, which read : —

MONROE, MICH., 10 P. M.

First time I've struck a telegraph office in over three weeks. Have followed those footprints, horseback, through the woods, a thousand miles to here, and they get stronger and bigger and fresher every day. Don't worry — inside of another week I'll have the elephant. This is dead sure.

DARLEY, *Detective.*

The chief ordered three cheers for "Darley, one of the finest minds on the force," and then commanded that he be telegraphed to come home and receive his share of the reward.

So ended that marvellous episode of the stolen elephant. The newspapers were pleasant with praises once more, the next day, with one contemptible exception. This sheet said, "Great is the detective ! He may be a little slow in finding a little thing like a mislaid elephant, — he may hunt him all day and sleep with his rotting carcass all night for three weeks, but he will find him at last — if he can get the man who mislaid him to show him the place ! "

Poor Hassan was lost to me forever. The cannonshots had wounded him fatally, he had crept to that unfriendly place in the fog, and there, surrounded by his enemies and in constant danger of detection, he had wasted away with hunger and suffering till death gave him peace.

The compromise cost me $100,000; my detective expenses were $42,000 more; I never applied for a place again under my government; I am a ruined man and a wanderer in the earth, — but my admiration for that man, whom I believe to be the greatest detective the world has ever produced, remains undimmed to this day, and will so remain unto the end.

SOME RAMBLING NOTES OF AN IDLE EXCURSION.

I.

ALL the journeyings I had ever done had been purely in the way of business. The pleasant May weather suggested a novelty, namely, a trip for pure recreation, the bread-and-butter element left out. The Reverend said he would go, too : a good man, one of the best of men, although a clergyman. By eleven at night we were in New Haven and on board the New York boat. We bought our tickets, and then went wandering around, here and there, in the solid comfort of being free and idle, and of putting distance between ourselves and the mails and telegraphs.

After a while I went to my state-room and undressed, but the night was too enticing for bed. We were moving down the bay now, and it was pleasant to stand at the window and take the cool night-breeze and watch the gliding lights on shore. Presently, two elderly men sat down under that window and began a conversation. Their talk was properly no business of mine, yet I was feeling friendly toward the world and willing to be entertained. I soon gathered that they were brothers, that they were from a small Connecticut vil-

lage, and that the matter in hand concerned the cemetery. Said one, —

"Now, John, we talked it all over amongst ourselves,
and this is what we 've done. You see, everybody was
a-movin' from the old buryin' ground, and our folks
was most about left to theirselves, as you may say.
They was crowded, too, as you know; lot wa' n't big
enough in the first place ; and last year, when Seth's
wife died, we could n't hardly tuck her in. She sort
o' overlaid Deacon Shorb's lot, and he soured on her,
so to speak, and on the rest of us, too. So we talked
it over, and I was for a lay-out in the new simitery
on the hill. They wa' n't unwilling, if it was cheap.
Well, the two best and biggest plots was No. 8 and
No. 9, — both of a size; nice comfortable room for
twenty-six, — twenty-six full-growns, that is ; but you
reckon in children and other shorts, and strike an
everage, and I should say you might lay in thirty,
or may be thirty-two or three, pretty genteel, — no
crowdin' to signify."

"That 's a plenty, William. Which one did you
buy ? "

"Well, I 'm a-comin' to that, John. You see, No. 8
was thirteen dollars, No. 9 fourteen — "

"I see. So 's 't you took No. 8."

"You wait. I took No. 9. And I 'll tell you for
why. In the first place, Deacon Shorb wanted it.
Well, after the way he 'd gone on about Seth's wife
overlappin' his prem'ses, I 'd 'a' beat him out of that
No. 9 if I 'd 'a' had to stand two dollars extra,
let alone one. That 's the way I felt about it. Says

I, what's a dollar, any way? Life's on'y a pilgrimage, says I; we ain't here for good, and we can't take it with us, says I. So I just dumped it down, knowin' the Lord don't suffer a good deed to go for nothin', and cal'latin' to take it out o' somebody in the course o' trade. Then there was another reason, John. No. 9's a long way the handiest lot in the simitery, and the likeliest for situation. It lays right on top of a knoll in the dead centre of the buryin' ground; and you can see Millport from there, and Tracy's, and Hopper Mount, and a raft o' farms, and so on. There ain't no better outlook from a buryin' plot in the State. Si Higgins says so, and I reckon he ought to know. Well, and that ain't all. 'Course Shorb had to take No. 8; wa'n't no help for't. Now, No. 8 jines on to No. 9, but it's on the slope of the hill, and every time it rains it'll soak right down on to the Shorbs. Si Higgins says 't when the deacon's time comes, he better take out fire and marine insurance both on his remains."

Here there was the sound of a low, placid, duplicate chuckle of appreciation and satisfaction.

"Now, John, here's a little rough draught of the ground, that I've made on a piece of paper. Up here in the left-hand corner we've bunched the departed; took them from the old grave-yard and stowed them one along side o' t' other, on a first-come-first-served plan, no partialities, with Gran'ther Jones for a starter, on'y because it happened so, and windin' up indiscriminate with Seth's twins. A little crowded towards the end of the lay-out, may be, but we reckoned 't wa'n't best to scatter the twins. Well, next comes the livin'. Here, where it 's marked A, we 're goin' to put Mariar and her family, when they 're called; B, that 's for Brother Hosea and his'n; C, Calvin and tribe. What 's left is these two lots here, — just the gem of the whole patch for general style and outlook : they 're for me and my folks, and you and yourn. Which of them would you ruther be buried in ? "

" I swan you 've took me mighty unexpected, William ! It sort of started the shivers. Fac⁺ is, I was thinkin' so busy about makin' things comfortable for the others, I had n't thought about being buried myself."

" Life 's on'y a fleetin' show, John, as the sayin' is. We 've all got to go, sooner or later. To go with a clean record 's the main thing. Fact is, it 's the on'y thing worth strivin' for, John."

" Yes, that 's so, William, that 's so ; there ain't no getting around it. Which of these lots would you recommend ? "

" Well, it depends, John. Are you particular about outlook ? "

" I don't say I am, William ; I don't say I ain't. Reely, I don't know. But mainly, I reckon, I 'd set store by a south exposure."

" That 's easy fixed, John. They 're both south exposure. They take the sun, and the Shorbs get the shade."

" How about sile, William ? "

" D 's a sandy sile, E 's mostly loom."

" You may gimme E, then, William ; a sandy sile caves in, more or less, and costs for repairs."

"All right ; set your name down here, John, under E. Now, if you don't mind payin' me your share of the fourteen dollars, John, while we're on the business, everything 's fixed."

After some higgling and sharp bargaining the money was paid, and John bade his brother good-night and took his leave. There was silence for some moments ; then a soft chuckle welled up from the lonely William, and he muttered : " I declare for 't, if I have n't made a mistake ! It 's D that 's mostly loom, not E. And John 's booked for a sandy sile, after all."

There was another soft chuckle, and William departed to his rest, also.

The next day, in New York, was a hot one. Still we managed to get more or less entertainment out of it. Toward the middle of the afternoon we arrived on board the stanch steamship Bermuda, with bag and baggage, and hunted for a shady place. It was blazing summer weather, until we were half way down the harbor. Then I buttoned my coat closely ; half an hour later I put on a spring overcoat and buttoned that. As we passed the light-ship I added an ulster and tied a handkerchief around the collar to hold it snug to my neck. So rapidly had the summer gone and winter come again !

By nightfall we were far out at sea, with no land in sight. No telegrams could come here, no letters, no news. This was an uplifting thought. It was still more uplifting to reflect that the millions of harassed people on shore behind us were suffering just as usual.

The next day brought us into the midst of the Atlantic solitudes, — out of smoke-colored soundings into fathomless deep blue; no ships visible anywhere over the wide ocean; no company but Mother Cary's chickens wheeling, darting, skimming the waves in the sun. There were some sea-faring men among the passengers, and conversation drifted into matters concerning ships and sailors. One said that "true as the needle to the pole" was a bad figure, since the needle seldom pointed to the pole. He said a ship's compass was not faithful to any particular point, but was the most fickle and treacherous of the servants of man. It was forever changing. It changed every day in the year; consequently the amount of the daily variation had to be ciphered out and allowance made for it, else the mariner would go utterly astray. Another said there was a vast fortune waiting for the genius who should invent a compass that would not be affected by the local influences of an iron ship. He said there was only one creature more fickle than a wooden ship's compass, and that was the compass of an iron ship. Then came reference to the well-known fact that an experienced mariner can look at the compass of a new iron vessel, thousands of miles from her birthplace, and tell which way her head was pointing when she was in process of building.

Now an ancient whale-ship master fell to talking about the sort of crews they used to have in his early days. Said he, —

"Sometimes we'd have a batch of college students. Queer lot. Ignorant? Why, they didn't know the

cat-heads from the main brace. But if you took them
for fools you'd get bit, sure. They'd learn more in a
month than another man would in a year. We had
one, once, in the Mary Ann, that came aboard with
gold spectacles on. And besides, he was rigged out
from main truck to keelson in the nobbiest clothes
that ever saw a fo'castle. He had a chest full, too:
cloaks, and broadcloth coats, and velvet vests: everything swell, you know; and didn't the salt water fix
them out for him? I guess not! Well, going to sea,
the mate told him to go aloft and help shake out the
fore-to'gallants'l. Up he shins to the foretop, with his
spectacles on, and in a minute down he comes again,
looking insulted. Says the mate, 'What did you come
down for?' Says the chap, 'P'r'aps you didn't notice
that there ain't any ladders above there.' You see
we hadn't any shrouds above the foretop. The men
bursted out in a laugh such as I guess you never heard
the like of. Next night, which was dark and rainy,
the mate ordered this chap to go aloft about something, and I'm dummed if he didn't start up with an
umbrella and a lantern! But no matter; he made a
mighty good sailor before the voyage was done, and
we had to hunt up something else to laugh at. Years
afterwards, when I had forgot all about him, I comes
into Boston, mate of a ship, and was loafing around
town with the second mate, and it so happened that
we stepped into the Revere House, thinking may be we
would chance the salt-horse in that big dining-room
for a flyer, as the boys say. Some fellows were talking just at our elbow, and one says, 'Yonder's the new

governor of Massachusetts, — at that table over there, with the ladies.' We took a good look, my mate and I, for we had n't either of us ever seen a governor before. I looked and looked at that face, and then all of a sudden it popped on me! But I did n't give any sign. Says I, 'Mate, I 've a notion to go over and shake hands with him.' Says he, 'I think I see you doing it, Tom.' Says I, 'Mate, I 'm a-going to do it.' Says he, 'Oh, yes, I guess so! May be you don't want to bet you will, Tom?' Says I, 'I don't mind going a V on it, mate.' Says he, 'Put it up.' 'Up she goes,' says I, planking the cash. This surprised him. But he covered it, and says, pretty sarcastic, 'Had n't you better take your grub with the governor and the ladies, Tom?' Says I, 'Upon second thoughts, I will.' Says he, 'Well, Tom, you *are* a dum fool.' Says I, 'May be I am, may be I ain't; but the main question is, do you want to risk two and a half that I won't do it?' 'Make it a V,' says he. 'Done,' says I. I started, him a-giggling and slapping his hand on his thigh, he felt so good. I went over there and leaned my knuckles on the table a minute and looked the governor in the face, and says I, 'Mister Gardner, don't you know me?' He stared, and I stared, and he stared. Then all of a sudden he sings out, 'Tom Bowling, by the holy poker! Ladies, it 's old Tom Bowling, that you 've heard me talk about, — shipmate of mine in the Mary Ann.' He rose up and shook hands with me ever so hearty — I sort of glanced around and took a realizing sense of my mate's saucer eyes, — and then says the governor, 'Plant yourself,

Tom, plant yourself; you can't cat your anchor again till you've had a feed with me and the ladies!' I planted myself alongside the governor, and canted my eye around towards my mate. Well, sir, his dead-lights were bugged out like tompions; and his mouth stood that wide open that you could have laid a ham in it without him noticing it."

There was great applause at the conclusion of the old captain's story; then, after a moment's silence, a grave, pale young man said, —

"Had you ever met the governor before?"

The old captain looked steadily at this inquirer a while, and then got up and walked aft without making any reply. One passenger after another stole a furtive glance at the inquirer, but failed to make him out, and so gave him up. It took some little work to get the talk-machinery to running smoothly again after this derangement; but at length a conversation sprang up about that important and jealously guarded instrument, a ship's time-keeper, its exceeding delicate accuracy, and the wreck and destruction that have sometimes resulted from its varying a few seemingly trifling moments from the true time; then, in due course, my comrade, the Reverend, got off on a yarn, with a fair wind and everything drawing. It was a true story, too, — about Captain Rounceville's shipwreck, — true in every detail. It was to this effect : —

Captain Rounceville's vessel was lost in mid-Atlantic, and likewise his wife and his two little children. Captain Rounceville and seven seamen escaped with life, but with little else. A small, rudely constructed raft was to be their home for eight days. They had neither provisions nor water. They had scarcely any clothing ; no one had a coat but the captain. This coat was changing hands all the time, for the weather was very cold. Whenever a man became exhausted with the cold, they put the coat on him and laid him down between two shipmates until the garment and their bodies had warmed life into him again. Among the sailors was a Portuguese who knew no English. He seemed to have no thought of his own calamity, but was concerned only about the captain's bitter loss of wife and children. By day, he would look his dumb compassion in the captain's face ; and by night, in the darkness and the driving spray and rain, he would seek out the captain and try to comfort him with caressing pats on the shoulder. One day, when hunger and thirst were making their sure inroads upon the men's strength and spirits, a floating barrel was seen at a distance. It seemed a great find, for doubtless it contained food of some sort. A brave fellow swam to it, and after long and exhausting effort got it to the raft. It was eagerly opened. It was a barrel of magnesia ! On the fifth day an onion was spied. A sailor swam off and got it. Although perishing with hunger, he brought it in its integrity and put it into the captain's hand. The history of the sea teaches that among starving, shipwrecked men selfishness is rare, and a wonder-compelling magnanimity the rule. The onion was equally divided into eight parts, and eaten with deep thanksgivings. On the eighth day a distant ship was sighted. Attempts were made to hoist an oar, with

Captain Rounceville's coat on it for a signal. There were many failures, for the men were but skeletons now, and strengthless. At last success was achieved, but the signal brought no help. The ship faded out of sight and left despair behind her. By and by another ship appeared, and passed so near that the castaways, every eye eloquent with gratitude, made ready to welcome the boat that would be sent to save them. But this ship also drove on, and left these men staring their unutterable surprise and dismay into each other's ashen faces. Late in the day, still another ship came up out of the distance, but the men noted with a pang that her course was one which would not bring her nearer. Their remnant of life was nearly spent; their lips and tongues were swollen, parched, cracked with eight days' thirst; their bodies starved; and here was their last chance gliding relentlessly from them; they would not be alive when the next sun rose. For a day or two past the men had lost their voices, but now Captain Rounceville whispered, "Let us pray." The Portuguese patted him on the shoulder in sign of deep approval. All knelt at the base of the oar that was waving the signal-coat aloft, and bowed their heads. The sea was tossing; the sun rested, a red, rayless disk, on the sea-line in the west. When the men presently raised their heads they would have roared a hallelujah if they had had a voice : the ship's sails lay wrinkled and flapping against her masts, she was going about ! Here was rescue at last, and in the very last instant of time that was left for it. No, not rescue yet, — only the imminent prospect of it. The red disk

sank under the sea and darkness blotted out the ship.
By and by came a pleasant sound, — oars moving in a
boat's rowlocks. Nearer it came, and nearer, — within
thirty steps, but nothing visible. Then a deep voice :
"Hol-*lo!*" The castaways could not answer; their
swollen tongues refused voice. The boat skirted round
and round the raft, started away — the agony of it ! —
returned, rested the oars, close at hand, listening, no
doubt. The deep voice again : "Hol-*lo!* Where are
ye, shipmates ? " Captain Rounceville whispered to
his men, saying: "Whisper your best, boys ! now —
all at once ! " So they sent out an eightfold whisper
in hoarse concert : "Here ! " There was life in it if it
succeeded ; death if it failed. After that supreme moment Captain Rounceville was conscious of nothing
until he came to himself on board the saving ship.
Said the Reverend, concluding, —

"There was one little moment of time in which that
raft could be visible from that ship, and only one. If
that one little fleeting moment had passed unfruitful,
those men's doom was sealed. As close as that does
God shave events foreordained from the beginning of
the world. When the sun reached the water's edge
that day, the captain of that ship was sitting on deck
reading his prayer-book. The book fell; he stooped
to pick it up, and happened to glance at the sun. In
that instant that far-off raft appeared for a second
against the red disk, its needle-like oar and diminutive
signal cut sharp and black against the bright surface,
and in the next instant was thrust away into the dusk
again. But that ship, that captain, and that pregnant

instant had had their work appointed for them in the dawn of time and could not fail of the performance. The chronometer of God never errs!"

There was deep, thoughtful silence for some moments. Then the grave, pale young man said, —

"What is the chronometer of God?"

------◆------

II.

AT dinner, six o'clock, the same people assembled whom we had talked with on deck and seen at luncheon and breakfast this second day out, and at dinner the evening before. That is to say, three journeying ship-masters, a Boston merchant, and a returning Bermudian who had been absent from his Bermuda thirteen years; these sat on the starboard side. On the port side sat the Reverend in the seat of honor; the pale young man next to him; I next; next to me an aged Bermudian, returning to his sunny islands after an absence of twenty-seven years. Of course our captain was at the head of the table, the purser at the foot of it. A small company, but small companies are pleasantest.

No racks upon the table; the sky cloudless, the sun brilliant, the blue sea scarcely ruffled : then what had become of the four married couples, the three bachelors, and the active and obliging doctor from the rural districts of Pennsylvania ? — for all these were on deck when we sailed down New York harbor. This is the explanation. I quote from my note-book : —

Thursday, 3.30 P. M. Under way, passing the Battery. The large party, of four married couples, three bachelors, and a cheery, exhilarating doctor from the wilds of Pennsylvania, are evidently travelling together. All but the doctor grouped in camp-chairs on deck.

Passing principal fort. The doctor is one of those people who has an infallible preventive of sea-sickness; is flitting from friend to friend administering it and saying, "Don't you be afraid; I *know* this medicine; absolutely infallible; prepared under my own supervision." Takes a dose himself, intrepidly.

4.15 P. M. Two of those ladies have struck their colors, notwithstanding the "infallible." They have gone below. The other two begin to show distress.

5 P. M. Exit one husband and one bachelor. These still had their infallible in cargo when they started, but arrived at the companion-way without it.

5.10. Lady No. 3, two bachelors, and one married man have gone below with their own opinion of the infallible.

5.20. Passing Quarantine Hulk. The infallible has done the business for all the party except the Scotchman's wife and the author of that formidable remedy.

Nearing the Light-Ship. Exit the Scotchman's wife, head drooped on stewardess's shoulder.

Entering the open sea. Exit doctor!

The rout seems permanent; hence the smallness of the company at table since the voyage began. Our captain is a grave, handsome Hercules of thirty-five, with a brown hand of such majestic size that one cannot eat for admiring it and wondering if a single kid or calf could furnish material for gloving it.

Conversation not general; drones along between couples. One catches a sentence here and there. Like this, from Bermudian of thirteen years' absence : "It is the nature of women to ask trivial, irrelevant, and pursuing questions, — questions that pursue you from a beginning in nothing to a run-to-cover in no-where." Reply of Bermudian of twenty-seven years' absence : "Yes ; and to think they have logical, ana-lytical minds and argumentative ability. You see 'em begin to whet up whenever they smell argument in the air." Plainly these be philosophers.

Twice since we left port our engines have stopped for a couple of minutes at a time. Now they stop again. Says the pale young man, meditatively, "There ! — that engineer is sitting down to rest again."

Grave stare from the captain, whose mighty jaws cease to work, and whose harpooned potato stops in mid-air on its way to his open, paralyzed mouth. Presently says he in measured tones, "Is it your idea that the engineer of this ship propels her by a crank turned by his own hands ?"

The pale young man studies over this a moment, then lifts up his guileless eyes, and says, "Don't he ?"

Thus gently falls the death-blow to further conversa-tion, and the dinner drags to its close in a reflective silence, disturbed by no sounds but the murmurous wash of the sea and the subdued clash of teeth.

After a smoke and a promenade on deck, where is no motion to discompose our steps, we think of a game of whist. We ask the brisk and capable stewardess from Ireland if there are any cards in the ship.

"Bless your soul, dear, indeed there is. Not a whole pack, true for ye, but not enough missing to signify."

However, I happened by accident to bethink me of a new pack in a morocco case, in my trunk, which I had placed there by mistake, thinking it to be a flask of something. So a party of us conquered the tedium of the evening with a few games and were ready for bed at six bells, mariner's time, the signal for putting out the lights.

There was much chat in the smoking-cabin on the upper deck after luncheon to-day, mostly whaler yarns from those old sea-captains. Captain Tom Bowling was garrulous. He had that garrulous attention to minor detail which is born of secluded farm life or life at sea on long voyages, where there is little to do and time no object. He would sail along till he was right in the most exciting part of a yarn, and then say, "Well, as I was saying, the rudder was fouled, ship driving before the gale, head-on, straight for the iceberg, all hands holding their breath, turned to stone, top-hamper giving way, sails blown to ribbons, first one stick going, then another, boom! smash! crash! duck your head and stand from under! when up comes Johnny Rogers, capstan bar in hand, eyes a-blazing, hair a-flying . . . no, 't wa' n't Johnny Rogers . . . lemme see . . . seems to me Johnny Rogers wa' n't along that voyage; he was along *one* voyage, I know that mighty well, but somehow it seems to me that he signed the articles for this voyage, but — but — whether he come along or not, or got left, or something happened — "

And so on and so on, till the excitement all cooled down and nobody cared whether the ship struck the iceberg or not.

In the course of his talk he rambled into a criticism upon New England degrees of merit in ship-building. Said he, " You get a vessel built away down Maine-way ; Bath, for instance ; what's the result? First thing you do, you want to heave her down for repairs, — *that's* the result ! Well, sir, she hain't been hove down a week till you can heave a dog through her seams. You send that vessel to sea, and what's the result? She wets her oakum the first trip ! Leave it to any man if 't ain't so. Well, you let *our* folks build you a vessel — down New Bedford-way. What's the result? Well, sir, you might take that ship and heave her down, and keep her hove down six months, and she 'll never shed a tear !"

Everybody, landsmen and all, recognized the descriptive neatness of that figure, and applauded, which greatly pleased the old man. A moment later, the meek eyes of the pale young fellow heretofore mentioned came up slowly, rested upon the old man's face a moment, and the meek mouth began to open.

" Shet your head ! " shouted the old mariner.

It was a rather startling surprise to everybody, but it was effective in the matter of its purpose. So the conversation flowed on instead of perishing.

There was some talk about the perils of the sea, and a landsman delivered himself of the customary nonsense about the poor mariner wandering in far oceans, tempest-tossed, pursued by dangers, every storm-blast and thunderbolt in the home skies moving the friends by snug firesides to compassion for that poor mariner, and prayers for his succor. Captain Bowling put up with this for a while, and then burst out with a new view of the matter.

" Come, belay there ! I have read this kind of rot all my life in poetry and tales and such like rubbage. Pity for the poor mariner ! sympathy for the poor mariner ! All right enough, but not in the way the poetry puts it. Pity for the mariner's wife ! all right again, but not in the way the poetry puts it. Look-a-here ! whose life 's the safest in the whole world ? The poor mariner's. You look at the statistics, you 'll see. So don't you fool away any sympathy on the poor mariner's dangers and privations and sufferings. Leave that to the poetry muffs. Now you look at the other side a minute. Here is Captain Brace, forty years old, been at sea thirty. On his way now to take command of his ship and sail south from Bermuda. Next week he 'll be under way : easy times ; comfortable quarters ; passengers, sociable company ; just enough to do to keep his mind healthy and not tire him ; king over his ship, boss of everything and everybody ; thirty years' safety to learn him that his profession ain't a dangerous one. Now you look back at his home. His wife 's a feeble woman ; she 's a stranger in New York ; shut up in blazing hot or freezing cold lodgings, according to the season ; don't know anybody hardly ; no company but her lonesomeness and her thoughts ; husband gone six months at a time. She has borne eight children ; five of them she has buried without her husband ever setting eyes on them. She watched them all the long nights till they died, — he comfortable on the sea ; she followed them to the grave, she heard the clods fall that broke her heart, — he comfortable on the sea ; she mourned at home, weeks and weeks, missing them every day and every hour, — he cheerful at sea, knowing nothing about it. Now look at it a minute, — turn it over in your mind and size it : five children born, she among strangers, and him not by to hearten her ; buried, and him not by to comfort her ; think of that ! Sympathy for the poor mariner's perils is rot ; give it to his wife's hard lines, where it belongs ! Poetry makes out that all the wife worries about is the dangers her husband's running. She's got substantialer things to worry over, I tell you. Poetry's always pitying the poor mariner on account of his perils at sea ; better a blamed sight pity him for the nights he can't sleep for thinking of how he had to leave his wife in her very birth pains, lonesome and friendless, in the thick of disease and trouble and death. If there's one thing that can make me madder than another, it's this sappy, damned maritime poetry ! "

Captain Brace was a patient, gentle, seldom-speaking man, with a pathetic something in his bronzed face that had been a mystery up to this time, but stood interpreted now, since we had heard his story. He had voyaged eighteen times to the Mediterranean, seven times to India, once to the arctic pole in a discovery-ship, and "between times" had visited all the remote seas and ocean corners of the globe. But he said that twelve years ago, on account of his family, he "settled down," and ever since then had ceased to roam. And what do you suppose was this simple-hearted, life-long wanderer's idea of settling down and ceasing to roam? Why, the making of two five-month voyages a year between Surinam and Boston for sugar and molasses!

Among other talk, to-day, it came out that whale-ships carry no doctor. The captain adds the doctor-ship to his own duties. He not only gives medicines, but sets broken limbs after notions of his own, or saws them off and sears the stump when amputation seems best. The captain is provided with a medicine-chest, with the medicines numbered instead of named. A book of directions goes with this. It describes diseases and symptoms, and says, "Give a teaspoonful of No. 9 once an hour," or "Give ten grains of No. 12 every half hour," etc. One of our sea-captains came across a skipper in the North Pacific who was in a state of great surprise and perplexity. Said he, —

"There's something rotten about this medicine-chest business. One of my men was sick, — nothing much the matter. I looked in the book : it said, give him a teaspoonful of No. 15. I went to the medicine-chest, and I see I was out of No. 15. I judged I'd got to get up a combination somehow that would fill the bill; so I hove into the fellow half a teaspoonful of No. 8 and half a teaspoonful of No. 7, and I'll be hanged if it didn't kill him in fifteen minutes! There's something about this medicine-chest system that's too many for me!"

There was a good deal of pleasant gossip about old Captain "Hurricane" Jones, of the Pacific Ocean, — peace to his ashes! Two or three of us present had known him; I, particularly well, for I had made four sea-voyages with him. He was a very remarkable man. He was born in a ship; he picked up what little education he had among his shipmates; he began life in the forecastle, and climbed grade by grade to the captaincy. More than fifty years of his sixty-five were spent at sea. He had sailed all oceans, seen all lands, and borrowed a tint from all climates. When a man has been fifty years at sea he necessarily knows nothing of men, nothing of the world but its surface, nothing of the world's thought, nothing of the world's learning but its A B C, and that blurred and distorted by the unfocused lenses of an untrained mind. Such a man is only a gray and bearded child. That is what old Hurricane Jones was, — simply an innocent, lovable old infant. When his spirit was in repose he was as sweet and gentle as a girl; when his wrath was up he was a hurricane that made his nickname seem tamely descriptive. He was formidable in a fight, for he was of powerful build and dauntless courage. He was frescoed from head to heel with pictures and mottoes tattooed in red and blue India ink. I was with him one voyage when he got his last vacant space tattooed; this vacant space was around his left ankle. During three days he stumped about the ship with his ankle bare and swollen, and this legend gleaming red and angry out from a clouding of India ink : "Virtue is its own R'd." (There was a lack of room.) He was deeply and sincerely pious, and swore like a fish-woman. He considered swearing blameless, because sailors would not understand an order unillumined by it. He was a profound Biblical scholar, — that is, he thought he was. He believed everything in the Bible, but he had his own methods of arriving at his beliefs. He was of the "advanced" school of thinkers, and applied natural laws to the interpretation of all miracles, somewhat on the plan of the people who make the six days of creation six geological epochs, and so forth. Without being aware of it, he was a rather severe satire on modern scientific religionists. Such a man as I have been describing is rabidly fond of disquisition and argument ; one knows that without being told it.

One trip the captain had a clergyman on board, but did not know he was a clergyman, since the passenger list did not betray the fact. He took a great liking to this Rev. Mr. Peters, and talked with him a great deal : told him yarns, gave him toothsome scraps of personal history, and wove a glittering streak of profanity through his garrulous fabric that was refreshing to a spirit weary of the dull neutralities of undecorated speech. One day the captain said, "Peters, do you ever read the Bible ?"

"Well — yes."

"I judge it ain't often, by the way you say it. Now, you tackle it in dead earnest once, and you'll find it'll pay. Don't you get discouraged, but hang right on. First, you won't understand it; but by and by things will begin to clear up, and then you would n't lay it down to eat."

"Yes, I have heard that said."

"And it's so, too. There ain't a book that begins with it. It lays over 'em all, Peters. There's some pretty tough things in it, — there ain't any getting around that, — but you stick to them and think them out, and when once you get on the inside everything's plain as day."

"The miracles, too, captain?"

"Yes, sir! the miracles, too. Every one of them. Now, there's that business with the prophets of Baal; like enough that stumped you?"

"Well, I don't know but — "

"Own up, now; it stumped you. Well, I don't wonder. You had n't had any experience in ravelling such things out, and naturally it was too many for you. Would you like to have me explain that thing to you, and show you how to get at the meat of these matters?"

"Indeed, I would, captain, if you don't mind."

Then the captain proceeded as follows: "I'll do it with pleasure. First, you see, I read and read, and thought and thought, till I got to understand what sort of people they were in the old Bible times, and then after that it was all clear and easy. Now, this was the way I put it up, concerning Isaac[1] and the prophets of Baal. There was some mighty sharp men

[1] This is the captain's own mistake.

amongst the public characters of that old ancient day, and Isaac was one of them. Isaac had his failings, — plenty of them, too; it ain't for me to apologize for Isaac; he played it on the prophets of Baal, and like enough he was justifiable, considering the odds that was against him. No, all I say is, 't wa' n't any miracle, and that I 'll show you so 's 't you can see it yourself.

"Well, times had been getting rougher and rougher for prophets, — that is, prophets of Isaac's denomination. There was four hundred and fifty prophets of Baal in the community, and only one Presbyterian; that is, if Isaac *was* a Presbyterian, which I reckon he was, but it don't say. Naturally, the prophets of Baal took all the trade. Isaac was pretty low-spirited, I reckon, but he was a good deal of a man, and no doubt he went a-prophesying around, letting on to be doing a land-office business, but 't wa' n't any use; he could n't run any opposition to amount to anything. By and by things got desperate with him; he sets his head to work and thinks it all out, and then what does he do? Why, he begins to throw out hints that the other parties are this and that and t' other, — nothing very definite, may be, but just kind of undermining their reputation in a quiet way. This made talk, of course, and finally got to the king. The king asked Isaac what he meant by his talk. Says Isaac, 'Oh, nothing particular; only, can they pray down fire from heaven on an altar? It ain't much, may be, your majesty, only can they *do* it? That 's the idea.' So the king was a good deal disturbed, and he went to the prophets of Baal, and they said, pretty airy, that if he had an altar ready, *they* were ready; and they intimated he better get it insured, too.

"So next morning all the children of Israel and their parents and the other people gathered themselves together. Well, here was that great crowd of prophets of Baal packed together on one side, and Isaac walking up and down all alone on the other, putting up his job. When time was called, Isaac let on to be comfortable and indifferent; told the other team to take the first innings. So they went at it, the whole four hundred and fifty, praying around the altar, very hopeful, and doing their level best. They prayed an hour, — two hours, — three hours, — and so on, plumb till noon. It wa' n't any use; they had n't took a trick. Of course they felt kind of ashamed before all those people, and well they might. Now, what would a magnanimous man do? Keep still, would n't he? Of course. What did Isaac do? He gravelled the prophets of Baal every way he could think of. Says he, 'You don't speak up loud enough; your god 's asleep, like enough, or may be he 's taking a walk; you want to holler, you know,' — or words to that effect; I don't recollect the exact language. Mind, I don't apologize for Isaac; he had his faults.

"Well, the prophets of Baal prayed along the best they knew how all the afternoon, and never raised a spark. At last, about sundown, they were all tuckered out, and they owned up and quit.

"What does Isaac do, now? He steps up and says to some friends of his, there, 'Pour four barrels of water on the altar!' Everybody was astonished; for the other side had prayed at it dry, you know, and got whitewashed. They poured it on. Says he, 'Heave on four more barrels.' Then he says, 'Heave on four more.' Twelve barrels, you see, altogether. The water ran all over the altar, and all down the sides, and filled up a trench around it that would hold a couple of hogsheads, — 'measures,' it says; I reckon it means about a hogshead. Some of the people were going to put on their things and go, for they allowed he was crazy. They did n't know Isaac. Isaac knelt down and began to pray : he strung along, and strung along, about the heathen in distant lands, and about the sister churches, and about the state and the country at large, and about those that's in authority in the government, and all the usual programme, you know, till everybody had got tired and gone to thinking about something else, and then, all of a sudden, when nobody was noticing, he outs with a match and rakes it on the under side of his leg, and pff! up the whole thing blazes like a house afire ! Twelve barrels of *water ?* *Petroleum,* sir, PETROLEUM ! that 's what it was ! "

" Petroleum, captain ? "

" Yes, sir ; the country was full of it. Isaac knew all about that. You read the Bible. Don't you worry about the tough places. They ain't tough when you come to think them out and throw light on them. There ain't a thing in the Bible but what is true ; all you want is to go prayerfully to work and cipher out how 't was done."

At eight o'clock on the third morning out from New

York, land was sighted. Away across the sunny waves one saw a faint dark stripe stretched along under the horizon, — or pretended to see it, for the credit of his eyesight. Even the Reverend said he saw it, a thing which was manifestly not so. But I never have seen any one who was morally strong enough to confess that he could not see land when others claimed that they could.

By and by the Bermuda Islands were easily visible. The principal one lay upon the water in the distance, a long, dull-colored body, scalloped with slight hills and valleys. We could not go straight at it, but had to travel all the way around it, sixteen miles from shore, because it is fenced with an invisible coral reef. At last we sighted buoys, bobbing here and there, and then we glided into a narrow channel among them, "raised the reef," and came upon shoaling blue water that soon further shoaled into pale green, with a surface scarcely rippled. Now came the resurrection hour : the berths gave up their dead. Who are these pale spectres in plug hats and silken flounces that file up the companion-way in melancholy procession and step upon the deck ? These are they which took the infallible preventive of sea-sickness in New York harbor and then disappeared and were forgotten. Also there came two or three faces not seen before until this moment. One's impulse is to ask, " Where did *you* come aboard ? "

We followed the narrow channel a long time, with land on both sides, — low hills that might have been green and grassy, but had a faded look instead. How-

ever, the land-locked water was lovely, at any rate,
with its glittering belts of blue and green where
moderate soundings were, and its broad splotches of
rich brown where the rocks lay near the surface.
Everybody was feeling so well that even the grave,
pale young man (who, by a sort of kindly common consent, had come latterly to be referred to as " the Ass ")
received frequent and friendly notice, — which was
right enough, for there was no harm in him.

At last we steamed between two island points whose
rocky jaws allowed only just enough room for the
vessel's body, and now before us loomed Hamilton
on her clustered hillsides and summits, the whitest
mass of terraced architecture that exists in the world,
perhaps.

It was Sunday afternoon, and on the pier were
gathered one or two hundred Bermudians, half of
them black, half of them white, and all of them nob-
bily dressed, as the poet says.

Several boats came off to the ship, bringing citizens.
One of these citizens was a faded, diminutive old gentleman, who approached our most ancient passenger
with a childlike joy in his twinkling eyes, halted before him, folded his arms, and said, smiling with all
his might and with all the simple delight that was in
him, " You don't know me, John ! Come, out with it,
now ; you know you don't ! "

The ancient passenger scanned him perplexedly,
scanned the napless, threadbare costume of venerable
fashion that had done Sunday-service no man knows
how many years, contemplated the marvellous stove-

pipe hat of still more ancient and venerable pattern, with its poor pathetic old stiff brim canted up "gallusly" in the wrong places, and said, with a hesitation that indicated strong internal effort to "place" the gentle old apparition, "Why . . . let me see . . . plague on it . . . there's *something* about you that . . . er . . . er . . . but I've been gone from Bermuda for twenty-seven years, and . . . hum, hum . . . I don't seem to get at it, somehow, but there's something about you that is just as familiar to me as — "

"Likely it might be his hat," murmured the Ass, with innocent, sympathetic interest.

———•———

III.

So the Reverend and I had at last arrived at Hamilton, the principal town in the Bermuda Islands. A wonderfully white town; white as snow itself. White as marble; white as flour. Yet looking like none of these, exactly. Never mind, we said; we shall hit upon a figure by and by that will describe this peculiar white.

It was a town that was compacted together upon the sides and tops of a cluster of small hills. Its outlying borders fringed off and thinned away among the cedar forests, and there was no woody distance of curving coast, or leafy islet sleeping upon the dimpled, painted sea, but was flecked with shining white points, — half-concealed houses peeping out of the foliage.

The architecture of the town was mainly Spanish, inherited from the colonists of two hundred and fifty years ago. Some ragged-topped cocoa-palms, glimpsed here and there, gave the land a tropical aspect.

There was an ample pier of heavy masonry; upon this, under shelter, were some thousands of barrels containing that product which has carried the fame of Bermuda to many lands, the potato. With here and there an onion. That last sentence is facetious; for they grow at least two onions in Bermuda to one potato. The onion is the pride and joy of Bermuda. It is her jewel, her gem of gems. In her conversation, her pulpit, her literature, it is her most frequent and eloquent figure. In Bermudian metaphor it stands for perfection, — perfection absolute.

The Bermudian weeping over the departed exhausts praise when he says, " He was an onion ! " The Bermudian extolling the living hero bankrupts applause when he says, " He is an onion ! " The Bermudian setting his son upon the stage of life to dare and do for himself climaxes all counsel, supplication, admonition, comprehends all ambition, when he says, " Be an onion ! "

When parallel with the pier, and ten or fifteen steps outside it, we anchored. It was Sunday, bright and sunny. The groups upon the pier — men, youths, and boys — were whites and blacks in about equal proportion. All were well and neatly dressed, many of them nattily, a few of them very stylishly. One would have to travel far before he would find another town of twelve thousand inhabitants that could represent itself so respectably, in the matter of clothes, on a freight-pier, without premeditation or effort. The women and young girls, black and white, who occasionally passed by, were nicely clad, and many were elegantly and fashionably so. The men did not affect summer clothing much, but the girls and women did, and their white garments were good to look at, after so many months of familiarity with sombre colors.

Around one isolated potato barrel stood four young gentlemen, two black, two white, becomingly dressed, each with the head of a slender cane pressed against his teeth, and each with a foot propped up on the barrel. Another young gentleman came up, looked longingly at the barrel, but saw no rest for his foot there, and turned pensively away to seek another barrel. He wandered here and there, but without result. Nobody sat upon a barrel, as is the custom of the idle in other lands, yet all the isolated barrels were humanly occupied. Whosoever had a foot to spare put it on a barrel, if all the places on it were not already taken. The habits of all peoples are determined by their circumstances. The Bermudians lean upon barrels because of the scarcity of lamp-posts.

Many citizens came on board and spoke eagerly to the officers, — inquiring about the Turco-Russian war news, I supposed. However, by listening judiciously I found that this was not so. They said, "What is the price of onions?" or, "How's onions?" Naturally enough this was their first interest; but they dropped into the war the moment it was satisfied.

We went ashore and found a novelty of a pleasant

nature : there were no hackmen, hacks, or omnibuses
on the pier or about it anywhere, and nobody offered
his services to us, or molested us in any way. I said
it was like being in heaven. The Reverend rebukingly
and rather pointedly advised me to make the most of
it, then. We knew of a boarding-house, and what we
needed now was somebody to pilot us to it. Presently
a little barefooted colored boy came along, whose rag-
gedness was conspicuously un-Bermudian. His rear
was so marvellously bepatched with colored squares
and triangles that one was half persuaded he had got
it out of an atlas. When the sun struck him right, he
was as good to follow as a lightning-bug. We hired
him and dropped into his wake. He piloted us through
one picturesque street after another, and in due course
deposited us where we belonged. He charged nothing
for his map, and but a trifle for his services ; so the
Reverend doubled it. The little chap received the
money with a beaming applause in his eye which
plainly said, "This man's an onion ! "

We had brought no letters of introduction; our
names had been misspelt in the passenger list ; nobody knew whether we were honest folk or otherwise.
So we were expecting to have a good private time in
case there was nothing in our general aspect to close
boarding-house doors against us. We had no trouble.
Bermuda has had but little experience of rascals, and is
not suspicious. We got large, cool, well-lighted rooms
on a second floor, overlooking a bloomy display of
flowers and flowering shrubs, — calla and annunciation
lilies, lantanas, heliotrope, jessamine, roses, pinks,

double geraniums, oleanders, pomegranates, blue morn-
ing-glories of a great size, and many plants that were
unknown to me.

We took a long afternoon walk, and soon found out
that that exceedingly white town was built of blocks of
white coral. Bermuda is a coral island, with a six-
inch crust of soil on top of it, and every man has a
quarry on his own premises. Everywhere you go you
see square recesses cut into the hillsides, with perpendicular walls unmarred by crack or crevice, and perhaps you fancy that a house grew out of the ground
there, and has been removed in a single piece from the
mould. If you do, you err. But the material for a
house has been quarried there. They cut right down
through the coral, to any depth that is convenient, —
ten to twenty feet, — and take it out in great square
blocks. This cutting is done with a chisel that has a
handle twelve or fifteen feet long, and is used as one
uses a crowbar when he is drilling a hole, or a dasher
when he is churning. Thus soft is this stone. Then
with a common handsaw they saw the great blocks into
handsome, huge bricks that are two feet long, a foot wide,
and about six inches thick. These stand loosely piled
during a month to harden ; then the work of building
begins. The house is built of these blocks ; it is roofed
with broad coral slabs an inch thick, whose edges lap
upon each other, so that the roof looks like a succession of shallow steps or terraces ; the chimneys are
built of the coral blocks, and sawed into graceful and
picturesque patterns ; the ground-floor veranda is
paved with coral blocks ; also the walk to the gate ;

the fence is built of coral blocks, — built in massive panels, with broad capstones and heavy gate-posts, and the whole trimmed into easy lines and comely shape with the saw. Then they put a hard coat of whitewash, as thick as your thumb nail, on the fence and all over the house, roof, chimneys, and all; the sun comes out and shines on this spectacle, and it is time for you to shut your unaccustomed eyes, lest they be put out. It is the whitest white you can conceive of, and the blindingest. A Bermuda house does not look like marble; it is a much intenser white than that; and besides, there is a dainty, indefinable something else about its look that is not marble-like. We put in a great deal of solid talk and reflection over this matter of trying to find a figure that would describe the unique white of a Bermuda house, and we contrived to hit upon it at last. It is exactly the white of the icing of a cake, and has the same unemphasized and scarcely perceptible polish. The white of marble is modest and retiring compared with it.

After the house is cased in its hard scale of whitewash, not a crack, or sign of a seam, or joining of the blocks, is detectable, from base-stone to chimney-top; the building looks as if it had been carved from a single block of stone, and the doors and windows sawed out afterwards. A white marble house has a cold, tomb-like, unsociable look, and takes the conversation out of a body and depresses him. Not so with a Bermuda house. There is something exhilarating, even hilarious, about its vivid whiteness when the sun plays upon it. If it be of picturesque shape and graceful contour, — and many of the Bermudian dwellings are, — it will so fascinate you that you will keep your eyes on it until they ache. One of those clean-cut, fanciful chimneys, — too pure and white for this world, — with one side glowing in the sun and the other touched with a soft shadow, is an object that will charm one's gaze by the hour. I know of no other country that has chimneys worthy to be gazed at and gloated over. One of those snowy houses, half-concealed and half-glimpsed through green foliage, is a pretty thing to see; and if it takes one by surprise and suddenly, as he turns a sharp corner of a country road, it will wring an exclamation from him, sure.

Wherever you go, in town or country, you find those snowy houses, and always with masses of bright-colored flowers about them, but with no vines climbing their walls; vines cannot take hold of the smooth, hard whitewash. Wherever you go, in the town or along the country roads, among little potato farms and patches or expensive country-seats, these stainless white dwellings, gleaming out from flowers and foliage, meet you at every turn. The least little bit of a cottage is as white and blemishless as the stateliest mansion. Nowhere is there dirt or stench, puddle or hog-wallow, neglect, disorder, or lack of trimness and neatness. The roads, the streets, the dwellings, the people, the clothes, — this neatness extends to everything that falls under the eye. It is the tidiest country in the world. And very much the tidiest, too.

Considering these things, the question came up, Where do the poor live? No answer was arrived at.

Therefore, we agreed to leave this conundrum for future statesmen to wrangle over.

What a bright and startling spectacle one of those blazing white country palaces, with its brown-tinted window caps and ledges, and green shutters, and its wealth of caressing flowers and foliage, would be in black London! And what a gleaming surprise it would be in nearly any American city one could mention, too!

Bermuda roads are made by cutting down a few inches into the solid white coral — or a good many feet, where a hill intrudes itself — and smoothing off the surface of the road-bed. It is a simple and easy process. The grain of the coral is coarse and porous; the road-bed has the look of being made of coarse white sugar. Its excessive cleanness and whiteness are a trouble in one way: the sun is reflected into your eyes with such energy as you walk along, that you want to sneeze all the time. Old Captain Tom Bowling found another difficulty. He joined us in our walk, but kept wandering unrestfully to the roadside. Finally he explained. Said he, "Well, I chew, you know, and the road's so plaguy clean."

We walked several miles that afternoon in the bewildering glare of the sun, the white roads, and the white buildings. Our eyes got to paining us a good deal. By and by a soothing, blessed twilight spread its cool balm around. We looked up in pleased surprise and saw that it proceeded from an intensely black negro who was going by. We answered his military salute in the grateful gloom of his near presence, and then passed on into the pitiless white glare again.

The colored women whom we met usually bowed and spoke ; so did the children. The colored men commonly gave the military salute. They borrow this fashion from the soldiers, no doubt; England has kept a garrison here for generations. The younger men's custom of carrying small canes is also borrowed from the soldiers, I suppose, who always carry a cane, in Bermuda as everywhere else in Britain's broad dominions.

The country roads curve and wind hither and thither in the delightfulest way, unfolding pretty surprises at every turn: billowy masses of oleander that seem to float out from behind distant projections like the pink cloud-banks of sunset ; sudden plunges among cottages and gardens, life and activity, followed by as sudden plunges into the sombre twilight and stillness of the woods ; flitting visions of white fortresses and beacon towers pictured against the sky on remote hill-tops ; glimpses of shining green sea caught for a moment through opening headlands, then lost again ; more woods and solitude ; and by and by another turn lays bare, without warning, the full sweep of the inland ocean, enriched with its bars of soft color, and graced with its wandering sails.

Take any road you please, you may depend upon it you will not stay in it half a mile. Your road is every-thing that a road ought to be : it is bordered with trees, and with strange plants and flowers ; it is shady and pleasant, or sunny and still pleasant ; it carries you by the prettiest and peacefulest and most home-like of homes, and through stretches of forest that lie in a deep hush sometimes, and sometimes are alive with the music of birds; it curves always, which is a continual promise, whereas straight roads reveal everything at a glance and kill interest. Your road is all this, and yet you will not stay in it half a mile, for the reason that little seductive, mysterious roads are always branching out from it on either hand, and as these curve sharply also and hide what is beyond, you cannot resist the temptation to desert your own chosen road and explore them. You are usually paid for your trouble; consequently, your walk inland always turns out to be one of the most crooked, involved, purposeless, and interesting experiences a body can imagine. There is enough of variety. Sometimes you are in the level open, with marshes thick grown with flag-lances that are ten feet high on the one hand, and potato and onion orchards on the other; next, you are on a hill-top, with the ocean and the Islands spread around you; presently the road winds through a deep cut, shut in by perpendicular walls thirty or forty feet high, marked with the oddest and abruptest stratum lines, suggestive of sudden and eccentric old upheavals, and garnished with here and there a clinging adventurous flower, and here and there a dangling vine; and by and by your way is along the sea edge, and you may look down a fathom or two through the transparent water and watch the diamond-like flash and play of the light upon the rocks and sands on the bottom until you are tired of it, — if you are so constituted as to be able to get tired of it.

You may march the country roads in maiden meditation, fancy free, by field and farm, for no dog will plunge out at you from unsuspected gate, with breath-taking surprise of ferocious bark, notwithstanding it is a Christian land and a civilized. We saw upwards of a million cats in Bermuda, but the people are very ab-stemious in the matter of dogs. Two or three nights we prowled the country far and wide, and never once were accosted by a dog. It is a great privilege to visit such a land. The cats were no offence when properly distributed, but when piled they obstructed travel.

As we entered the edge of the town that Sunday afternoon, we stopped at a cottage to get a drink of water. The proprietor, a middle-aged man with a good face, asked us to sit down and rest. His dame brought chairs, and we grouped ourselves in the shade of the trees by the door. Mr. Smith — that was not his name, but it will answer — questioned us about ourselves and our country, and we answered him truthfully, as a general thing, and questioned him in return. It was all very simple and pleasant and so-ciable. Rural, too; for there was a pig and a small donkey and a hen anchored out, close at hand, by cords to their legs, on a spot that purported to be grassy. Presently, a woman passed along, and although she coldly said nothing she changed the drift of our talk. Said Smith: —

"She did n't look this way, you noticed? Well, she is our next neighbor on one side, and there's another family that's our next neighbors on the other side; but there's a general coolness all around now, and we don't speak. Yet these three families, one generation and another, have lived here side by side and been as friendly as weavers for a hundred and fifty years, till about a year ago."

"Why, what calamity could have been powerful enough to break up so old a friendship?"

"Well, it was too bad, but it couldn't be helped. It happened like this: About a year or more ago, the rats got to pestering my place a good deal, and I set up a steel-trap in the back yard. Both of these neighbors run considerable to cats, and so I warned them about the trap, because their cats were pretty sociable around here nights, and they might get into trouble without my intending it. Well, they shut up their cats for a while, but you know how it is with people; they got careless, and sure enough one night the trap took Mrs. Jones's principal tomcat into camp, and finished him up. In the morning Mrs. Jones comes here with the corpse in her arms, and cries and takes on the same as if it was a child. It was a cat by the name of Yelverton, — Hector G. Yelverton, — a troublesome old rip, with no more principle than an Injun, though you couldn't make *her* believe it. I said all a man could to comfort her, but no, nothing would do but I must pay for him. Finally, I said I warn't investing in cats now as much as I was, and with that she walked off in a huff, carrying the remains with her. That closed our intercourse with the Joneses. Mrs. Jones joined another church and took her tribe with her. She said she would not hold fellowship with assassins. Well, by and by comes

Mrs. Brown's turn, — she that went by here a minute ago. She had a disgraceful old yellow cat that she thought as much of as if he was twins, and one night he tried that trap on his neck, and it fitted him so, and was so sort of satisfactory, that he laid down and curled up and stayed with it. Such was the end of Sir John Baldwin."

"Was that the name of the cat?"

"The same. There's cats around here with names that would surprise you. Maria" (to his wife), "what was that cat's name that eat a keg of ratsbane by mistake over at Hooper's, and started home and got struck by lightning and took the blind staggers and fell in the well and was most drowned before they could fish him out?"

"That was that colored Deacon Jackson's cat. I only remember the last end of its name, which was Hold-The-Fort-For-I-Am-Coming Jackson."

"Sho! that ain't the one. That's the one that eat up an entire box of Seidlitz powders, and then had n't any more judgment than to go and take a drink. He was considered to be a great loss, but I never could see it. Well, no matter about the names. Mrs. Brown wanted to be reasonable, but Mrs. Jones would n't let her. She put her up to going to law for damages. So to law she went, and had the face to claim seven shillings and sixpence. It made a great stir. All the neighbors went to court. Everybody took sides. It got hotter and hotter, and broke up all the friendships for three hundred yards around, — friendships that had lasted for generations and generations.

"Well, I proved by eleven witnesses that the cat was of a low character and very ornery, and warn't worth a cancelled postage-stamp, any way, taking the average of cats here ; but I lost the case. What could I expect? The system is all wrong here, and is bound to make revolution and bloodshed some day. You see, they give the magistrate a poor little starvation salary, and then turn him loose on the public to gouge for fees and costs to live on. What is the natural result? Why he never looks into the justice of a case, — never once. All he looks at is which client has got the money. So this one piled the fees and costs and everything on to me. I could pay specie, don't you see? and he knew mighty well that if he put the verdict on to Mrs. Brown, where it belonged, he'd have to take his swag in currency."

"Currency? Why, has Bermuda a currency?"

"Yes, — onions. And they were forty per cent discount, too, then, because the season had been over as much as three months. So I lost my case. I had to pay for that cat. But the general trouble the case made was the worst thing about it. Broke up so much good feeling. The neighbors don't speak to each other now. Mrs. Brown had named a child after me. But she changed its name right away. She is a Baptist. Well, in the course of baptizing it over again, it got drowned. I was hoping we might get to be friendly again some time or other, but of course this drowning the child knocked that all out of the question. It would have saved a world of heart-break and ill blood if she had named it dry."

I knew by the sigh that this was honest. All this trouble and all this destruction of confidence in the purity of the bench on account of a seven-shilling lawsuit about a cat! Somehow, it seemed to "size" the country.

At this point we observed that an English flag had just been placed at half-mast on a building a hundred yards away. I and my friends were busy in an instant trying to imagine whose death, among the island dignitaries, could command such a mark of respect as this. Then a shudder shook them and me at the same moment, and I knew that we had jumped to one and the same conclusion : " The governor has gone to England ; it is for the British admiral ! "

At this moment Mr. Smith noticed the flag. He said with emotion, —

" That 's on a boarding-house. I judge there 's a boarder dead."

A dozen other flags within view went to half-mast.

" It 's a boarder, sure," said Smith.

" But would they half-mast the flags here for a boarder, Mr. Smith ? "

" Why, certainly they would, if he was *dead.*"

That seemed to size the country again.

IV.

THE early twilight of a Sunday evening in Hamilton, Bermuda, is an alluring time. There is just enough of whispering breeze, fragrance of flowers, and sense of repose to raise one's thoughts heavenward; and just enough amateur piano music to keep him reminded of the other place. There are many venerable pianos in Hamilton, and they all play at twilight. Age enlarges and enriches the powers of some musical instruments, — notably those of the violin, — but it seems to set a piano's teeth on edge. Most of the music in vogue there is the same that those pianos prattled in their innocent infancy; and there is something very pathetic about it when they go over it now, in their asthmatic second childhood, dropping a note here and there, where a tooth is gone.

We attended evening service at the stately Episcopal church on the hill, where were five or six hundred people, half of them white and the other half black, according to the usual Bermudian proportions; and all well dressed, — a thing which is also usual in Bermuda and to be confidently expected. There was good music, which we heard, and doubtless a good sermon, but there was a wonderful deal of coughing, and so only the high parts of the argument carried over it. As we came out, after service, I overheard one young girl say to another, —

"Why, you don't mean to say you pay duty on

gloves and laces! I only pay postage; have them done up and sent in the 'Boston Advertiser.'"

There are those who believe that the most difficult thing to create is a woman who can comprehend that it is wrong to smuggle; and that an impossible thing to create is a woman who will not smuggle, whether or no, when she gets a chance. But these may be errors.

We went wandering off toward the country, and were soon far down in the lonely black depths of a road that was roofed over with the dense foliage of a double rank of great cedars. There was no sound of any kind, there; it was perfectly still. And it was so dark that one could detect nothing but sombre outlines. We strode farther and farther down this tunnel, cheering the way with chat.

Presently the chat took this shape: " How insensibly the character of a people and of a government makes its impress upon a stranger, and gives him a sense of security or of insecurity without his taking deliberate thought upon the matter or asking anybody a question! We have been in this land half a day; we have seen none but honest faces; we have noted the British flag flying, which means efficient government and good order; so without inquiry we plunge unarmed and with perfect confidence into this dismal place, which in almost any other country would swarm with thugs and garroters — "

'Sh! What was that? Stealthy footsteps! Low voices! We gasp, we close up together, and wait. A vague shape glides out of the dusk and confronts us. A voice speaks — demands money!

" A shilling, gentlemen, if you please, to help build the new Methodist church."

Blessed sound! Holy sound! We contribute with thankful avidity to the new Methodist church, and are happy to think how lucky it was that those little colored Sunday-school scholars did not seize upon everything we had with violence, before we recovered from our momentary helpless condition. By the light of cigars we write down the names of weightier philanthropists than ourselves on the contribution-cards, and then pass on into the farther darkness, saying, What sort of a government do they call this, where they allow little black pious children, with contribution-cards, to plunge out upon peaceable strangers in the dark and scare them to death?

We prowled on several hours, sometimes by the seaside, sometimes inland, and finally managed to get lost, which is a feat that requires talent in Bermuda. I had on new shoes. They were No. 7's when I started, but were not more than 5's now, and still diminishing. I walked two hours in those shoes after that, before we reached home. Doubtless I could have the reader's sympathy for the asking. Many people have never had the headache or the toothache, and I am one of those myself; but everybody has worn tight shoes for two or three hours, and known the luxury of taking them off in a retired place and seeing his feet swell up and obscure the firmament. Once when I was a callow, bashful cub, I took a plain, unsentimental country girl to a comedy one night. I had known her a day; she seemed divine; I wore my new boots. At

6

the end of the first half-hour she said, "Why do you
fidget so with your feet?" I said, "Did I?" Then
I put my attention there and kept still. At the end
of another half-hour she said, "Why do you say, 'Yes,
oh yes!' and 'Ha, ha, oh, certainly! very true!' to
everything I say, when half the time those are entirely
irrelevant answers?" I blushed, and explained that
I had been a little absent-minded. At the end of
another half-hour she said, "Please, why do you grin
so steadfastly at vacancy, and yet look so sad?" I
explained that I always did that when I was reflecting.
An hour passed, and then she turned and contemplated
me with her earnest eyes and said, "Why do you cry
all the time?" I explained that very funny comedies
always made me cry. At last human nature sur-
rendered, and I secretly slipped my boots off. This
was a mistake. I was not able to get them on any
more. It was a rainy night; there were no omnibuses
going our way; and as I walked home, burning up
with shame, with the girl on one arm and my boots
under the other, I was an object worthy of some compassion, — especially in those moments of martyrdom
when I had to pass through the glare that fell upon
the pavement from street lamps. Finally, this child
of the forest said, "Where are your boots?" and being
taken unprepared, I put a fitting finish to the follies
of the evening with the stupid remark, "The higher
classes do not wear them to the theatre."

The Reverend had been an army chaplain during
the war, and while we were hunting for a road that
would lead to Hamilton he told a story about two

dying soldiers which interested me in spite of my feet.
He said that in the Potomac hospitals rough pine
coffins were furnished by government, but that it was
not always possible to keep up with the demand ; so,
when a man died, if there was no coffin at hand he
was buried without one.   One night, late, two soldiers
lay dying in a ward.   A man came in with a coffin on
his shoulder, and stood trying to make up his mind
which of these two poor fellows would be likely to need
it first.   Both of them begged for it with their fading
eyes, — they were past talking.   Then one of them
protruded a wasted hand from his blankets and made
a feeble beckoning sign with the fingers, to signify,
"Be a good fellow; put it under my bed, please."
The man did it, and left.   The lucky soldier painfully
turned himself in his bed until he faced the other war-
rior, raised himself partly on his elbow, and began to
work up a mysterious expression of some kind in his
face.   Gradually, irksomely, but surely and steadily,
it developed, and at last it took definite form as a
pretty successful *wink*.   The sufferer fell back exhausted with his labor, but bathed in glory.   Now
entered a personal friend of No. 2, the despoiled soldier.
No. 2 pleaded with him with eloquent eyes, till presently he understood, and removed the coffin from
under No. 1's bed and put it under No. 2's.   No. 2
indicated his joy, and made some more signs; the
friend understood again, and put his arm under No.
2's shoulders and lifted him partly up.   Then the dying hero turned the dim exultation of his eye upon
No. 1, and began a slow and labored work with his

hands; gradually he lifted one hand up toward his face; it grew weak and dropped back again; once more he made the effort, but failed again. He took a rest; he gathered all the remnant of his strength, and this time he slowly but surely carried his thumb to the side of his nose, spread the gaunt fingers wide in triumph, and dropped back dead. That picture sticks by me yet. The "situation" is unique.

The next morning, at what seemed a very early hour, the little white table-waiter appeared suddenly in my room and shot a single word out of himself: "Breakfast!"

This was a remarkable boy in many ways. He was about eleven years old; he had alert, intent black eyes; he was quick of movement; there was no hesitation, no uncertainty about him anywhere; there was a military decision in his lip, his manner, his speech, that was an astonishing thing to see in a little chap like him; he wasted no words; his answers always came so quick and brief that they seemed to be part of the question that had been asked instead of a reply to it. When he stood at table with his fly-brush, rigid, erect, his face set in a cast-iron gravity, he was a statue till he detected a dawning want in somebody's eye; then he pounced down, supplied it, and was instantly a statue again. When he was sent to the kitchen for anything, he marched upright till he got to the door; he turned hand-springs the rest of the way.

"Breakfast!"

I thought I would make one more effort to get some conversation out of this being.

" Have you called the Reverend, or are — "

" Yes s'r ! "

" Is it early, or is — "

" Eight-five ! "

" Do you have to do all the 'chores,' or is there somebody to give you a l— "

" Colored girl ! "

" Is there only one parish in this island, or are there — "

" Eight ! "

" Is the big church on the hill a parish church, or is it — "

" Chapel-of-ease ! "

" Is taxation here classified into poll, parish, town, and — "

" Don't know ! "

Before I could cudgel another question out of my head, he was below, hand-springing across the back yard. He had slid down the balusters, head-first. I gave up trying to provoke a discussion with him. The essential element of discussion had been left out of him ; his answers were so final and exact that they did not leave a doubt to hang conversation on. I suspect that there is the making of a mighty man or a mighty rascal in this boy, — according to circumstances, — but they are going to apprentice him to a carpenter. It is the way the world uses its opportunities.

During this day and the next we took carriage drives about the island and over to the town of St. George's, fifteen or twenty miles away. Such hard, excellent roads to drive over are not to be found elsewhere out

of Europe. An intelligent young colored man drove
us, and acted as guide-book. In the edge of the town
we saw five or six mountain-cabbage palms (atrocious
name!) standing in a straight row, and equidistant
from each other. These were not the largest or the
tallest trees I have ever seen, but they were the state
liest, the most majestic. That row of them must be
the nearest that nature has ever come to counterfeit-
ing a colonnade. These trees are all the same height,
say sixty feet; the trunks as gray as granite, with a
very gradual and perfect taper; without sign of branch
or knot or flaw; the surface not looking like bark, but
like granite that has been dressed and not polished.
Thus all the way up the diminishing shaft for fifty
feet; then it begins to take the appearance of being
closely wrapped, spool-fashion, with gray cord, or of
having been turned in a lathe. Above this point there
is an outward swell, and thence upwards, for six feet
or more, the cylinder is a bright, fresh green, and is
formed of wrappings like those of an ear of green
Indian corn. Then comes the great, spraying palm
plume, also green. Other palm-trees always lean out
of the perpendicular, or have a curve in them. But
the plumb-line could not detect a deflection in any
individual of this stately row; they stand as straight
as the colonnade of Baalbec; they have its great
height, they have its gracefulness, they have its dignity; in moonlight or twilight, and shorn of their
plumes, they would duplicate it.

The birds we came across in the country were singularly tame; even that wild creature, the quail, would

pick around in the grass at ease while we inspected it and talked about it at leisure. A small bird of the canary species had to be stirred up with the butt-end of the whip before it would move, and then it moved only a couple of feet. It is said that even the suspicious flea is tame and sociable in Bermuda, and will allow himself to be caught and caressed without misgivings. This should be taken with allowance, for doubtless there is more or less brag about it. In San Francisco they used to claim that their native flea could kick a child over, as if it were a merit in a flea to be able to do that; as if the knowledge of it trumpeted abroad ought to entice immigration. Such a thing in nine cases out of ten would be almost sure to deter a thinking man from coming.

We saw no bugs or reptiles to speak of, and so I was thinking of saying in print, in a general way, that there were none at all; but one night after I had gone to bed, the Reverend came into my room carrying something, and asked, " Is this your boot ? " I said it was, and he said he had met a spider going off with it. Next morning he stated that just at dawn the same spider raised his window and was coming in to get a shirt, but saw him and fled.

I inquired, " Did he get the shirt ? "

" No."

" How did you know it was a shirt he was after ? "

" I could see it in his eye."

We inquired around, but could hear of no Bermudian spider capable of doing these things. Citizens said that their largest spiders could not more than spread their legs over an ordinary saucer, and that they had always been considered honest. Here was testimony of a clergyman against the testimony of mere worldlings, — interested ones, too. On the whole, I judged it best to lock up my things.

Here and there on the country roads we found lemon, papaia, orange, lime, and fig trees; also several sorts of palms, among them the cocoa, the date, and the palmetto. We saw some bamboos forty feet high, with stems as thick as a man's arm. Jungles of the mangrove-tree stood up out of swamps, propped on their interlacing roots as upon a tangle of stilts. In dryer places the noble tamarind sent down its grateful cloud of shade. Here and there the blossomy tamarisk adorned the roadside. There was a curious gnarled and twisted black tree, without a single leaf on it. It might have passed itself off for a dead apple-tree but for the fact that it had a star-like, red-hot flower sprinkled sparsely over its person. It had the scattery red glow that a constellation might have when glimpsed through smoked glass. It is possible that our constellations have been so constructed as to be invisible through smoked glass; if this is so it is a great mistake.

We saw a tree that bears grapes, and just as calmly and unostentatiously as a vine would do it. We saw an India-rubber tree, but out of season, possibly, so there were no shoes on it, nor suspenders, nor anything that a person would properly expect to find there. This gave it an impressively fraudulent look. There was exactly one mahogany-tree on the island. I know this to be reliable, because I saw a man who said he had counted it many a time and could not be mistaken. He was a man with a hare lip and a pure heart, and everybody said he was as true as steel. Such men are all too few.

One's eye caught near and far the pink cloud of the oleander and the red blaze of the pomegranate blossom. In one piece of wild wood the morning-glory vines had wrapped the trees to their very tops, and decorated them all over with couples and clusters of great blue bells, — a fine and striking spectacle, at a little distance. But the dull cedar is everywhere, and its is the prevailing foliage. One does not appreciate how dull it is until the varnished, bright green attire of the infrequent lemon-tree pleasantly intrudes its contrast. In one thing Bermuda is eminently tropical, — was in May, at least, — the unbrilliant, slightly faded, unrejoicing look of the landscape. For forests arrayed in a blemishless magnificence of glowing green foliage that seems to exult in its own existence and can move the beholder to an enthusiasm that will make him either shout or cry, one must go to countries that have malignant winters.

We saw scores of colored farmers digging their crops of potatoes and onions, their wives and children helping, — entirely contented and comfortable, if looks go for anything. We never met a man, or woman, or child anywhere in this sunny island who seemed to be unprosperous, or discontented, or sorry about anything. This sort of monotony became very tiresome presently, and even something worse. The spectacle of an entire nation grovelling in contentment is an infuriating thing. We felt the lack of something in this community, — a vague, an undefinable, an elusive something, and yet a lack. But after considerable thought we made out what it was, — tramps. Let them go there, right now, in a body. It is utterly virgin soil. Passage is cheap. Every true patriot in America will help buy tickets. Whole armies of these excellent beings can be spared from our midst and our polls; they will find a delicious climate and a green, kind-hearted people. There are potatoes and onions for all, and a generous welcome for the first batch that arrives, and elegant graves for the second.

It was the Early Rose potato the people were digging. Later in the year they have another crop, which they call the Garnet. We buy their potatoes (retail) at fifteen dollars a barrel; and those colored farmers buy ours for a song, and live on them. Havana might exchange cigars with Connecticut in the same advantageous way, if she thought of it.

We passed a roadside grocery with a sign up, "Potatoes Wanted." An ignorant stranger, doubtless. He could not have gone thirty steps from his place without finding plenty of them.

In several fields the arrowroot crop was already sprouting. Bermuda used to make a vast annual profit out of this staple before fire-arms came into such general use.

The island is not large. Somewhere in the interior a man ahead of us had a very slow horse. I suggested that we had better go by him; but the driver said the man had but a little way to go. I waited to see, wondering how he could know. Presently the man did turn down another road. I asked, "How did you know he would?"

"Because I knew the man, and where he lived."

I asked him, satirically, if he knew everybody in the island; he answered, very simply, that he did. This gives a body's mind a good substantial grip on the dimensions of the place.

At the principal hotel in St. George's, a young girl, with a sweet, serious face, said we could not be furnished with dinner, because we had not been expected, and no preparation had been made. Yet it was still an hour before dinner time. We argued, she yielded not; we supplicated, she was serene. The hotel had not been expecting an inundation of two people, and so it seemed that we should have to go home dinnerless. I said we were not very hungry; a fish would do. My little maid answered, it was not the market-day for fish. Things began to look serious; but presently the boarder who sustained the hotel came in, and when the case was laid before him he was cheerfully willing to divide. So we had much pleasant chat at table about St. George's chief industry, the repairing of damaged ships; and in between we had a soup that had something in it that seemed to taste like the hereafter, but it proved to be only pepper of a particularly vivacious kind. And we had an iron-clad chicken that was deliciously cooked, but not in the right way. Baking was not the thing to convince his sort. He ought to have been put through a quartz mill until the "tuck" was taken out of him, and then boiled till we came again. We got a good deal of sport out of him, but not enough sustenance to leave the victory on our side. No matter; we had potatoes and a pie and a sociable good time. Then a ramble through the town, which is a quaint one, with interesting, crooked streets, and narrow, crooked lanes, with here and there a grain of dust. Here, as in Hamilton, the dwellings had Venetian blinds of a very sensible pattern. They were not double shutters, hinged at the sides, but a single broad shutter, hinged at the top; you push it outward, from the bottom, and fasten it at any angle required by the sun or desired by yourself.

All about the island one sees great white scars on the hill-slopes. These are dished spaces where the soil has been scraped off and the coral exposed and glazed with hard whitewash. Some of these are a quarter-acre in size. They catch and carry the rainfall to reservoirs; for the wells are few and poor, and there are no natural springs and no brooks.

They say that the Bermuda climate is mild and equable, with never any snow or ice, and that one may be very comfortable in spring clothing the year round, there. We had delightful and decided summer weather in May, with a flaming sun that permitted the thinnest of raiment, and yet there was a constant breeze; consequently we were never discomforted by heat. At four or five in the afternoon the mercury began to go down, and then it became necessary to change to thick garments. I went to St. George's in the morning clothed in the thinnest of linen, and reached home at

five in the afternoon with two overcoats on. The
nights are said to be always cool and bracing. We
had mosquito nets, and the Reverend said the mosquitoes persecuted him a good deal. I often heard
him slapping and banging at these imaginary creatures
with as much zeal as if they had been real. There
are no mosquitoes in the Bermudas in May.

The poet Thomas Moore spent several months in
Bermuda more than seventy years ago. He was sent
out to be registrar of the admiralty. I am not quite
clear as to the function of a registrar of the admiralty
of Bermuda, but I think it is his duty to keep a record
of all the admirals born there. I will inquire into this.
There was not much doing in admirals, and Moore got
tired and went away. A reverently preserved souvenir
of him is still one of the treasures of the islands. I
gathered the idea, vaguely, that it was a jug, but was
persistently thwarted in the twenty-two efforts I made
to visit it. However, it was no matter, for I found
afterwards that it was only a chair.

There are several "sights" in the Bermudas, of
course, but they are easily avoided. This is a great
advantage, — one cannot have it in Europe. Bermuda
is the right country for a jaded man to "loaf" in.
There are no harassments; the deep peace and quiet
of the country sink into one's body and bones and give
his conscience a rest, and chloroform the legion of
invisible small devils that are always trying to whitewash his hair. A good many Americans go there
about the first of March and remain until the early
spring weeks have finished their villanies at home.

The Bermudians are hoping soon to have telegraphic communication with the world. But even after they shall have acquired this curse it will still be a good country to go to for a vacation, for there are charming little islets scattered about the enclosed sea where one could live secure from interruption. The telegraph boy would have to come in a boat, and one could easily kill him while he was making his landing.

We had spent four days in Bermuda,—three bright ones out of doors and one rainy one in the house, we being disappointed about getting a yacht for a sail; and now our furlough was ended, and we entered into the ship again and sailed homeward.

Among the passengers was a most lean and lank and forlorn invalid, whose weary look and patient eyes and sorrowful mien awoke every one's kindly interest and stirred every one's compassion. When he spoke — which was but seldom — there was a gentleness in his tones that made each hearer his friend. The second night of the voyage — we were all in the smoking cabin at the time — he drifted, little by little, into the general conversation. One thing brought on another, and so, in due course, he happened to fall into the biographical vein, and the following strange narrative was the result.

THE INVALID'S STORY.[1]

I seem sixty and married, but these effects are due to my condition and sufferings, for I am a bachelor,

---

[1] Left out of these "Rambling Notes," when originally published in the "Atlantic Monthly," because it was feared that the

and only forty-one. It will be hard for you to believe that I, who am now but a shadow, was a hale, hearty man two short years ago, — a man of iron, a very athlete! — yet such is the simple truth. But stranger still than this fact is the way in which I lost my health. I lost it through helping to take care of a box of guns on a two-hundred-mile railway journey one winter's night. It is the actual truth, and I will tell you about it.

I belong in Cleveland, Ohio. One winter's night, two years ago, I reached home just after dark, in a driving snow-storm, and the first thing I heard when I entered the house was that my dearest boyhood friend and schoolmate, John B. Hackett, had died the day before, and that his last utterance had been a desire that I would take his remains home to his poor old father and mother in Wisconsin. I was greatly shocked and grieved, but there was no time to waste in emotions; I must start at once. I took the card, marked "Deacon Levi Hackett, Bethlehem, Wisconsin," and hurried off through the whistling storm to the railway station. Arrived there I found the long white-pine box which had been described to me; I fastened the card to it with some tacks, saw it put safely aboard the express car, and then ran into the eating-room to provide myself with a sandwich and some cigars. When I returned, presently, there was my coffin-box *back again,* apparently, and a young fellow examining around it, with a card in his hand, and some tacks and

story was not true, and at that time there was no way of proving that it was not. — M. T.

a hammer! I was astonished and puzzled. He began
to nail on his card, and I rushed out to the express
car, in a good deal of a state of mind, to ask for an
explanation. But no — there was my box, all right, in
the express car; it had n't been disturbed. [The fact
is that without my suspecting it a prodigious mistake
had been made. I was carrying off a box of *guns*
which that young fellow had come to the station to
ship to a rifle company in Peoria, Illinois, and *he* had
got my corpse!] Just then the conductor sung out
"All aboard," and I jumped into the express car
and got a comfortable seat on a bale of buckets. The
expressman was there, hard at work, — a plain man of
fifty, with a simple, honest, good-natured face, and a
breezy, practical heartiness in his general style. As
the train moved off a stranger skipped into the car
and set a package of peculiarly mature and capable
Limburger cheese on one end of my coffin-box — I
mean my box of guns. That is to say, I know *now*
that it was Limburger cheese, but at that time I never
had heard of the article in my life, and of course
was wholly ignorant of its character. Well, we sped
through the wild night, the bitter storm raged on, a
cheerless misery stole over me, my heart went down,
down, down! The old expressman made a brisk
remark or two about the tempest and the arctic
weather, slammed his sliding doors to, and bolted
them, closed his window down tight, and then went
bustling around, here and there and yonder, setting
things to rights, and all the time contentedly humming "Sweet By and By," in a low tone, and flatting

a good deal. Presently I began to detect a most evil and searching odor stealing about on the frozen air. This depressed my spirits still more, because of course I attributed it to my poor departed friend. There was something infinitely saddening about his calling himself to my remembrance in this dumb pathetic way, so it was hard to keep the tears back. Moreover, it distressed me on account of the old expressman, who, I was afraid, might notice it. However, he went humming tranquilly on, and gave no sign; and for this I was grateful. Grateful, yes, but still uneasy; and soon I began to feel more and more uneasy every minute, for every minute that went by that odor thickened up the more, and got to be more and more gamey and hard to stand. Presently, having got things arranged to his satisfaction, the expressman got some wood and made up a tremendous fire in his stove. This distressed me more than I can tell, for I could not but feel that it was a mistake. I was sure that the effect would be deleterious upon my poor departed friend. Thompson — the expressman's name was Thompson, as I found out in the course of the night — now went poking around his car, stopping up whatever stray cracks he could find, remarking that it did n't make any difference what kind of a night it was outside, he calculated to make *us* comfortable, anyway. I said nothing, but I believed he was not choosing the right way. Meantime he was humming to himself just as before; and meantime, too, the stove was getting hotter and hotter, and the place closer and closer. I felt myself growing pale and qualmish, but

7

grieved in silence and said nothing. Soon I noticed that the "Sweet By and By" was gradually fading cut; next it ceased altogether, and there was an ominous stillness. After a few moments Thompson said, —

"Pfew! I reckon it ain't no cinnamon 't I've loaded up thish-yer stove with!"

He gasped once or twice, then moved toward the cof— gun-box, stood over that Limburger cheese part of a moment, then came back and sat down near me, looking a good deal impressed. After a contemplative pause, he said, indicating the box with a gesture, —

"Friend of yourn?"

"Yes," I said with a sigh.

"He's pretty ripe, *ain't* he!"

Nothing further was said for perhaps a couple of minutes, each being busy with his own thoughts; then Thompson said, in a low, awed voice, —

"Sometimes it's uncertain whether they're really gone or not, — *seem* gone, you know — body warm, joints limber — and so, although you *think* they're gone, you don't really know. I've had cases in my car. It's perfectly awful, becuz *you* don't know what minute they'll rise right up and look at you!" Then, after a pause, and slightly lifting his elbow toward the box, — "But *he* ain't in no trance! No, sir, I go bail for *him!*"

We sat some time, in meditative silence, listening to the wind and the roar of the train; then Thompson said, with a good deal of feeling, —

"Well-a-well, we've all got to go, they ain't no getting around it. Man that is born of woman is of few

days and far between, as Scriptur' says. Yes, you look
at it any way you want to, it's awful solemn and cu-
r'us: they ain't *nobody* can get around it; *all's* got to
go — just *everybody*, as you may say. One day you're
hearty and strong " — here he scrambled to his feet
and broke a pane and stretched his nose out at it a
moment or two, then sat down again while I struggled
up and thrust my nose out at the same place, and this
we kept on doing every now and then — " and next
day he's cut down like the grass, and the places which
knowed him then knows him no more forever, as Scriptur' says. Yes-'ndeedy, it's awful solemn and cur'us;
but we've all got to go, one time or another; they ain't
no getting around it."

There was another long pause; then, —

" What did he die of?"

I said I didn't know.

" How long has he ben dead?"

It seemed judicious to enlarge the facts to fit the
probabilities; so I said, —

" Two or three days."

But it did no good; for Thompson received it with
an injured look which plainly said, " Two or three *years*,
you mean." Then he went right along, placidly ignor-
ing my statement, and gave his views at considerable
length upon the unwisdom of putting off burials too
long. Then he lounged off toward the box, stood a
moment, then came back on a sharp trot and visited
the broken pane, observing, —

" 'T would 'a' ben a dum sight better, all around, if
they'd started him along last summer."

Thompson sat down and buried his face in his red silk handkerchief, and began to slowly sway and rock his body like one who is doing his best to endure the almost unendurable. By this time the fragrance — if you may call it fragrance — was just about suffocating, as near as you can come at it. Thompson's face was turning gray; I knew mine had n't any color left in it. By and by Thompson rested his forehead in his left hand, with his elbow on his knee, and sort of waved his red handkerchief towards the box with his other hand, and said, —

"I 've carried a many a one of 'em, — some of 'em considerable overdue, too, — but, lordy, he just lays over 'em all ! — and does it *easy.* Cap., they was heliotrope to *him !*"

This recognition of my poor friend gratified me, in spite of the sad circumstances, because it had so much the sound of a compliment.

Pretty soon it was plain that something had got to be done. I suggested cigars. Thompson thought it was a good idea. He said, —

"Likely it 'll modify him some."

We puffed gingerly along for a while, and tried hard to imagine that things were improved. But it was n't any use. Before very long, and without any consultation, both cigars were quietly dropped from our nerveless fingers at the same moment. Thompson said, with a sigh, —

"No, Cap., it don't modify him worth a cent. Fact is, it makes him worse, becuz it appears to stir up his ambition. What do you reckon we better do, now ?"

I was not able to suggest anything; indeed, I had to be swallowing and swallowing, all the time, and did not like to trust myself to speak. Thompson fell to maundering, in a desultory and low-spirited way, about the miserable experiences of this night; and he got to referring to my poor friend by various titles, — sometimes military ones, sometimes civil ones ; and I noticed that as fast as my poor friend's effectiveness grew, Thompson promoted him accordingly, — gave him a bigger title. Finally he said, —

"I 've got an idea. Suppos'n' we buckle down to it and give the Colonel a bit of a shove towards t' other end of the car ? — about ten foot, say. He would n't have so much influence, then, don't you reckon ?"

I said it was a good scheme. So we took in a good fresh breath at the broken pane, calculating to hold it till we got through ; then we went there and bent down over that deadly cheese and took a grip on the box. Thompson nodded " All ready," and then we threw ourselves forward with all our might ; but Thompson slipped, and slumped down with his nose on the cheese, and his breath got loose. He gagged and gasped, and floundered up and made a break for the door, pawing the air and saying, hoarsely, " Don't hender me ! — gimme the road ! I 'm a-dying ; gimme the road !" Out on the cold platform I sat down and held his head a while, and he revived. Presently he said, —

" Do you reckon we started the Gen'rul any ?"

I said no ; we had n't budged him.

" Well, then, *that* idea 's up the flume. We got to

think up something else. He's suited wher' he is, I reckon; and if that's the way he feels about it, and has made up his mind that he don't wish to be disturbed, you bet you he's a-going to have his own way in the business. Yes, better leave him right wher' he is, long as he wants it so; becuz he holds all the trumps, don't you know, and so it stands to reason that the man that lays out to alter his plans for him is going to get left."

But we could n't stay out there in that mad storm; we should have frozen to death. So we went in again and shut the door, and began to suffer once more and take turns at the break in the window. By and by, as we were starting away from a station where we had stopped a moment Thompson pranced in cheerily, and exclaimed, —

"We're all right, now! I reckon we've got the Commodore this time. I judge I've got the stuff here that'll take the tuck out of him."

It was carbolic acid. He had a carboy of it. He sprinkled it all around everywhere; in fact he drenched everything with it, rifle-box, cheese, and all. Then we sat down, feeling pretty hopeful. But it was n't for long. You see the two perfumes began to mix, and then — well, pretty soon we made a break for the door; and out there Thompson swabbed his face with his bandanna and said in a kind of disheartened way, —

"It ain't no use. We can't buck agin *him*. He just utilizes everything we put up to modify him with, and gives it his own flavor and plays it back on us. Why, Cap., don't you know, it's as much as a hundred

times worse in there now than it was when he first
got a-going. I never *did* see one of 'em warm up to
his work so, and take such a dumnation interest in it.
No, sir, I never did, as long as I 've ben on the road;
and I 've carried a many a one of 'em, as I was telling you."

We went in again, after we were frozen pretty stiff;
but my, we could n't *stay* in, now. So we just waltzed
back and forth, freezing, and thawing, and stifling, by
turns. In about an hour we stopped at another station; and as we left it Thompson came in with a bag,
and said, —

"Cap., I 'm a-going to chance him once more, —
just this once; and if we don't fetch him this time, the
thing for us to do, is to just throw up the sponge and
withdraw from the canvass. That 's the way *I* put
it up."

He had brought a lot of chicken feathers, and dried
apples, and leaf tobacco, and rags, and old shoes, and
sulphur, and assafœtida, and one thing or another; and
he piled them on a breadth of sheet iron in the middle
of the floor, and set fire to them. When they got well
started, I could n't see, myself, how even the corpse
could stand it. All that went before was just simply
poetry to that smell, — but mind you, the original smell
stood up out of it just as sublime as ever, — fact is,
these other smells just seemed to give it a better hold;
and my, how rich it was! I did n't make these reflec-
tions there — there was n't time — made them on the
platform. And breaking for the platform, Thompson
got suffocated and fell; and before I got him dragged

out, which I did by the collar, I was mighty near gone myself. When we revived, Thompson said dejectedly, —

"We got to stay out here, Cap. We got to do it. They ain't no other way. The Governor wants to travel alone, and he's fixed so he can outvote us."

And presently he added, —

"And don't you know, we're *pisoned*. It's *our* last trip, you can make up your mind to it. Typhoid fever is what's going to come of this. I feel it a-coming right now. Yes, sir, we're elected, just as sure as you're born."

We were taken from the platform an hour later, frozen and insensible, at the next station, and I went straight off into a virulent fever, and never knew anything again for three weeks. I found out, then, that I had spent that awful night with a harmless box of rifles and a lot of innocent cheese; but the news was too late to save *me;* imagination had done its work, and my health was permanently shattered; neither Bermuda nor any other land can ever bring it back to me. This is my last trip; I am on my way home to die.

We made the run home to New York quarantine in three days and five hours, and could have gone right along up to the city if we had had a health permit. But health permits are not granted after seven in the evening, partly because a ship cannot be inspected and overhauled with exhaustive thoroughness except in daylight, and partly because health officers are liable to catch cold if they expose themselves to the night air. Still, you can *buy* a permit after hours for five dollars extra, and the officer will do the inspecting next week. Our ship and passengers lay under expense and in humiliating captivity all night, under the very nose of the little official reptile who is supposed to protect New York from pestilence by his vigilant "inspections." This imposing rigor gave everybody a solemn and awful idea of the beneficent watchfulness of our government, and there were some who wondered if anything finer could be found in other countries.

In the morning we were all a-tiptoe to witness the intricate ceremony of inspecting the ship. But it was a disappointing thing. The health officer's tug ranged alongside for a moment, our purser handed the lawful three-dollar permit fee to the health officer's bootblack, who passed us a folded paper in a forked stick, and away we went. The entire "inspection" did not occupy thirteen seconds.

The health officer's place is worth a hundred thousand dollars a year to him. His system of inspection is perfect, and therefore cannot be improved on ; but it seems to me that his system of collecting his fees might be amended. For a great ship to lie idle all night is a most costly loss of time ; for her passengers to have to do the same thing works to them the same damage, with the addition of an amount of exasperation and bitterness of soul that the spectacle of that health officer's ashes on a shovel could hardly sweeten. Now why would it not be better and simpler to let the ships pass in unmolested, and the fees and permits be exchanged once a year by post ?

THE FACTS CONCERNING THE RECENT CAR-
NIVAL OF CRIME IN CONNECTICUT.

———◆———

I WAS feeling blithe, almost jocund. I put a match
to my cigar, and just then the morning's mail was
handed in. The first superscription I glanced at was
in a handwriting that sent a thrill of pleasure through
and through me. It was Aunt Mary's; and she was
the person I loved and honored most in all the world,
outside of my own household. She had been my boyhood's idol; maturity, which is fatal to so many en-
chantments, had not been able to dislodge her from
her pedestal; no, it had only justified her right to
be there, and placed her dethronement permanently
among the impossibilities. To show how strong her
influence over me was, I will observe that long after
everybody else's "*do*-stop-smoking" had ceased to
affect me in the slightest degree, Aunt Mary could
still stir my torpid conscience into faint signs of life
when she touched upon the matter. But all things
have their limit, in this world. A happy day came at
last, when even Aunt Mary's words could no longer
move me. I was not merely glad to see that day
arrive; I was more than glad — I was grateful; for
when its sun had set, the one alloy that was able to
mar my enjoyment of my aunt's society was gone.

The remainder of her stay with us that winter was in every way a delight. Of course she pleaded with me just as earnestly as ever, after that blessed day, to quit my pernicious habit, but to no purpose whatever; the moment she opened the subject I at once became calmly, peacefully, contentedly indifferent — absolutely, adamantinely indifferent. Consequently the closing weeks of that memorable visit melted away as pleasantly as a dream, they were so freighted, for me, with tranquil satisfaction. I could not have enjoyed my pet vice more if my gentle tormentor had been a smoker herself, and an advocate of the practice. Well, the sight of her handwriting reminded me that I was getting very hungry to see her again. I easily guessed what I should find in her letter. I opened it. Good! just as I expected; she was coming! Coming this very day, too, and by the morning train; I might expect her any moment.

I said to myself, "I am thoroughly happy and content, now. If my most pitiless enemy could appear before me at this moment, I would freely right any wrong I may have done him."

Straightway the door opened, and a shrivelled, shabby dwarf entered. He was not more than two feet high. He seemed to be about forty years old. Every feature and every inch of him was a trifle out of shape; and so, while one could not put his finger upon any particular part and say, "This is a conspicuous deformity," the spectator perceived that this little person was a deformity as a whole, — a vague, general, evenly blended, nicely adjusted deformity. There was a foxlike cunning in the face and the sharp little eyes, and also alertness and malice. And yet, this vile bit of human rubbish seemed to bear a sort of remote and ill-defined resemblance to me! It was dully perceptible in the mean form, the countenance, and even the clothes, gestures, manner, and attitudes of the creature. He was a far-fetched, dim suggestion of a burlesque upon me, a caricature of me in little. One thing about him struck me forcibly, and most unpleasantly : he was covered all over with a fuzzy, greenish mould, such as one sometimes sees upon mildewed bread. The sight of it was nauseating.

He stepped along with a chipper air, and flung himself into a doll's chair in a very free and easy way, without waiting to be asked. He tossed his hat into the waste basket. He picked up my old chalk pipe from the floor, gave the stem a wipe or two on his knee, filled the bowl from the tobacco-box at his side, and said to me in a tone of pert command, —

"Gimme a match !"

I blushed to the roots of my hair; partly with indignation, but mainly because it somehow seemed to me that this whole performance was very like an exaggeration of conduct which I myself had sometimes been guilty of in my intercourse with familiar friends, — but never, never with strangers, I observed to myself. I wanted to kick the pygmy into the fire, but some incomprehensible sense of being legally and legitimately under his authority forced me to obey his order. He applied the match to the pipe, took a contemplative whiff or two, and remarked, in an irritatingly familiar way, —

"Seems to me it's devilish odd weather for this time of year."

I flushed again, and in anger and humiliation as before; for the language was hardly an exaggeration of some that I have uttered in my day, and moreover was delivered in a tone of voice and with an exasperating drawl that had the seeming of a deliberate travesty of my style. Now there is nothing I am quite so sensitive about as a mocking imitation of my drawling infirmity of speech. I spoke up sharply and said, —

"Look here, you miserable ash-cat! you will have to give a little more attention to your manners, or I will throw you out of the window!"

The manikin smiled a smile of malicious content and security, puffed a whiff of smoke contemptuously toward me, and said, with a still more elaborate drawl, —

"Come — go gently, now; don't put on *too* many airs with your betters."

This cool snub rasped me all over, but it seemed to subjugate me, too, for a moment. The pygmy contemplated me awhile with his weasel eyes, and then said, in a peculiarly sneering way, —

"You turned a tramp away from your door this morning."

I said crustily, —

"Perhaps I did, perhaps I didn't. How do *you* know?"

"Well, I know. It isn't any matter *how* I know."

"Very well. Suppose I *did* turn a tramp away from the door — what of it?"

"Oh, nothing; nothing in particular. Only you lied to him."

"I *did n't!* That is, I — "

"Yes, but you did; you lied to him."

I felt a guilty pang, — in truth I had felt it forty times before that tramp had travelled a block from my door, — but still I resolved to make a show of feeling slandered; so I said, —

"This is a baseless impertinence. I said to the tramp — "

"There — wait. You were about to lie again. *I* know what you said to him. You said the cook was gone down town and there was nothing left from breakfast. Two lies. You knew the cook was behind the door, and plenty of provisions behind *her*."

This astonishing accuracy silenced me; and it filled me with wondering speculations, too, as to how this cub could have got his information. Of course he could have culled the conversation from the tramp, but by what sort of magic had he contrived to find out about the concealed cook? Now the dwarf spoke again : —

"It was rather pitiful, rather small, in you to refuse to read that poor young woman's manuscript the other day, and give her an opinion as to its literary value; and she had come so far, too, and *so* hopefully. Now *was n't* it?"

I felt like a cur! And I had felt so every time the thing had recurred to my mind, I may as well confess. I flushed hotly and said, —

"Look here, have you nothing better to do than prowl around prying into other people's business? Did that girl tell you that?"

"Never mind whether she did or not. The main thing is, you did that contemptible thing. And you felt ashamed of it afterwards. Aha! you feel ashamed of it *now!*"

This with a sort of devilish glee. With fiery earnestness I responded, —

"I told that girl, in the kindest, gentlest way, that I could not consent to deliver judgment upon *any* one's manuscript, because an individual's verdict was worthless. It might underrate a work of high merit and lose it to the world, or it might overrate a trashy production and so open the way for its infliction upon the world. I said that the great public was the only tribunal competent to sit in judgment upon a literary effort, and therefore it must be best to lay it before that tribunal in the outset, since in the end it must stand or fall by that mighty court's decision any way."

"Yes, you said all that. So you did, you juggling, small-souled shuffler! And yet when the happy hopefulness faded out of that poor girl's face, when you saw her furtively slip beneath her shawl the scroll she had so patiently and honestly scribbled at, — so ashamed of her darling now, so proud of it before, — when you saw the gladness go out of her eyes and the tears come there, when she crept away so humbly who had come so —"

"Oh, peace! peace! peace! Blister your merciless tongue, have n't all these thoughts tortured me enough, without *your* coming here to fetch them back again?"

Remorse! remorse! It seemed to me that it would

eat the very heart out of me! And yet that small fiend only sat there leering at me with joy and contempt, and placidly chuckling. Presently he began to speak again. Every sentence was an accusation, and every accusation a truth. Every clause was freighted with sarcasm and derision, every slow-dropping word burned like vitriol. The dwarf reminded me of times when I had flown at my children in anger and punished them for faults which a little inquiry would have taught me that others, and not they, had committed. He reminded me of how I had disloyally allowed old friends to be traduced in my hearing, and been too craven to utter a word in their defence. He reminded me of many dishonest things which I had done; of many which I had procured to be done by children and other irresponsible persons; of some which I had planned, thought upon, and longed to do, and been kept from the performance by fear of consequences only. With exquisite cruelty he recalled to my mind, item by item, wrongs and unkindnesses I had inflicted and humiliations I had put upon friends since dead, "who died thinking of those injuries, maybe, and grieving over them," he added, by way of poison to the stab.

"For instance," said he, "take the case of your younger brother, when you two were boys together, many a long year ago. He always lovingly trusted in you with a fidelity that your manifold treacheries were not able to shake. He followed you about like a dog, content to suffer wrong and abuse if he might only be with you; patient under these injuries so long as it was your hand that inflicted them. The latest picture you have of him in health and strength must be such a comfort to you! You pledged your honor that if he would let you blindfold him no harm should come to him; and then, giggling and choking over the rare fun of the joke, you led him to a brook thinly glazed with ice, and pushed him in; and how you did laugh! Man, you will never forget the gentle, reproachful look he gave you as he struggled shivering out, if you live a thousand years! Oho! you see it now, you see it *now !*"

"Beast, I have seen it a million times, and shall see it a million more! and may you rot away piecemeal, and suffer till doomsday what I suffer now, for bringing it back to me again!"

The dwarf chuckled contentedly, and went on with his accusing history of my career. I dropped into a moody, vengeful state, and suffered in silence under the merciless lash. At last this remark of his gave me a sudden rouse :—

"Two months ago, on a Tuesday, you woke up, away in the night, and fell to thinking, with shame, about a peculiarly mean and pitiful act of yours toward a poor ignorant Indian in the wilds of the Rocky Mountains in the winter of eighteen hundred and —"

"Stop a moment, devil! Stop! Do you mean to tell me that even my very *thoughts* are not hidden from you?"

"It seems to look like that. Did n't you think the thoughts I have just mentioned?"

"If I did n't, I wish I may never breathe again!

Look here, friend — look me in the eye. Who *are* you?"

"Well, who do you think?"

"I think you are Satan himself. I think you are the devil."

"No."

"No? Then who *can* you be?"

"Would you really like to know?"

"*Indeed* I would."

"Well, I am your *Conscience!*"

In an instant I was in a blaze of joy and exultation. I sprang at the creature, roaring, —

"Curse you, I have wished a hundred million times that you were tangible, and that I could get my hands on your throat once! Oh, but I will wreak a deadly vengeance on —"

Folly! Lightning does not move more quickly than my Conscience did! He darted aloft so suddenly that in the moment my fingers clutched the empty air he was already perched on the top of the high book-case, with his thumb at his nose in token of derision. I flung the poker at him, and missed. I fired the boot-jack. In a blind rage I flew from place to place, and snatched and hurled any missile that came handy; the storm of books, inkstands, and chunks of coal gloomed the air and beat about the manikin's perch relentlessly, but all to no purpose; the nimble figure dodged every shot; and not only that, but burst into a cackle of sarcastic and triumphant laughter as I sat down exhausted. While I puffed and gasped with fatigue and excitement, my Conscience talked to this effect : —

"My good slave, you are curiously witless — no, I mean characteristically so. In truth, you are always consistent, always yourself, always an ass. Otherwise it must have occurred to you that if you attempted this murder with a sad heart and a heavy conscience, I would droop under the burdening influence instantly. Fool, I should have weighed a ton, and could not have budged from the floor ; but instead, you are so cheerfully anxious to kill me that your conscience is as light as a feather ; hence I am away up here out of your reach. I can almost respect a mere ordinary sort of fool ; but *you* — pah ! "

I would have given anything, then, to be heavy-hearted, so that I could get this person down from there and take his life, but I could no more be heavy-hearted over such a desire than I could have sorrowed over its accomplishment. So I could only look longingly up at my master, and rave at the ill-luck that denied me a heavy conscience the one only time that I had ever wanted such a thing in my life. By and by I got to musing over the hour's strange adventure, and of course my human curiosity began to work. I set myself to framing in my mind some questions for this fiend to answer. Just then one of my boys entered, leaving the door open behind him, and exclaimed, —

"My ! what *has* been going on, here ? The bookcase is all one riddle of — "

I sprang up in consternation, and shouted, —

"Out of this ! Hurry ! Jump ! Fly ! Shut the door ! Quick, or my Conscience will get away ! "

The door slammed to, and I locked it. I glanced up and was grateful, to the bottom of my heart, to see that my owner was still my prisoner. I said, —

"Hang you, I might have lost you! Children are the heedlessest creatures. But look here, friend, the boy did not seem to notice you at all; how is that?"

"For a very good reason. I am invisible to all but you."

I made mental note of that piece of information with a good deal of satisfaction. I could kill this miscreant now, if I got a chance, and no one would know it. But this very reflection made me so light-hearted that my Conscience could hardly keep his seat, but was like to float aloft toward the ceiling like a toy balloon. I said, presently, —

"Come, my Conscience, let us be friendly. Let us fly a flag of truce for a while. I am suffering to ask you some questions."

"Very well. Begin."

"Well, then, in the first place, why were you never visible to me before?"

"Because you never asked to see me before; that is, you never asked in the right spirit and the proper form before. You were just in the right spirit this time, and when you called for your most pitiless enemy I was that person by a very large majority, though you did not suspect it."

"Well, did that remark of mine turn you into flesh and blood?"

"No. It only made me visible to you. I am unsubstantial, just as other spirits are."

This remark prodded me with a sharp misgiving. If he was unsubstantial, how was I going to kill him? But I dissembled, and said persuasively, —

"Conscience, it isn't sociable of you to keep at such a distance. Come down and take another smoke."

This was answered with a look that was full of derision, and with this observation added : —

"Come where you can get at me and kill me? The invitation is declined with thanks."

"All right," said I to myself; "so it seems a spirit *can* be killed, after all; there will be one spirit lacking in this world, presently, or I lose my guess." Then I said aloud, —

"Friend — "

"There ; wait a bit. I am not your friend, I am your enemy ; I am not your equal, I am your master. Call me 'my lord,' if you please. You are too familiar."

"I don't like such titles. I am willing to call you *sir*. That is as far as — "

"We will have no argument about this. Just obey ; that is all. Go on with your chatter."

"Very well, my lord, — since nothing but my lord will suit you, — I was going to ask you how long you will be visible to me?"

"Always!"

I broke out with strong indignation : "This is simply an outrage. That is what I think of it. You have dogged, and dogged, and *dogged* me, all the days of my life, invisible. That was misery enough ; now to have such a looking thing as you tagging after me like another shadow all the rest of my days is an intolerable prospect. You have my opinion, my lord; make the most of it."

" My lad, there was never so pleased a conscience in this world as I was when you made me visible. It gives me an inconceivable advantage. *Now*, I can look you straight in the eye, and call you names, and leer at you, jeer at you, sneer at you; and *you* know what eloquence there is in visible gesture and expression, more especially when the effect is heightened by audible speech. I shall always address you henceforth in your o-w-n s-n-i-v-e-l-l-i-n-g d-r-a-w-l — baby ! "

I let fly with the coal-hod. No result. My lord said, —

" Come, come ! Remember the flag of truce ! "

" Ah, I forgot that. I will try to be civil; and *you* try it, too, for a novelty. The idea of a *civil* conscience ! It is a good joke ; an excellent joke. All the consciences *I* have ever heard of were nagging, badgering, fault-finding, execrable savages ! Yes ; and always in a sweat about some poor little insignificant trifle or other — destruction catch the lot of them, *I* say ! I would trade mine for the small-pox and seven kinds of consumption, and be glad of the chance. Now tell me, why *is* it that a conscience can't haul a man over the coals once, for an offence, and then let him alone ? Why is it that it wants to keep on pegging at him, day and night and night and day, week in and week out, forever and ever, about the same old thing ? There is no sense in that, and no reason in it. I think a conscience that will act like that is meaner than the very dirt itself."

"Well, *we* like it; that suffices."

"Do you do it with the honest intent to improve a man?"

That question produced a sarcastic smile, and this reply:—

"No, sir. Excuse me. We do it simply because it is 'business.' It is our trade. The *purpose* of it *is* to improve the man, but *we* are merely disinterested agents. We are appointed by authority, and have n't anything to say in the matter. We obey orders and leave the consequences where they belong. But I am willing to admit this much: we *do* crowd the orders a trifle when we get a chance, which is most of the time. We enjoy it. We are instructed to remind a man a few times of an error; and I don't mind acknowledging that we try to give pretty good measure. And when we get hold of a man of a peculiarly sensitive nature, oh, but we do haze him! I have known consciences to come all the way from China and Russia to see a person of that kind put through his paces, on a special occasion. Why, I knew a man of that sort who had accidentally crippled a mulatto baby; the news went abroad, and I wish you may never commit another sin if the consciences did n't flock from all over the earth to enjoy the fun and help his master exercise him. That man walked the floor in torture for forty-eight hours, without eating or sleeping, and then blew his brains out. The child was perfectly well again in three weeks."

"Well, you are a precious crew, not to put it too strong. I think I begin to see, now, why you have always been a trifle inconsistent with me. In your anxiety to get all the juice you can out of a sin, you make a man repent of it in three or four different ways. For instance, you found fault with me for lying to that tramp, and I suffered over that. But it was only yesterday that I told a tramp the square truth, to wit, that, it being regarded as bad citizenship to encourage vagrancy, I would give him nothing. What did you do *then?* Why, you made me say to myself, 'Ah, it would have been so much kinder and more blameless to ease him off with a little white lie, and send him away feeling that if he could not have bread, the gentle treatment was at least something to be grateful for!' Well, I suffered all day about *that.* Three days before, I had fed a tramp, and fed him freely, supposing it a virtuous act. Straight off you said, 'O false citizen, to have fed a tramp!' and I suffered as usual. I gave a tramp work; you objected to it, — *after* the contract was made, of course; you never speak up beforehand. Next, I *refused* a tramp work; you objected to *that.* Next, I proposed to kill a tramp; you kept me awake all night, oozing remorse at every pore. Sure I was going to be right *this* time, I sent the next tramp away with my benediction; and I wish you may live as long as I do, if you did n't make me smart all night again because I did n't kill him. Is there *any* way of satisfying that malignant invention which is called a conscience?"

"Ha, ha! this is luxury! Go on!"

"But come, now, answer me that question. *Is* there any way?"

"Well, none that I propose to tell *you*, my son. Ass! I don't care *what* act you may turn your hand to, I can straightway whisper a word in your ear and make you think you have committed a dreadful meanness. It is my *business* — and my joy — to make you repent of *every*thing you do. If I have fooled away any opportunities it was not intentional; I beg to assure you it was not intentional!"

"Don't worry; you have n't missed a trick that *I* know of. I never did a thing in all my life, virtuous or otherwise, that I did n't repent of within twenty-four hours. In church last Sunday I listened to a charity sermon. My first impulse was to give three hundred and fifty dollars; I repented of that and reduced it a hundred; repented of that and reduced it another hundred; repented of that and reduced it another hundred; repented of that and reduced the remaining fifty to twenty-five; repented of that and came down to fifteen; repented of that and dropped to two dollars and a half; when the plate came around at last, I repented once more and contributed ten cents. Well, when I got home, I did wish to goodness I had that ten cents back again! You never *did* let me get through a charity sermon without having something to sweat about."

"Oh, and I never shall, I never shall. You can always depend on me."

"I think so. Many and many 's the restless night l 've wanted to take you by the neck. If I could only get hold of you now!"

"Yes, no doubt. But I am not an ass; I am only

the saddle of an ass. But go on, go on. You enter-
tain me more than I like to confess."

"I am glad of that. (You will not mind my lying
a little, to keep in practice.) Look here; not to be too
personal, I think you are about the shabbiest and most
contemptible little shrivelled-up reptile that can be
imagined. I am grateful enough that you are invisible to other people, for I should die with shame to be
seen with such a mildewed monkey of a conscience
as *you* are. Now if you were five or six feet high,
and — "

"Oh, come! who is to blame?"

"*I* don't know."

"Why, you are; nobody else."

"Confound you, I was n't consulted about your personal appearance."

"I don't care, you had a good deal to do with it,
nevertheless. When you were eight or nine years old,
I was seven feet high, and as pretty as a picture."

"I wish you had died young! So you have grown
the wrong way, have you?"

"Some of us grow one way and some the other.
You had a large conscience once; if you 've a small
conscience now, I reckon there are reasons for it.
However, both of us are to blame, you and I. You
see, you used to be conscientious about a great many
things; morbidly so, I may say. It was a great many
years ago. You probably do not remember it, now.
Well, I took a great interest in my work, and I so
enjoyed the anguish which certain pet sins of yours
afflicted you with, that I kept pelting at you until I

rather overdid the matter. You began to rebel. Of course I began to lose ground, then, and shrivel a little, — diminish in stature, get mouldy, and grow deformed. The more I weakened, the more stubbornly you fastened on to those particular sins; till at last the places on my person that represent those vices became as callous as shark skin. Take smoking, for instance. I played that card a little too long, and I lost. When people plead with you at this late day to quit that vice, that old callous place seems to enlarge and cover me all over like a shirt of mail. It exerts a mysterious, smothering effect; and presently I, your faithful hater, your devoted Conscience, go sound asleep! Sound? It is no name for it. I couldn't hear it thunder at such a time. You have some few other vices — perhaps eighty, or maybe ninety — that affect me in much the same way."

"This is flattering; you must be asleep a good part of your time."

"Yes, of late years. I should be asleep *all* the time, but for the help I get."

"Who helps you?"

"Other consciences. Whenever a person whose conscience I am acquainted with tries to plead with you about the vices you are callous to, I get my friend to give his client a pang concerning some villany of his own, and that shuts off his meddling and starts him off to hunt personal consolation. My field of usefulness is about trimmed down to tramps, budding authoresses, and that line of goods, now; but don't you worry — I'll harry you on *them* while they last! Just you put your trust in me."

"I think I can. But if you had only been good enough to mention these facts some thirty years ago, I should have turned my particular attention to him, and I think that by this time I should not only have had you pretty permanently asleep on the entire list of human vices, but reduced to the size of a homœopathic pill, at that. That is about the style of conscience *I* am pining for. If I only had you shrunk down to a homœopathic pill, and could get my hands on you, would I put you in a glass case for a keepsake? No, sir. I would give you to a yellow dog! That is where *you* ought to be — you and all your tribe. You are not fit to be in society, in my opinion. Now another question. Do you know a good many consciences in this section?"

"Plenty of them."

"I would give anything to see some of them! Could you bring them here? And would they be visible to me?"

"Certainly not."

"I suppose I ought to have known that, without asking. But no matter, you can describe them. Tell me about my neighbor Thompson's conscience, please."

"Very well. I know him intimately; have known him many years. I knew him when he was eleven feet high and of a faultless figure. But he is very rusty and tough and misshapen, now, and hardly ever interests himself about anything. As to his present size — well, he sleeps in a cigar box."

"Likely enough. There are few smaller, meaner men in this region than Hugh Thompson. Do you know Robinson's conscience?"

"Yes. He is a shade under four and a half feet high; used to be a blonde; is a brunette, now, but still shapely and comely."

"Well, Robinson is a good fellow. Do you know Tom Smith's conscience?"

"I have known him from childhood. He was thirteen inches high, and rather sluggish, when he was two years old — as nearly all of us are, at that age. He is thirty-seven feet high, now, and the stateliest figure in America. His legs are still racked with growing-pains, but he has a good time, nevertheless. Never sleeps. He is the most active and energetic member of the New England Conscience Club; is president of it. Night and day you can find him pegging away at Smith, panting with his labor, sleeves rolled up, countenance all alive with enjoyment. He has got his victim splendidly dragooned, now. He can make poor Smith imagine that the most innocent little thing he does is an odious sin; and then he sets to work and almost tortures the soul out of him about it."

"Smith is the noblest man in all this section, and the purest; and yet is always breaking his heart because he cannot be good! Only a conscience *could* find pleasure in heaping agony upon a spirit like that. Do you know my aunt Mary's conscience?"

"I have seen her at a distance, but am not acquainted with her. She lives in the open air altogether, because no door is large enough to admit her."

"I can believe that. Let me see. Do you know the conscience of that publisher who once stole some sketches of mine for a 'series' of his, and then left me to pay the law expenses I had to incur in order to choke him off?"

"Yes. He has a wide fame. He was exhibited, a month ago, with some other antiquities, for the benefit of a recent Member of the Cabinet's conscience, that was starving in exile. Tickets and fares were high, but I travelled for nothing by pretending to be the conscience of an editor, and got in for half price by representing myself to be the conscience of a clergyman. However, the publisher's conscience, which was to have been the main feature of the entertainment, was a failure — as an exhibition. He was there, but what of that? The management had provided a microscope with a magnifying power of only thirty thousand diameters, and so nobody got to see him, after all. There was great and general dissatisfaction, of course, but — "

Just here there was an eager footstep on the stair ; I opened the door, and my aunt Mary burst into the room. It was a joyful meeting, and a cheery bombardment of questions and answers concerning family matters ensued. By and by my aunt said, —

"But I am going to abuse you a little now. You promised me, the day I saw you last, that you would look after the needs of the poor family around the corner as faithfully as I had done it myself. Well, I found out by accident that you failed of your promise. *Was* that right?"

In simple truth, I never had thought of that family a second time! And now such a splintering pang of guilt shot through me! I glanced up at my Conscience. Plainly, my heavy heart was affecting him. His body was drooping forward; he seemed about to fall from the book-case. My aunt continued : —

"And think how you have neglected my poor *protégée* at the almshouse, you dear, hard-hearted promise-breaker!" I blushed scarlet, and my tongue was tied. As the sense of my guilty negligence waxed sharper and stronger, my Conscience began to sway heavily back and forth; and when my aunt, after a little pause, said in a grieved tone, "Since you never once went to see her, maybe it will not distress you now to know that that poor child died, months ago, utterly friendless and forsaken!" my Conscience could no longer bear up under the weight of my sufferings, but tumbled headlong from his high perch and struck the floor with a dull, leaden thump. He lay there writhing with pain and quaking with apprehension, but straining every muscle in frantic efforts to get up. In a fever of expectancy I sprang to the door, locked it, placed my back against it, and bent a watchful gaze upon my struggling master. Already my fingers were itching to begin their murderous work.

"Oh, what *can* be the matter!" exclaimed my aunt, shrinking from me, and following with her frightened eyes the direction of mine. My breath was coming in short, quick gasps now, and my excitement was almost uncontrollable. My aunt cried out, —

"Oh, do not look so! You appall me! Oh, what can the matter be? What is it you see? Why do you stare so? Why do you work your fingers like that?"

"Peace, woman!" I said, in a hoarse whisper. "Look elsewhere; pay no attention to me; it is nothing — nothing. I am often this way. It will pass in a moment. It comes from smoking too much."

My injured lord was up, wild-eyed with terror, and trying to hobble toward the door. I could hardly breathe, I was so wrought up. My aunt wrung her hands, and said, —

"Oh, I knew how it would be; I knew it would come to this at last! Oh, I implore you to crush out that fatal habit while it may yet be time! You must not, you shall not be deaf to my supplications longer!" My struggling Conscience showed sudden signs of weariness! "Oh, promise me you will throw off this hateful slavery of tobacco!" My Conscience began to reel drowsily, and grope with his hands — enchanting spectacle! "I beg you, I beseech you, I implore you! Your reason is deserting you! There is madness in your eye! It flames with frenzy! Oh, hear me, hear me, and be saved! See, I plead with you on my very knees!" As she sank before me my Conscience reeled again, and then drooped languidly to the floor, blinking toward me a last supplication for mercy, with heavy eyes. "Oh, promise, or you are lost! Promise, and be redeemed! Promise! Promise and live!" With a long-drawn sigh my conquered Conscience closed his eyes and fell fast asleep!

With an exultant shout I sprang past my aunt, and in an instant I had my life-long foe by the throat. After so many years of waiting and longing, he was

mine at last. I tore him to shreds and fragments. I
rent the fragments to bits. I cast the bleeding rubbish
into the fire, and drew into my nostrils the grateful
incense of my burnt-offering. At last, and forever, my
Conscience was dead!

I was a free man! I turned upon my poor aunt,
who was almost petrified with terror, and shouted, —

"Out of this with your paupers, your charities, your
reforms, your pestilent morals! You behold before
you a man whose life-conflict is done, whose soul is at
peace; a man whose heart is dead to sorrow, dead to
suffering, dead to remorse; a man WITHOUT A CON-
SCIENCE! In my joy I spare you, though I could
throttle you and never feel a pang! Fly!"

She fled. Since that day my life is all bliss. Bliss,
unalloyed bliss. Nothing in all the world could persuade me to have a conscience again. I settled all
my old outstanding scores, and began the world anew.
I killed thirty-eight persons during the first two weeks
— all of them on account of ancient grudges. I burned
a dwelling that interrupted my view. I swindled a
widow and some orphans out of their last cow, which
is a very good one, though not thoroughbred, I believe. I have also committed scores of crimes, of
various kinds, and have enjoyed my work exceedingly,
whereas it would formerly have broken my heart and
turned my hair gray, I have no doubt.

In conclusion I wish to state, by way of advertisement, that medical colleges desiring assorted tramps
for scientific purposes, either by the gross, by cord

9

measurement, or per ton, will do well to examine the lot in my cellar before purchasing elsewhere, as these were all selected and prepared by myself, and can be had at a low rate, because I wish to clear out my stock and get ready for the spring trade.

ABOUT MAGNANIMOUS–INCIDENT LITERATURE.

———◆———

ALL my life, from boyhood up, I have had the habit of reading a certain set of anecdotes, written in the quaint vein of The World's ingenious Fabulist, for the lesson they taught me and the pleasure they gave me. They lay always convenient to my hand, and whenever I thought meanly of my kind I turned to them, and they banished that sentiment; whenever I felt myself to be selfish, sordid, and ignoble I turned to them, and they told me what to do to win back my self-respect. Many times I wished that the charming anecdotes had not stopped with their happy climaxes, but had continued the pleasing history of the several benefactors and beneficiaries. This wish rose in my breast so persistently that at last I determined to satisfy it by seeking out the sequels of those anecdotes myself. So I set about it, and after great labor and tedious research accomplished my task. I will lay the result before you, giving you each anecdote in its turn, and following it with its sequel as I gathered it through my investigations.

THE GRATEFUL POODLE.

One day a benevolent physician (who had read the books) having found a stray poodle suffering from a broken leg, conveyed the poor creature to his home, and after setting and bandaging the injured limb gave the little outcast its liberty again, and thought no more about the matter. But how great was his surprise, upon opening his door one morning, some days later, to find the grateful poodle patiently waiting there, and in its company another stray dog, one of whose legs, by some accident, had been broken. The kind physician at once relieved the distressed animal, nor did he forget to admire the inscrutable goodness and mercy of God, who had been willing to use so humble an instrument as the poor outcast poodle for the inculcating of, etc., etc., etc.

SEQUEL.

The next morning the benevolent physician found the two dogs, beaming with gratitude, waiting at his door, and with them two other dogs, — cripples. The cripples were speedily healed, and the four went their way, leaving the benevolent physician more overcome by pious wonder than ever. The day passed, the morning came. There at the door sat now the four reconstructed dogs, and with them four others requiring reconstruction. This day also passed, and another morning came ; and now sixteen dogs, eight of them newly crippled, occupied the sidewalk, and the people were going around. By noon the broken legs were all set, but the pious wonder in the good physician's breast was beginning to get mixed with involuntary profanity. The sun rose once more, and exhibited thirty-two dogs, sixteen of them with broken legs, occupying the sidewalk and half of the street; the human spectators took up the rest of the room. The cries of the wounded, the songs of the healed brutes, and the comments of the on-looking citizens made great and inspiring cheer, but traffic was interrupted in that street. The good physician hired a couple of assistant surgeons and got through his benevolent work before dark, first taking the precaution to cancel his church membership, so that he might express himself with the latitude which the case required.

But some things have their limits. When once more the morning dawned, and the good physician looked out upon a massed and far-reaching multitude of clamorous and beseeching dogs, he said, "I might as well acknowledge it, I have been fooled by the books; they only tell the pretty part of the story, and then stop. Fetch me the shot-gun; this thing has gone along far enough."

He issued forth with his weapon, and chanced to step upon the tail of the original poodle, who promptly bit him in the leg. Now the great and good work which this poodle had been engaged in had engendered in him such a mighty and augmenting enthusiasm as to turn his weak head at last and drive him mad. A month later, when the benevolent physician lay in the death throes of hydrophobia, he called his weeping friends about him, and said, —

"Beware of the books. They tell but half of the story. Whenever a poor wretch asks you for help, and you feel a doubt as to what result may flow from your benevolence, give yourself the benefit of the doubt and kill the applicant."

And so saying he turned his face to the wall and gave up the ghost.

THE BENEVOLENT AUTHOR.

A poor and young literary beginner had tried in vain to get his manuscripts accepted. At last, when the horrors of starvation were staring him in the face, he laid his sad case before a celebrated author, beseech-ing his counsel and assistance. This generous man immediately put aside his own matters and proceeded to peruse one of the despised manuscripts. Having completed his kindly task, he shook the poor young man cordially by the hand, saying, "I perceive merit in this; come again to me on Monday." At the time specified, the celebrated author, with a sweet smile, but saying nothing, spread open a magazine which was damp from the press. What was the poor young man's astonishment to discover upon the printed page his own article. "How can I ever," said he, falling upon his knees and bursting into tears, "testify my gratitude for this noble conduct!" The celebrated author was the renowned Snodgrass; the poor young beginner thus rescued from obscurity and starvation was the afterwards equally renowned Snagsby. Let this pleasing incident admonish us to turn a charitable ear to all beginners that need help.

SEQUEL.

The next week Snagsby was back with five rejected manuscripts. The celebrated author was a little surprised, because in the books the young struggler had needed but one lift, apparently. However, he ploughed through these papers, removing unnecessary flowers and digging up some acres of adjective-stumps, and then succeeded in getting two of the articles accepted.

A week or so drifted by, and the grateful Snagsby arrived with another cargo. The celebrated author had felt a mighty glow of satisfaction within himself the first time he had successfully befriended the poor young struggler, and had compared himself with the generous people in the books with high gratification; but he was beginning to suspect now that he had struck upon something fresh in the noble-episode line. His enthusiasm took a chill. Still, he could not bear to repulse this struggling young author, who clung to him with such pretty simplicity and trustfulness.

· Well, the upshot of it all was that the celebrated author presently found himself permanently freighted with the poor young beginner. All his mild efforts to unload his cargo went for nothing. He had to give daily counsel, daily encouragement; he had to keep on procuring magazine acceptances, and then revamping the manuscripts to make them presentable. When the young aspirant got a start at last, he rode into sudden fame by describing the celebrated author's private life with such a caustic humor and such minuteness of blistering detail that the book sold a prodigious edition, and broke the celebrated author's heart with mortification. With his latest gasp he said, " Alas, the books deceived me ; they do not tell the whole story. Beware of the struggling young author, my friends. Whom God sees fit to starve, let not man presumptuously rescue to his own undoing."

THE GRATEFUL HUSBAND.

One day a lady was driving through the principal street of a great city with her little boy, when the horses took fright and dashed madly away, hurling the coachman from his box and leaving the occupants of the carriage paralyzed with terror. But a brave youth who was driving a grocery wagon threw himself before the plunging animals, and succeeded in arresting their flight at the peril of his own.[1] The grateful lady took his number, and upon arriving at her home she related the heroic act to her husband (who had read the books), who listened with streaming eyes to the moving recital, and who, after returning thanks, in conjunction with his restored loved ones, to Him who suffereth not even a sparrow to fall to the ground unnoticed, sent for the brave young person, and, placing a check for five hundred dollars in his hand, said, " Take this as a reward for your noble act, William Ferguson, and if ever you shall need a friend, remember that Thompson McSpadden has a grateful heart." Let us learn from this that a good deed cannot fail to benefit the doer, however humble he may be.

[1] This is probably a misprint. — M. T.

SEQUEL.

William Ferguson called the next week and asked Mr. McSpadden to use his influence to get him a higher employment, he feeling capable of better things than driving a grocer's wagon. Mr. McSpadden got him an under-clerkship at a good salary.

Presently William Ferguson's mother fell sick, and William — Well, to cut the story short, Mr. McSpadden consented to take her into his house. Before long she yearned for the society of her younger children; so Mary and Julia were admitted also, and little Jimmy, their brother. Jimmy had a pocket-knife, and he wandered into the drawing-room with it one day, alone, and reduced ten thousand dollars' worth of furniture to an indeterminable value in rather less than three quarters of an hour. A day or two later he fell downstairs and broke his neck, and seventeen of his family's relatives came to the house to attend the funeral. This made them acquainted, and they kept the kitchen occupied after that, and likewise kept the McSpaddens busy hunting up situations of various sorts for them, and hunting up more when they wore these out. The old woman drank a good deal and swore a good deal; but the grateful McSpaddens knew it was their duty to reform her, considering what her son had done for them, so they clave nobly to their generous task. William came often and got decreasing sums of money, and asked for higher and more lucrative employments, — which the grateful McSpadden more or less promptly procured for him. McSpadden consented also, after some demur, to fit William for college ; but when the first vacation came and the hero requested to be sent to Europe for his health, the persecuted McSpadden rose against the tyrant and revolted. He plainly and squarely refused. William Ferguson's mother was so astounded that she let her gin-bottle drop, and her profane lips refused to do their office. When she recovered she said in a half-gasp, " Is this your gratitude ? Where would your wife and boy be now, but for my son ? "

William said, " Is this your gratitude ? Did I save your wife's life or not ? tell me that ! "

Seven relations swarmed in from the kitchen and each said, " And this is his gratitude ! "

William's sisters stared, bewildered, and said, " And this is his grat— " but were interrupted by their mother, who burst into tears and exclaimed, " To think that my sainted little Jimmy threw away his life in the service of such a reptile ! "

Then the pluck of the revolutionary McSpadden rose to the occasion, and he replied with fervor, " Out of my house, the whole beggarly tribe of you ! I was beguiled by the books, but shall never be beguiled again, — once is sufficient for me." And turning to William he shouted, " Yes, you did save my wife's life, and the next man that does it shall die in his tracks ! "

Not being a clergyman, I place my text at the end of my sermon instead of at the beginning. Here it is, from Mr. Noah Brooks's Recollections of President Lincoln, in " Scribner's Monthly " : —

" J. H. Hackett, in his part of Falstaff, was an actor who gave Mr. Lincoln great delight. With his usual desire to signify to others his sense of obligation, Mr. Lincoln wrote a genial little note to the actor, expressing his pleasure at witnessing his performance. Mr. Hackett, in reply, sent a book of some sort; perhaps it was one of his own authorship. He also wrote several notes to the President. One night, quite late, when the episode had passed out of my mind, I went to the White House in answer to a message. Passing into the President's office, I noticed, to my surprise, Hackett sitting in the anteroom as if waiting for an audience. The President asked me if any one was outside. On being told, he said, half sadly, ' Oh, I can't see him, I can't see him ; I was in hopes he had gone away.' Then he added, ' Now this just illustrates the difficulty of having pleasant friends and acquaintances in this place. You know how I liked Hackett as an actor, and how I wrote to tell him so. He sent me that book, and there I thought the matter would end. He is a master of his place in the profession, I suppose, and well fixed in it ; but just because we had a little friendly correspondence, such as any two men might have, he wants something. What do you suppose he wants ?' I could not guess, and Mr. Lincoln added, ' Well, he wants to be consul to London. Oh, dear ! ' "

I will observe, in conclusion, that the William Ferguson incident occurred, and within my personal knowledge, — though I have changed the nature of the details, to keep William from recognizing himself in it.

All the readers of this article have in some sweet and gushing hour of their lives played the rôle of Magnanimous-Incident hero. I wish I knew how many there are among them who are willing to talk about that episode and like to be reminded of the consequences that flowed from it.

PUNCH, BROTHERS, PUNCH.

———◆———

WILL the reader please to cast his eye over the following verses, and see if he can discover anything harmful in them?

> "Conductor, when you receive a fare,
> Punch in the presence of the passenjare!
> A blue trip slip for an eight-cent fare,
> A buff trip slip for a six-cent fare,
> A pink trip slip for a three-cent fare,
> Punch in the presence of the passenjare!
>
> CHORUS.
> Punch, brothers! punch with care!
> Punch in the presence of the passenjare!"

I came across these jingling rhymes in a newspaper, a little while ago, and read them a couple of times. They took instant and entire possession of me. All through breakfast they went waltzing through my brain; and when, at last, I rolled up my napkin, I could not tell whether I had eaten anything or not. I had carefully laid out my day's work the day before, —a thrilling tragedy in the novel which I am writing. I went to my den to begin my deed of blood. I took up my pen, but all I could get it to say was, "Punch

in the presence of the passenjare." I fought hard for
an hour, but it was useless. My head kept humming,
"A blue trip slip for an eight-cent fare, a buff trip slip
for a six-cent fare," and so on and so on, without peace
or respite. The day's work was ruined — I could see
that plainly enough. I gave up and drifted down
town, and presently discovered that my feet were
keeping time to that relentless jingle. When I could
stand it no longer I altered my step. But it did no
good; those rhymes accommodated themselves to the
new step and went on harassing me just as before. I
returned home, and suffered all the afternoon; suffered
all through an unconscious and unrefreshing dinner;
suffered, and cried, and jingled all through the evening;
went to bed and rolled, tossed, and jingled right along,
the same as ever; got up at midnight frantic, and tried
to read; but there was nothing visible upon the whirling page except "Punch! punch in the presence of the
passenjare." By sunrise I was out of my mind, and
everybody marvelled and was distressed at the idiotic
burden of my ravings, — "Punch! oh, punch! punch
in the presence of the passenjare!"

Two days later, on Saturday morning, I arose, a tot-
tering wreck, and went forth to fulfil an engagement
with a valued friend, the Rev. Mr. ——, to walk to
the Talcott Tower, ten miles distant. He stared at
me, but asked no questions. We started. Mr. ——
talked, talked, talked — as is his wont. I said nothing; I heard nothing. At the end of a mile, Mr. ——
said, —

"Mark, are you sick? I never saw a man look so

haggard and worn and absent-minded. Say some-thing; do!"

Drearily, without enthusiasm, I said: "Punch, brothers, punch with care! Punch in the presence of the passenjare!"

My friend eyed me blankly, looked perplexed, then said, —

"I do not think I get your drift, Mark. There does not seem to be any relevancy in what you have said, certainly nothing sad; and yet — maybe it was the way you *said* the words — I never heard anything that sounded so pathetic. What is — "

But I heard no more. I was already far away with my pitiless, heart-breaking "blue trip slip for an eight-cent fare, buff trip slip for a six-cent fare, pink trip slip for a three-cent fare; punch in the presence of the passenjare." I do not know what occurred during the other nine miles. However, all of a sudden Mr. —— laid his hand on my shoulder and shouted, —

"Oh, wake up! wake up! wake up! Don't sleep all day! Here we are at the Tower, man! I have talked myself deaf and dumb and blind, and never got a response. Just look at this magnificent autumn landscape! Look at it! look at it! Feast your eyes on it! You have travelled; you have seen boasted landscapes elsewhere. Come, now, deliver an honest opinion. What do you say to this?"

I sighed wearily, and murmured, —

"A buff trip slip for a six-cent fare, a pink trip slip for a three-cent fare, punch in the presence of the passenjare."

Rev. Mr. —— stood there, very grave, full of concern, apparently, and looked long at me; then he said, —

"Mark, there is something about this that I cannot understand. Those are about the same words you said before; there does not seem to be anything in them, and yet they nearly break my heart when you say them. Punch in the — how is it they go?"

I began at the beginning and repeated all the lines. My friend's face lighted with interest. He said, —

"Why, what a captivating jingle it is! It is almost music. It flows along so nicely. I have nearly caught the rhymes myself. Say them over just once more, and then I'll have them, sure."

I said them over. Then Mr. —— said them. He made one little mistake, which I corrected. The next time and the next he got them right. Now a great burden seemed to tumble from my shoulders. That torturing jingle departed out of my brain, and a grateful sense of rest and peace descended upon me. I was light-hearted enough to sing; and I did sing for half an hour, straight along, as we went jogging homeward. Then my freed tongue found blessed speech again, and the pent talk of many a weary hour began to gush and flow. It flowed on and on, joyously, jubilantly, until the fountain was empty and dry. As I wrung my friend's hand at parting, I said, —

"Have n't we had a royal good time! But now I remember, you have n't said a word for two hours. Come, come, out with something!"

The Rev. Mr. —— turned a lack-lustre eye upon

me, drew a deep sigh, and said, without animation, without apparent consciousness, —

"Punch, brothers, punch with care ! Punch in the presence of the passenjare ! "

A pang shot through me as I said to myself, "Poor fellow, poor fellow ! *he* has got it, now."

I did not see Mr. —— for two or three days after that. Then, on Tuesday evening, he staggered into my presence and sank dejectedly into a seat. He was pale, worn ; he was a wreck. He lifted his faded eyes to my face and said, —

"Ah, Mark, it was a ruinous investment that I made in those heartless rhymes. They have ridden me like a nightmare, day and night, hour after hour, to this very moment. Since I saw you I have suffered the torments of the lost. Saturday evening I had a sudden call, by telegraph, and took the night train for Boston. The occasion was the death of a valued old friend who had requested that I should preach his funeral sermon. I took my seat in the cars and set myself to framing the discourse. But I never got beyond the opening paragraph ; for then the train started and the car-wheels began their 'clack, clack — clack-clack-clack ! clack, clack — clack-clack-clack ! ' and right away those odious rhymes fitted themselves to that accompaniment. For an hour I sat there and set a syllable of those rhymes to every separate and distinct clack the car-wheels made. Why, I was as fagged out, then, as if I had been chopping wood all day. My skull was splitting with headache. It seemed to me that I must go mad if I sat there any

10

longer ; so I undressed and went to bed. I stretched myself out in my berth, and — well, you know what the result was. The thing went right along, just the same. 'Clack-clack-clack, a blue trip slip, clack-clack-clack, for an eight-cent fare; clack-clack-clack, a buff trip slip, clack-clack-clack, for a six-cent fare, and so on, and so on, and so on — *punch,* in the presence of the passenjare !' Sleep? Not a single wink ! I was almost a lunatic when I got to Boston. Don't ask me about the funeral. I did the best I could, but every solemn individual sentence was meshed and tangled and woven in and out with 'Punch, brothers, punch with care, punch in the presence of the passenjare.' And the most distressing thing was that my *delivery* dropped into the undulating rhythm of those pulsing rhymes, and I could actually catch absent-minded people nodding *time* to the swing of it with their stupid heads. And, Mark, you may believe it or not, but before I got through, the entire assemblage were placidly bobbing their heads in solemn unison, mourn- ers, undertaker, and all. The moment I had finished, I fled to the anteroom in a state bordering on frenzy. Of course it would be my luck to find a sorrowing and aged maiden aunt of the deceased there, who had arrived from Springfield too late to get into the church. She began to sob, and said, —

" 'Oh, oh, he is gone, he is gone, and I did n't see him before he died !'

" 'Yes !' I said, 'he *is* gone, he *is* gone, he *is* gone — oh, *will* this suffering never cease ! '

" ' *You* loved him, then ! Oh, you too loved him ! '

" 'Loved him ! Loved *who ?* '

" ' Why, my poor George ! my poor nephew ! '

" ' Oh — *him !* Yes — oh, yes, yes. Certainly — certainly. Punch — punch — oh, this misery will kill me ! '

" ' Bless you ! bless you, sir, for these sweet words ! *I*, too, suffer in this dear loss. Were you present during his last moments ? '

" ' Yes ! I — *whose* last moments ? '

" ' *His.* The dear departed's.'

" ' Yes ! Oh, yes — yes — *yes !* I suppose so, I think so, *I* don't know ! Oh, certainly — I was there — *I* was there ! '

" ' Oh, what a privilege ! what a precious privilege ! And his last words — oh, tell me, tell me his last words ! What did he say ? '

" ' He said — he said — oh, my head, my head, my head ! He said — he said — he never said *any*thing but Punch, punch, *punch* in the presence of the passenjare ! Oh, leave me, madam ! In the name of all that is generous, leave me to my madness, my misery, my despair ! — a buff trip slip for a six-cent fare, a pink trip slip for a three-cent fare — endu-rance *can* no fur-ther go ! — PUNCH in the presence of the passenjare ! " '

My friend's hopeless eyes rested upon mine a pregnant minute, and then he said impressively, —

" Mark, you do not say anything. You do not offer me any hope. But, ah me, it is just as well — it is just as well. You could not do me any good. The time has long gone by when words could comfort me. Something tells me that my tongue is doomed to wag forever to the jigger of that remorseless jingle. There — there it is coming on me again : a blue trip slip for an eight-cent fare, a buff trip slip for a — "

Thus murmuring faint and fainter, my friend sank into a peaceful trance and forgot his sufferings in a blessed respite.

How did I finally save him from the asylum ? I took him to a neighboring university and made him discharge the burden of his persecuting rhymes into the eager ears of the poor, unthinking students. How is it with *them*, now ? The result is too sad to tell. Why did I write this article ? It was for a worthy, even a noble, purpose. It was to warn you, reader, if you should come across those merciless rhymes, to avoid them — avoid them as you would a pestilence !

A CURIOUS EXPERIENCE.

———◆———

THIS is the story which the Major told me, as
nearly as I can recall it : —

In the winter of 1862–3, I was commandant of Fort
Trumbull, at New London, Conn.   Maybe our life
there was not so brisk as life at "the front"; still it
was brisk enough, in its way — one's brains did n't
cake together there for lack of something to keep them
stirring.   For one thing, all the Northern atmosphere
at that time was thick with mysterious rumors —
rumors to the effect that rebel spies were flitting
everywhere, and getting ready to blow up our Northern forts, burn our hotels, send infected clothing into
our towns, and all that sort of thing.   You remember
it.   All this had a tendency to keep us awake, and
knock the traditional dulness out of garrison life.
Besides, ours was a recruiting station — which is the
same as saying we had n't any time to waste in dozing,
or dreaming, or fooling around.   Why, with all our
watchfulness, fifty per cent of a day's recruits would
leak out of our hands and give us the slip the same
night.   The bounties were so prodigious that a recruit

could pay a sentinel three or four hundred dollars to let him escape, and still have enough of his bounty-money left to constitute a fortune for a poor man. Yes, as I said before, our life was not drowsy.

Well, one day I was in my quarters alone, doing some writing, when a pale and ragged lad of fourteen or fifteen entered, made a neat bow, and said, —

"I believe recruits are received here?"

"Yes."

"Will you please enlist me, sir?"

"Dear me, no! You are too young, my boy, and too small."

A disappointed look came into his face, and quickly deepened into an expression of despondency. He turned slowly away, as if to go; hesitated, then faced me again, and said, in a tone which went to my heart, —

"I have no home, and not a friend in the world. If you *could* only enlist me!"

But of course the thing was out of the question, and I said so as gently as I could. Then I told him to sit down by the stove and warm himself, and added, —

"You shall have something to eat presently. You are hungry?"

He did not answer; he did not need to; the gratitude in his big soft eyes was more eloquent than any words could have been. He sat down by the stove, and I went on writing. Occasionally I took a furtive glance at him. I noticed that his clothes and shoes, although soiled and damaged, were of good style and material. This fact was suggestive. To it I added the facts that his voice was low and musical; his eyes deep and melancholy; his carriage and address gentlemanly; evidently the poor chap was in trouble. As a result, I was interested.

However, I became absorbed in my work, by and by, and forgot all about the boy. I don't know how long this lasted; but, at length, I happened to look up. The boy's back was toward me, but his face was turned in such a way that I could see one of his cheeks — and down that cheek a rill of noiseless tears was flowing.

"God bless my soul!" I said to myself; "I forgot the poor rat was starving." Then I made amends for my brutality by saying to him, "Come along, my lad; you shall dine with *me;* I am alone to-day."

He gave me another of those grateful looks, and a happy light broke in his face. At the table he stood with his hand on his chair-back until I was seated, then seated himself. I took up my knife and fork and — well, I simply held them, and kept still; for the boy had inclined his head and was saying a silent grace. A thousand hallowed memories of home and my childhood poured in upon me, and I sighed to think how far I had drifted from religion and its balm for hurt minds, its comfort and solace and support.

As our meal progressed, I observed that young Wicklow — Robert Wicklow was his full name — knew what to do with his napkin; and — well, in a word, I observed that he was a boy of good breeding; never mind the details. He had a simple frankness, too, which won upon me. We talked mainly about himself, and I had no difficulty in getting his history out of him. When he spoke of his having been born and reared in Louisiana, I warmed to him decidedly, for I had spent some time down there. I knew all the "coast" region of the Mississippi, and loved it, and had not been long enough away from it for my interest in it to begin to pale. The very names that fell from his lips sounded good to me, — so good that I steered the talk in directions that would bring them out. Baton Rouge, Plaquemine, Donaldsonville, Sixty-mile Point, Bonnet-Carre, the Stock-Landing, Carrollton, the Steamship Landing, the Steamboat Landing, New Orleans, Tchoupitoulas Street, the Esplanade, the Rue des Bons Enfants, the St. Charles Hotel, the Tivoli Circle, the Shell Road, Lake Pontchartrain; and it was particularly delightful to me to hear once more of the "R. E. Lee," the "Natchez," the "Eclipse," the "General Quitman," the "Duncan F. Kenner," and other old familiar steamboats. It was almost as good as being back there, these names so vividly reproduced in my mind the look of the things they stood for. Briefly, this was little Wicklow's history : —

When the war broke out, he and his invalid aunt and his father were living near Baton Rouge, on a great and rich plantation which had been in the family for fifty years. The father was a Union man. He was persecuted in all sorts of ways, but clung to his principles. At last, one night, masked men burned his mansion down, and the family had to fly for their lives. They were hunted from place to place, and learned all there was to know about poverty, hunger, and distress.

The invalid aunt found relief at last : misery and exposure killed her ; she died in an open field, like a
tramp, the rain beating upon her and the thunder
booming overhead. Not long afterward, the father was
captured by an armed band ; and while the son begged
and pleaded, the victim was strung up before his face.
[At this point a baleful light shone in the youth's eyes,
and he said, with the manner of one who talks to himself : " If I cannot be enlisted, no matter — I shall
find a way — I shall find a way."] As soon as the
father was pronounced dead, the son was told that if
he was not out of that region within twenty-four hours,
it would go hard with him. That night he crept to the
riverside and hid himself near a plantation landing.
By and by the " Duncan F. Kenner," stopped there,
and he swam out and concealed himself in the yawl
that was dragging at her stern. Before daylight the
boat reached the Stock-Landing, and he slipped ashore.
He walked the three miles which lay between that
point and the house of an uncle of his in Good-Children
Street, in New Orleans, and then his troubles were over
for the time being. But this uncle was a Union man,
too, and before very long he concluded that he had
better leave the South. So he and young Wicklow
slipped out of the country on board a sailing vessel,
and in due time reached New York. They put up at
the Astor House. Young Wicklow had a good time
of it for a while, strolling up and down Broadway, and
observing the strange Northern sights ; but in the end
a change came, — and not for the better. The uncle
had been cheerful at first, but now he began to look

troubled and despondent ; moreover, he became moody and irritable ; talked of money giving out, and no way to get more, — "not enough left for one, let alone two." Then, one morning, he was missing — did not come to breakfast. The boy inquired at the office, and was told that the uncle had paid his bill the night before and gone away — to Boston, the clerk believed, but was not certain.

The lad was alone and friendless. He did not know what to do, but concluded he had better try to follow and find his uncle. He went down to the steamboat landing ; learned that the trifle of money in his pocket would not carry him to Boston ; however, it would carry him to New London ; so he took passage for that port, resolving to trust to Providence to furnish him means to travel the rest of the way. He had now been wandering about the streets of New London three days and nights, getting a bite and a nap here and there for charity's sake. But he had given up at last ; courage and hope were both gone. If he could enlist, nobody could be more thankful ; if he could not get in as a soldier, could n't he be a drummer-boy ? Ah, he would work *so* hard to please, and would be so grateful !

Well, there 's the history of young Wicklow, just as he told it to me, barring details. I said, —

"My boy, you 're among friends, now, — don't you be troubled any more." How his eyes glistened ! I called in Sergeant John Rayburn, — he was from Hartford ; lives in Hartford yet ; maybe you know him, — and said, "Rayburn, quarter this boy with the musicians. I am going to enroll him as a drummer-boy, and I want you to look after him and see that he is well treated."

Well, of course, intercourse between the commandant of the post and the drummer-boy came to an end, now; but the poor little friendless chap lay heavy on my heart, just the same. I kept on the lookout, hoping to see him brighten up and begin to be cheery and gay; but no, the days went by, and there was no change. He associated with nobody; he was always absent-minded, always thinking; his face was always sad. One morning Rayburn asked leave to speak to me privately. Said he, —

"I hope I don't offend, sir; but the truth is, the musicians are in such a sweat it seems as if somebody's *got* to speak."

"Why, what is the trouble?"

"It 's the Wicklow boy, sir. The musicians are down on him to an extent you can't imagine."

"Well, go on, go on. What has he been doing?"

"Prayin', sir."

"Praying!"

"Yes, sir; the musicians have n't any peace of their life for that boy's prayin'. First thing in the morning he 's at it; noons he 's at it; and nights — well, *nights* he just lays into 'em like all possessed! Sleep? Bless you, they *can't* sleep: he 's got the floor, as the sayin' is, and then when he once gets his supplication-mill agoin', there just simply ain't any let-up *to* him. He starts in with the band-master, and he prays for him; next he takes the head bugler, and he prays for him; next the bass drum, and he scoops *him* in; and so on,

right straight through the band, givin' them all a
show, and takin' that amount of interest in it which
would make you think he thought he warn't but a
little while for this world, and believed he could n't be
happy in heaven without he had a brass band along,
and wanted to pick 'em out for himself, so he could
depend on 'em to do up the national tunes in a style
suitin' to the place. Well, sir, heavin' boots at him
don't have no effect; it's dark in there; and, besides,
he don't pray fair, anyway, but kneels down behind
the big drum; so it don't make no difference if they
rain boots at him, *he* don't give a dern — warbles right
along, same as if it was applause. They sing out,
'Oh, dry up!' 'Give us a rest!' 'Shoot him!' 'Oh,
take a walk!' and all sorts of such things. But what
of it? It don't phaze him. *He* don't mind it." After
a pause: "Kind of a good little fool, too; gits up in
the mornin' and carts all that stock of boots back, and
sorts 'em out and sets each man's pair where they belong. And they 've been throwed at him so much
now, that he knows every boot in the band, — can sort
'em out with his eyes shut."

After another pause, which I forbore to interrupt, —

"But the roughest thing about it is, that when he's
done prayin', — when he ever *does* get done, — he pipes
up and begins to *sing*. Well, you know what a honey
kind of a voice he's got when he talks; you know how
it would persuade a cast-iron dog to come down off of
a doorstep and lick his hand. Now if you'll take my
word for it, sir, it ain't a circumstance to his singin'!

Flute music is harsh to that boy's singin'. Oh, he just gurgles it out so soft and sweet and low, there in the dark, that it makes you think you are in heaven."

"What is there 'rough' about that?"

"Ah, that's just it, sir. You hear him sing

    " 'Just as I am — poor, wretched, blind,'

— just you hear him sing that, once, and see if you don't melt all up and the water come into your eyes! I don't care *what* he sings, it goes plum straight home to you — it goes deep down to where you *live* — and it fetches you every time! Just you hear him sing : —

    " 'Child of sin and sorrow, filled with dismay,
      Wait not till to-morrow, yield thee to-day ;
        Grieve not that love
        Which, from above ' —

and so on. It makes a body feel like the wickedest, ungratefulest brute that walks. And when he sings them songs of his about home, and mother, and childhood, and old memories, and things that's vanished, and old friends dead and gone, it fetches everything before your face that you've ever loved and lost in all your life — and it's just beautiful, it's just divine to listen to, sir — but, Lord, Lord, the heart-break of it! The band — well, they all cry — every rascal of them blubbers, and don't try to hide it, either; and first you know, that very gang that's been slammin' boots at that boy will skip out of their bunks all of a sudden, and rush over in the dark and hug him! Yes, they do — and slobber all over him, and call him pet names, and beg him to forgive them. And just at that time, if a regiment was to offer to hurt a hair of that cub's head, they 'd go for that regiment, if it was a whole army corps ! "

Another pause.

" Is that all ? " said I.

" Yes, sir."

" Well, dear me, what is the complaint ? What do they want done ? "

" Done ? Why, bless you, sir, they want you to stop him from *singin'*."

" What an idea ! You said his music was divine."

" That 's just it. It 's *too* divine. Mortal man can't stand it. It stirs a body up so ; it turns a body inside out ; it racks his feelin's all to rags ; it makes him feel bad and wicked, and not fit for any place but perdition. It keeps a body in such an everlastin' state of repentin', that nothin' don't taste good and there ain't no comfort in life. And then the *cryin'*, you see — every mornin' they are ashamed to look one another in the face."

" Well, this is an odd case, and a singular complaint. So they really want the singing stopped ? "

" Yes, sir, that is the idea. They don't wish to ask too much ; they would like powerful well to have the prayin' shut down on, or leastways trimmed off around the edges ; but the main thing 's the singin.' If they can only get the singin' choked off, they think they can stand the prayin', rough as it is to be bullyragged so much that way."

I told the sergeant I would take the matter under consideration. That night I crept into the musicians' quarters and listened. The sergeant had not over-stated the case. I heard the praying voice pleading in the dark; I heard the execrations of the harassed men; I heard the rain of boots whiz through the air, and bang and thump around the big drum. The thing touched me, but it amused me, too. By and by, after an impressive silence, came the singing. Lord, the pathos of it, the enchantment of it! Nothing in the world was ever so sweet, so gracious, so tender, so holy, so moving. I made my stay very brief; I was beginning to experience emotions of a sort not proper to the commandant of a fortress.

Next day I issued orders which stopped the praying and singing. Then followed three or four days which were so full of bounty-jumping excitements and irrita-tions that I never once thought of my drummer-boy. But now comes Sergeant Rayburn, one morning, and says, —

"That new boy acts mighty strange, sir."

"How?"

"Well, sir, he's all the time writing."

"Writing? What does he write — letters?"

"I don't know, sir; but whenever he's off duty, he is always poking and nosing around the fort, all by himself, — blest if I think there's a hole or corner in it he has n't been into, — and every little while he outs with pencil and paper and scribbles something down."

This gave me a most unpleasant sensation. I wanted to scoff at it, but it was not a time to scoff at *anything* that had the least suspicious tinge about it. Things were happening all around us, in the North, then, that

warned us to be always on the alert, and always suspecting. I recalled to mind the suggestive fact that
this boy was from the South, — the extreme South,
Louisiana, — and the thought was not of a reassur-
ing nature, under the circumstances. Nevertheless, it
cost me a pang to give the orders which I now gave
to Rayburn. I felt like a father who plots to expose
his own child to shame and injury. I told Rayburn
to keep quiet, bide his time, and get me some of those
writings whenever he could manage it without the boy's
finding it out. And I charged him not to do anything
which might let the boy discover that he was being
watched. I also ordered that he allow the lad his
usual liberties, but that he be followed at a distance
when he went out into the town.

During the next two days, Rayburn reported to me
several times. No success. The boy was still writing,
but he always pocketed his paper with a careless air
whenever Rayburn appeared in his vicinity. He had
gone twice to an old deserted stable in the town, remained a minute or two, and come out again. One
could not pooh-pooh these things — they had an evil
look. I was obliged to confess to myself that I was
getting uneasy. I went into my private quarters and
sent for my second in command, — an officer of intelligence and judgment, son of General James Watson
Webb. He was surprised and troubled. We had a
long talk over the matter, and came to the conclusion
that it would be worth while to institute a secret search.
I determined to take charge of that myself. So I had
myself called at two in the morning; and, pretty soon

after, I was in the musicians' quarters, crawling along the floor on my stomach among the snorers. I reached my slumbering waif's bunk at last, without disturbing anybody, captured his clothes and kit, and crawled stealthily back again. When I got to my own quarters, I found Webb there, waiting and eager to know the result. We made search immediately. The clothes were a disappointment. In the pockets we found blank paper and a pencil; nothing else, except a jack-knife and such queer odds and ends and useless trifles as boys hoard and value. We turned to the kit hopefully. Nothing there but a rebuke for us! — a little Bible with this written on the fly-leaf: "Stranger, be kind to my boy, for his mother's sake."

I looked at Webb — he dropped his eyes ; he looked at me — I dropped mine. Neither spoke. I put the book reverently back in its place. Presently Webb got up and went away, without remark. After a little I nerved myself up to my unpalatable job, and took the plunder back to where it belonged, crawling on my stomach as before. It seemed the peculiarly appropriate attitude for the business I was in. I was most honestly glad when it was over and done with.

About noon next day Rayburn came, as usual, to report. I cut him short. I said, —

"Let this nonsense be dropped. We are making a bugaboo out of a poor little cub who has got no more harm in him than a hymn-book."

The sergeant looked surprised, and said, —

"Well, you know it was your orders, sir, and I 've got some of the writing."
11

"And what does it amount to? How did you get it?"

"I peeped through the key-hole, and see him writing. So when I judged he was about done, I made a sort of a little cough, and I see him crumple it up and throw it in the fire, and look all around to see if anybody was coming. Then he settled back as comfortable and careless as anything. Then I comes in, and passes the time of day pleasantly, and sends him of an errand. He never looked uneasy, but went right along. It was a coal-fire and new-built; the writing had gone over behind a chunk, out of sight; but I got it out; there it is; it ain't hardly scorched, you see."

I glanced at the paper and took in a sentence or two. Then I dismissed the sergeant and told him to send Webb to me. Here is the paper in full:—

"FORT TRUMBULL, the 8th.

"COLONEL,—I was mistaken as to the calibre of the three guns I ended my list with. They are 18-pounders; all the rest of the armament is as I stated. The garrison remains as before reported, except that the two light infantry companies that were to be detached for service at the front are to stay here for the present—can't find out for how long, just now, but will soon. We are satisfied that, all things considered, matters had better be postponed un—"

There it broke off—there is where Rayburn coughed and interrupted the writer. All my affection for the boy, all my respect for him and charity for his forlorn condition, withered in a moment under the blight of this revelation of cold-blooded baseness.

But never mind about that. Here was business, — business that required profound and immediate attention, too. Webb and I turned the subject over and over, and examined it all around. Webb said, —

"What a pity he was interrupted! Something is going to be postponed until — when? And what *is* the something? Possibly he would have mentioned it, the pious little reptile!"

"Yes," I said, "we have missed a trick. And who is '*we*,' in the letter? Is it conspirators inside the fort or outside?"

That "we" was uncomfortably suggestive. However, it was not worth while to be guessing around that, so we proceeded to matters more practical. In the first place, we decided to double the sentries and keep the strictest possible watch. Next, we thought of calling Wicklow in and making him divulge everything; but that did not seem wisest until other methods should fail. We must have some more of the writings; so we began to plan to that end. And now we had an idea: Wicklow never went to the post-office, — perhaps the deserted stable was his post-office. We sent for my confidential clerk — a young German named Sterne, who was a sort of natural detective — and told him all about the case, and ordered him to go to work on it. Within the hour we got word that Wicklow was writing again. Shortly afterward, word came that he had asked leave to go out into the town. He was detained awhile, and meantime Sterne hurried off and concealed himself in the stable. By and by he saw Wicklow saunter in, look about him, then hide something under some rubbish in a corner, and take leisurely leave again. Sterne pounced upon the hidden article — a letter — and brought it to us. It had no superscription and no signature. It repeated what we had already read, and then went on to say : —

"We think it best to postpone till the two companies are gone. I mean the four inside think so; have not communicated with the others — afraid of attracting attention. I say four because we have lost two; they had hardly enlisted and got inside when they were shipped off to the front. It will be absolutely necessary to have two in their places. The two that went were the brothers from Thirty-mile Point. I have something of the greatest importance to reveal, but must not trust it to this method of communication; will try the other."

"The little scoundrel!" said Webb; "who *could* have supposed he was a spy? However, never mind about that; let us add up our particulars, such as they are, and see how the case stands to date. First, we've got a rebel spy in our midst, whom we know; secondly, we've got three more in our midst whom we don't know; thirdly, these spies have been introduced among us through the simple and easy process of enlisting as soldiers in the Union army — and evidently two of them have got sold at it, and been shipped off to the front; fourthly, there are assistant spies 'outside' — number indefinite; fifthly, Wicklow has very important matter which he is afraid to communicate by the 'present method' — will 'try the other.' That is the case, as it now stands. Shall we collar Wicklow and make him confess? Or shall we catch the person who removes the letters from the stable and make *him* tell? Or shall we keep still and find out more?"

We decided upon the last course. We judged that we did not need to proceed to summary measures now, since it was evident that the conspirators were likely to wait till those two light infantry companies were out of the way. We fortified Sterne with pretty ample powers, and told him to use his best endeavors to find out Wicklow's "other method" of communication. We meant to play a bold game; and to this end we proposed to keep the spies in an unsuspecting state as long as possible. So we ordered Sterne to return to the stable immediately, and, if he found the coast clear, to conceal Wicklow's letter where it was before, and leave it there for the conspirators to get.

The night closed down without further event. It was cold and dark and sleety, with a raw wind blowing; still I turned out of my warm bed several times during the night, and went the rounds in person, to see that all was right and that every sentry was on the alert. I always found them wide awake and watchful; evidently whispers of mysterious dangers had been floating about, and the doubling of the guards had been a kind of indorsement of those rumors. Once, toward morning, I encountered Webb, breasting his way against the bitter wind, and learned then that he, also, had been the rounds several times to see that all was going right.

Next day's events hurried things up somewhat. Wicklow wrote another letter; Sterne preceded him to the stable and saw him deposit it ; captured it as soon as Wicklow was out of the way, then slipped out and followed the little spy at a distance, with a detective in plain clothes at his own heels, for we thought it judicious to have the law's assistance handy in case of need. Wicklow went to the railway station, and waited around till the train from New York came in, then stood scanning the faces of the crowd as they poured out of the cars. Presently an aged gentleman, with green goggles and a cane, came limping along, stopped in Wicklow's neighborhood, and began to look about him expectantly. In an instant Wicklow darted forward, thrust an envelope into his hand, then glided away and disappeared in the throng. The next instant Sterne had snatched the letter ; and as he hurried past the detective, he said : "Follow the old gentleman — don't lose sight of him." Then Sterne skurried out with the crowd, and came straight to the fort.

We sat with closed doors, and instructed the guard outside to allow no interruption.

First we opened the letter captured at the stable. It read as follows : —

"HOLY ALLIANCE, — Found, in the usual gun, commands from the Master, left there last night, which set aside the instructions heretofore received from the subordinate quarter. Have left in the gun the usual indication that the commands reached the proper hand — "

Webb, interrupting : "Is n't the boy under constant surveillance now ?"

I said yes ; he had been under strict surveillance ever since the capturing of his former letter.

"Then how could he put anything into a gun, or take anything out of it, and not get caught?"

"Well," I said, "I don't like the look of that very well."

"I don't, either," said Webb. "It simply means that there are conspirators among the very sentinels. Without their connivance in some way or other, the thing could n't have been done."

I sent for Rayburn, and ordered him to examine the batteries and see what he could find. The reading of the letter was then resumed: —

"The new commands are peremptory, and require that the MMMM shall be FFFFF at 3 o'clock to-morrow morning. Two hundred will arrive, in small parties, by train and otherwise, from various directions, and will be at appointed place at right time. I will distribute the sign to-day. Success is apparently sure, though something must have got out, for the sentries have been doubled, and the chiefs went the rounds last night several times. W. W. comes from southerly to-day and will receive secret orders — by the other method. All six of you must be in 166 at sharp 2 A. M. You will find B. B. there, who will give you detailed instructions. Password same as last time, only reversed — put first syllable last and last syllable first. REMEMBER XXXX. Do not forget. Be of good heart; before the next sun rises you will be heroes; your fame will be permanent; you will have added a deathless page to history. Amen."

"Thunder and Mars," said Webb, "but we are getting into mighty hot quarters, as I look at it!"

I said there was no question but that things were beginning to wear a most serious aspect. Said I, —

"A desperate enterprise is on foot, that is plain enough. To-night is the time set for it, — that, also, is plain. The exact nature of the enterprise — I mean the manner of it — is hidden away under those blind bunches of M's and F's, but the end and aim, I judge, is the surprise and capture of the post. We must move quick and sharp now. I think nothing can be gained by continuing our clandestine policy as regards Wicklow. We *must* know, and as soon as possible, too, where ' 166 ' is located, so that we can make a descent upon the gang there at 2 A. M. ; and doubtless the quickest way to get that information will be to force it out of that boy. But first of all, and before we make any important move, I must lay the facts before the War Department, and ask for plenary powers."

The despatch was prepared in cipher to go over the wires ; I read it, approved it, and sent it along.

We presently finished discussing the letter which was under consideration, and then opened the one which had been snatched from the lame gentleman. It contained nothing but a couple of perfectly blank sheets of note-paper ! It was a chilly check to our hot eagerness and expectancy. We felt as blank as the paper, for a moment, and twice as foolish. But it was for a moment only ; for, of course, we immediately afterward thought of "sympathetic ink." We held the paper close to the fire and watched for the characters to come out, under the influence of the heat ; but nothing appeared but some faint tracings, which we could make nothing of. We then called in the surgeon, and sent him off with orders to apply every test he was acquainted with till he got the right one, and report the contents of the letter to me the instant he brought them to the surface. This check was a confounded annoyance, and we naturally chafed under the delay; for we had fully expected to get out of that letter some of the most important secrets of the plot.

Now appeared Sergeant Rayburn, and drew from his pocket a piece of twine string about a foot long, with three knots tied in it, and held it up.

" I got it out of a gun on the water-front," said he. "I took the tompions out of all the guns and examined close; this string was the only thing that was in any gun."

So this bit of string was Wicklow's " sign " to signify that the "Master's" commands had not miscarried. I ordered that every sentinel who had served near that gun during the past twenty-four hours be put in confinement at once and separately, and not allowed to communicate with any one without my privity and consent.

A telegram now came from the Secretary of War. It read as follows : —

" Suspend *habeas corpus*. Put town under martial law. Make necessary arrests. Act with vigor and promptness. Keep the Department informed."

We were now in shape to go to work. I sent out and had the lame gentleman quietly arrested and as quietly brought into the fort; I placed him under guard, and forbade speech to him or from him. He was inclined to bluster at first, but he soon dropped that.

Next came word that Wicklow had been seen to give something to a couple of our new recruits; and that, as soon as his back was turned, these had been seized and confined. Upon each was found a small bit of paper, bearing these words and signs in pencil : —

EAGLE'S THIRD FLIGHT.

REMEMBER XXXX.

166.

In accordance with instructions, I telegraphed to the Department, in cipher, the progress made, and also described the above ticket. We seemed to be in a strong enough position now to venture to throw off the mask as regarded Wicklow; so I sent for him. I also sent for and received back the letter written in sympathetic ink, the surgeon accompanying it with the information that thus far it had resisted his tests, but that there were others he could apply when I should be ready for him to do so.

Presently Wicklow entered. He had a somewhat worn and anxious look, but he was composed and easy, and if he suspected anything it did not appear in his face or manner. I allowed him to stand there a moment or two, then I said pleasantly, —

"My boy, why do you go to that old stable so much?"

He answered, with simple demeanor and without embarrassment,—

"Well, I hardly know, sir; there is n't any particular reason, except that I like to be alone, and I amuse myself there."

"You amuse yourself there, do you?"

"Yes, sir," he replied, as innocently and simply as before.

"Is that all you do there?"

"Yes, sir," he said, looking up with childlike wonderment in his big soft eyes.

"You are *sure?*"

"Yes, sir, sure."

After a pause, I said,—

"Wicklow, why do you write so much?"

"I? I do not write much, sir."

"You don't?"

"No, sir. Oh, if you mean scribbling, I *do* scribble some, for amusement."

"What do you do with your scribblings?"

"Nothing, sir — throw them away."

"Never send them to anybody?"

"No, sir."

I suddenly thrust before him the letter to the "Colonel." He started slightly, but immediately composed himself. A slight tinge spread itself over his cheek.

"How came you to send *this* piece of scribbling, then?"

"I nev-never meant any harm, sir."

"Never meant any harm! You betray the armament and condition of the post, and mean no harm by it?"

He hung his head and was silent.

"Come, speak up, and stop lying. Whom was this letter intended for?"

He showed signs of distress, now; but quickly collected himself, and replied, in a tone of deep earnestness, —

"I will tell you the truth, sir — the whole truth. The letter was never intended for anybody at all. I wrote it only to amuse myself. I see the error and foolishness of it, now, — but it is the only offence, sir, upon my honor."

"Ah, I am glad of that. It is dangerous to be writing such letters. I hope you are sure this is the only one you wrote?"

"Yes, sir, perfectly sure."

His hardihood was stupefying. He told that lie with as sincere a countenance as any creature ever wore. I waited a moment to soothe down my rising temper, and then said, —

"Wicklow, jog your memory now, and see if you can help me with two or three little matters which I wish to inquire about."

"I will do my very best, sir."

"Then, to begin with — who is 'the Master'?"

It betrayed him into darting a startled glance at our faces, but that was all. He was serene again in a moment, and tranquilly answered, —

"I do not know, sir."

"You do not know?"

"I do not know."

"You are *sure* you do not know?"

He tried hard to keep his eyes on mine, but the strain was too great; his chin sunk slowly toward his breast and he was silent; he stood there nervously fumbling with a button, an object to command one's pity, in spite of his base acts. Presently I broke the stillness with the question, —

"Who are the 'Holy Alliance'?"

His body shook visibly, and he made a slight random gesture with his hands, which to me was like the appeal of a despairing creature for compassion. But he made no sound. He continued to stand with his face bent toward the ground. As we sat gazing at him, waiting for him to speak, we saw the big tears begin to roll down his cheeks. But he remained silent. After a little, I said, —

"You must answer me, my boy, and you must tell me the truth. Who are the Holy Alliance?"

He wept on in silence. Presently I said, somewhat sharply, —

"Answer the question!"

He struggled to get command of his voice; and then, looking up appealingly, forced the words out between his sobs, —

"Oh, have pity on me, sir! I cannot answer it, for I do not know."

"What!"

"Indeed, sir, I am telling the truth. I never have

heard of the Holy Alliance till this moment. On my honor, sir, this is so."

"Good heavens! Look at this second letter of yours; there, do you see those words, '*Holy Alliance*'? What do you say now?"

He gazed up into my face with the hurt look of one upon whom a great wrong has been wrought, then said, feelingly, —

"This is some cruel joke, sir; and how could they play it upon me, who have tried all I could to do right, and have never done harm to anybody? Some one has counterfeited my hand; I never wrote a line of this; I have never seen this letter before!"

"Oh, you unspeakable liar! Here, what do you say to *this?*" — and I snatched the sympathetic-ink letter from my pocket and thrust it before his eyes.

His face turned white! — as white as a dead person's. He wavered slightly in his tracks, and put his hand against the wall to steady himself. After a moment he asked, in so faint a voice that it was hardly audible, —

"Have you — read it?"

Our faces must have answered the truth before my lips could get out the false "yes," for I distinctly saw the courage come back into that boy's eyes. I waited for him to say something, but he kept silent. So at last I said, —

"Well, what have you to say as to the revelations in this letter?"

He answered, with perfect composure, —

"Nothing, except that they are entirely harmless and innocent; they can hurt nobody."

I was in something of a corner now, as I could n't disprove his assertion. I did not know exactly how to proceed. However, an idea came to my relief, and I said, —

"You are sure you know nothing about the Master and the Holy Alliance, and did not write the letter which you say is a forgery?"

"Yes, sir — sure."

I slowly drew out the knotted twine string and held it up without speaking. He gazed at it indifferently, then looked at me inquiringly. My patience was sorely taxed. However, I kept my temper down, and said in my usual voice, —

"Wicklow, do you see this?"

"Yes, sir."

"What is it?"

"It seems to be a piece of string."

"*Seems?* It *is* a piece of string. Do you recognize it?"

"No, sir," he replied, as calmly as the words could be uttered.

His coolness was perfectly wonderful! I paused now for several seconds, in order that the silence might add impressiveness to what I was about to say; then I rose and laid my hand on his shoulder, and said gravely, —

"It will do you no good, poor boy, none in the world. This sign to the 'Master,' this knotted string, found in one of the guns on the water-front — "

"Found *in* the gun! Oh, no, no, no! do not say *in* the gun, but in a crack in the tompion! — it *must*

have been in the crack!" and down he went on his
knees and clasped his hands and lifted up a face that
was pitiful to see, so ashy it was, and so wild with
terror.

"No, it was *in* the gun."

"Oh, something has gone wrong! My God, I am
lost!" and he sprang up and darted this way and that,
dodging the hands that were put out to catch him, and
doing his best to escape from the place. But of course
escape was impossible. Then he flung himself on his
knees again, crying with all his might, and clasped me
around the legs; and so he clung to me and begged
and pleaded, saying, "Oh, have pity on me! Oh, be
merciful to me! Do not betray me; they would not
spare my life a moment! Protect me, save me. I will
confess everything!"

It took us some time to quiet him down and modify
his fright, and get him into something like a rational
frame of mind. Then I began to question him, he
answering humbly, with downcast eyes, and from time
to time swabbing away his constantly flowing tears.

"So you are at heart a rebel?"

"Yes, sir."

"And a spy?"

"Yes, sir."

"And have been acting under distinct orders from
outside?"

"Yes, sir."

"Willingly?"

"Yes, sir."

"*Gladly*, perhaps?"

"Yes, sir; it would do no good to deny it. The South is my country; my heart is Southern, and it is all in her cause."

"Then the tale you told me of your wrongs and the persecution of your family was made up for the occasion?"

"They — they told me to say it, sir."

"And you would betray and destroy those who pitied and sheltered you. Do you comprehend how base you are, you poor misguided thing?"

He replied with sobs only.

"Well, let that pass. To business. Who is the 'Colonel,' and where is he?"

He began to cry hard, and tried to beg off from answering. He said he would be killed if he told. I threatened to put him in the dark cell and lock him up if he did not come out with the information. At the same time I promised to protect him from all harm if he made a clean breast. For all answer, he closed his mouth firmly and put on a stubborn air which I could not bring him out of. At last I started with him; but a single glance into the dark cell converted him. He broke into a passion of weeping and supplicating, and declared he would tell everything.

So I brought him back, and he named the "Colonel," and described him particularly. Said he would be found at the principal hotel in the town, in citizen's dress. I had to threaten him again, before he would describe and name the "Master." Said the Master would be found at No. 15 Bond Street, New York, passing under the name of R. F. Gaylord. I tele-

graphed name and description to the chief of police
of the metropolis, and asked that Gaylord be arrested
and held till I could send for him.

"Now," said I, "it seems that there are several of
the conspirators 'outside,'—presumably in New London.   Name and describe them."

He named and described three men and two women,
—all stopping at the principal hotel.   I sent out
quietly, and had them and the "Colonel" arrested
and confined in the fort.

"Next, I want to know all about your three fellow-
conspirators who are here in the fort."

He was about to dodge me with a falsehood, I
thought ; but I produced the mysterious bits of paper
which had been found upon two of them, and this had
a salutary effect upon him.   I said we had possession
of two of the men, and he must point out the third.
This frightened him badly, and he cried out, —

"Oh, please don't make me ; he would kill me on
the spot !"

I said that that was all nonsense ; I would have somebody near by to protect him, and, besides, the men
should be assembled without arms.   I ordered all the
raw recruits to be mustered, and then the poor trem-
bling little wretch went out and stepped along down the
line, trying to look as indifferent as possible.   Finally
he spoke a single word to one of the men, and before
he had gone five steps the man was under arrest.

As soon as Wicklow was with us again, I had those
three men brought in.   I made one of them stand forward, and said, —

"Now, Wicklow, mind, not a shade's divergence from the exact truth. Who is this man, and what do you know about him?"

Being "in for it," he cast consequences aside, fastened his eyes on the man's face, and spoke straight along without hesitation, — to the following effect.

"His real name is George Bristow. He is from New Orleans; was second mate of the coast-packet 'Capitol,' two years ago; is a desperate character, and has served two terms for manslaughter, — one for killing a deck-hand named Hyde with a capstan-bar, and one for killing a roustabout for refusing to heave the lead, which is no part of a roustabout's business. He is a spy, and was sent here by the Colonel, to act in that capacity. He was third mate of the 'St. Nicholas,' when she blew up in the neighborhood of Memphis, in '58, and came near being lynched for robbing the dead and wounded while they were being taken ashore in an empty wood-boat."

And so forth and so on — he gave the man's biography in full. When he had finished, I said to the man, —

"What have you to say to this?"

"Barring your presence, sir, it is the infernalest lie that ever was spoke!"

I sent him back into confinement, and called the others forward in turn. Same result. The boy gave a detailed history of each, without ever hesitating for a word or a fact; but all I could get out of either rascal was the indignant assertion that it was all a lie. They would confess nothing. I returned them to captivity, and brought out the rest of my prisoners, one by one. Wicklow told all about them — what towns in the South they were from, and every detail of their connection with the conspiracy.

But they all denied his facts, and not one of them confessed a thing. The men raged, the women cried. According to their stories, they were all innocent people from out West, and loved the Union above all things in this world. I locked the gang up, in disgust, and fell to catechising Wicklow once more.

"Where is No. 166, and who is B. B?"

But *there* he was determined to draw the line. Neither coaxing nor threats had any effect upon him. Time was flying — it was necessary to institute sharp measures. So I tied him up a-tiptoe by the thumbs. As the pain increased, it wrung screams from him which were almost more than I could bear. But I held my ground, and pretty soon he shrieked out, —

"Oh, *please* let me down, and I will tell!"

"No — you'll tell *before* I let you down."

Every instant was agony to him, now, so out it came :—

"No. 166, Eagle Hotel!" — naming a wretched tavern down by the water, a resort of common laborers, 'longshoremen, and less reputable folk.

So I released him, and then demanded to know the object of the conspiracy.

"To take the fort to-night," said he, doggedly and sobbing.

"Have I got all the chiefs of the conspiracy?"

"No. You've got all except those that are to meet at 166."

" What does ' Remember XXXX ' mean ? "

No reply.

" What is the password to No. 166 ? "

No reply.

" What do those bunches of letters mean, — ' FFFFF ' and ' MMMM ' ? Answer ! or you will catch it again."

" I never *will* answer ! I will die first. Now do what you please."

" Think what you are saying, Wicklow. Is it final ? "

He answered steadily, and without a quiver in his voice, —

" It is final. As sure as I love my wronged country and hate everything this Northern sun shines on, I will die before I will reveal those things."

I triced him up by the thumbs again. When the agony was full upon him, it was heart-breaking to hear the poor thing's shrieks, but we got nothing else out of him. To every question he screamed the same reply : " I can die, and I *will* die ; but I will never tell."

Well, we had to give it up. We were convinced that he certainly would die rather than confess. So we took him down and imprisoned him, under strict guard.

Then for some hours we busied ourselves with sending telegrams to the War Department, and with making preparations for a descent upon No. 166.

It was stirring times, that black and bitter night. Things had leaked out, and the whole garrison was on the alert. The sentinels were trebled, and nobody could move, outside or in, without being brought to a stand with a musket levelled at his head. However, Webb and I were less concerned now than we had previously been, because of the fact that the conspiracy must necessarily be in a pretty crippled condition, since so many of its principals were in our clutches.

I determined to be at No. 166 in good season, capture and gag B. B., and be on hand for the rest when they arrived. At about a quarter past one in the morning I crept out of the fortress with half a dozen stalwart and gamy U. S. regulars at my heels — and the boy Wicklow, with his hands tied behind him. I told him we were going to No. 166, and that if I found he had lied again and was misleading us, he would have to show us the right place or suffer the consequences.

We approached the tavern stealthily and reconnoitred. A light was burning in the small bar-room, the rest of the house was dark. I tried the front door; it yielded, and we softly entered, closing the door behind us. Then we removed our shoes, and I led the way to the bar-room. The German landlord sat there, asleep in his chair. I woke him gently, and told him to take off his boots and precede us; warning him at the same time to utter no sound. He obeyed without a murmur, but evidently he was badly frightened. I ordered him to lead the way to 166. We ascended two or three flights of stairs as softly as a file of cats; and then, having arrived near the farther end of a long hall, we came to a door through the glazed transom of which we could discern the glow of a dim light from within. The landlord felt for me in the dark and whispered me that that was 166. I tried the door — it was locked on the inside. I whispered an order to one of my biggest soldiers; we set our ample shoulders to the door and with one heave we burst it from its hinges. I caught a half-glimpse of a figure in a bed — saw its head dart toward the candle; out went the light, and we were in pitch darkness. With one big bound I lit on that bed and pinned its occupant down with my knees. My prisoner struggled fiercely, but I got a grip on his throat with my left hand, and that was a good assistance to my knees in holding him down. Then straightway I snatched out my revolver, cocked it, and laid the cold barrel warn-ingly against his cheek.

"Now somebody strike a light!" said I. "I 've got him safe."

It was done. The flame of the match burst up. I looked at my captive, and, by George, it was a young woman!

I let go and got off the bed, feeling pretty sheepish. Everybody stared stupidly at his neighbor. Nobody had any wit or sense left, so sudden and overwhelming had been the surprise. The young woman began to cry, and covered her face with the sheet. The land-lord said, meekly, —

"My daughter, she has been doing something that is not right, *nicht wahr ?*"

" "Your daughter? Is she your daughter?"

"Oh, yes, she is my daughter. She is just to-night come home from Cincinnati a little bit sick."

"Confound it, that boy has lied again. This is not the right 166; this is not B. B. Now, Wicklow, you will find the correct 166 for us, or — hello! where is that boy?"

Gone, as sure as guns! And, what is more, we failed to find a trace of him. Here was an awkward predicament. I cursed my stupidity in not tying him to one of the men; but it was of no use to bother about that now. What should I do in the present circumstances? — that was the question. That girl *might* be B. B., after all. I did not believe it, but still it would not answer to take unbelief for proof. So I finally put my men in a vacant room across the hall from 166, and told them to capture anybody and everybody that approached the girl's room, and to keep the landlord with them, and under strict watch, until further orders. Then I hurried back to the fort to see if all was right there yet.

Yes, all was right. And all remained right. I stayed up all night to make sure of that. Nothing happened. I was unspeakably glad to see the dawn come again, and be able to telegraph the Department that the Stars and Stripes still floated over Fort Trumbull.

An immense pressure was lifted from my breast. Still I did not relax vigilance, of course, nor effort either; the case was too grave for that. I had up my prisoners, one by one, and harried them by the hour, trying to get them to confess, but it was a failure. They only gnashed their teeth and tore their hair, and revealed nothing.

About noon came tidings of my missing boy. He

had been seen on the road, tramping westward, some eight miles out, at six in the morning. I started a cavalry lieutenant and a private on his track at once. They came in sight of him twenty miles out. He had climbed a fence and was wearily dragging himself across a slushy field toward a large old-fashioned mansion in the edge of a village. They rode through a bit of woods, made a detour, and closed up on the house from the opposite side; then dismounted and skurried into the kitchen. Nobody there. They slipped into the next room, which was also unoccupied; the door from that room into the front or sitting room was open. They were about to step through it when they heard a low voice; it was somebody praying. So they halted reverently, and the lieutenant put his head in and saw an old man and an old woman kneeling in a corner of that sitting-room. It was the old man that was praying, and just as he was finishing his prayer, the Wicklow boy opened the front door and stepped in. Both of those old people sprang at him and smothered him with embraces, shouting, —

"Our boy! our darling! God be praised. The lost is found! He that was dead is alive again!"

Well, sir, what do you think! That young imp was born and reared on that homestead, and had never been five miles away from it in all his life, till the fortnight before he loafed into my quarters and gulled me with that maudlin yarn of his! It's as true as gospel. That old man was his father — a learned old retired clergyman; and that old lady was his mother.

Let me throw in a word or two of explanation concerning that boy and his performances. It turned out that he was a ravenous devourer of dime novels and sensation-story papers — therefore, dark mysteries and gaudy heroisms were just in his line. Then he had read newspaper reports of the stealthy goings and comings of rebel spies in our midst, and of their lurid purposes and their two or three startling achievements, till his imagination was all aflame on that subject. His constant comrade for some months had been a Yankee youth of much tongue and lively fancy, who had served for a couple of years as "mud clerk" (that is, subordinate purser) on certain of the packet-boats plying between New Orleans and points two or three hundred miles up the Mississippi — hence his easy facility in handling the names and other details pertaining to that region. Now I had spent two or three months in that part of the country before the war; and I knew just enough about it to be easily taken in by that boy, whereas a born Louisianian would probably have caught him tripping before he had talked fifteen minutes. Do you know the reason he said he would rather die than explain certain of his treasonable enigmas? Simply because he *could n't* explain them! — they had no meaning; he had fired them out of his imagination without forethought or afterthought; and so, upon sudden call, he was n't able to invent an explanation of them. For instance, he could n't reveal what was hidden in the "sympathetic ink" letter, for the ample reason that there was n't anything hidden in it; it was blank paper only. He had n't put anything into a gun, and had never intended to — for his letters were all written to imaginary persons, and when he hid one in the stable he always removed the one he had put there the day before; so he was not acquainted with that knotted string, since he was seeing it for the first time when I showed it to him; but as soon as I had let him find out where it came from, he straightway adopted it, in his romantic fashion, and got some fine effects out of it. He invented Mr. "Gaylord;" there was n't any 15 Bond Street, just then — it had been pulled down three months before. He invented the "Colonel;" he invented the glib histories of those unfortunates whom I captured and confronted with him; he invented "B. B.;" he even invented No. 166, one may say, for he did n't know there *was* such a number in the Eagle Hotel until we went there. He stood ready to invent anybody or anything whenever it was wanted. If I called for "outside" spies, he promptly described strangers whom he had seen at the hotel, and whose names he had happened to hear. Ah, he lived in a gorgeous, mysterious, romantic world during those few stirring days, and I think it was *real* to him, and that he enjoyed it clear down to the bottom of his heart.

But he made trouble enough for us, and just no end of humiliation. You see, on account of him we had fifteen or twenty people under arrest and confinement in the fort, with sentinels before their doors. A lot of the captives were soldiers and such, and to them I did n't have to apologize; but the rest were first-class citizens, from all over the country, and no amount of apologies was sufficient to satisfy them. They just fumed and raged and made no end of trouble! And those two ladies, — one was an Ohio Congressman's wife, the other a Western bishop's sister, — well, the scorn and ridicule and angry tears they poured out on me made up a keepsake that was likely to make me remember them for a considerable time, — and I shall. That old lame gentleman with the goggles was a college president from Philadelphia, who had come up to attend his nephew's funeral. He had never seen young Wicklow before, of course. Well, he not only missed the funeral, and got jailed as a rebel spy, but Wicklow had stood up there in my quarters and coldly described him as a counterfeiter, nigger-trader, horse-thief, and fire-bug from the most notorious rascal-nest in Galveston; and this was a thing which that poor old gentleman could n't seem to get over at all.

And the War Department! But, O my soul, let's draw the curtain over that part!

NOTE. — I showed my manuscript to the Major, and he said : " Your unfamiliarity with military matters has betrayed you into some little mistakes. Still, they are picturesque ones — let them go; military men will smile at them, the rest won't detect them. You have got the main facts of the history right, and have set them down just about as they occurred." — M. T.

THE GREAT REVOLUTION IN
PITCAIRN.

———◆———

L ET me refresh the reader's memory a little. Nearly
a hundred years ago the crew of the British ship
"Bounty" mutinied, set the captain and his officers
adrift upon the open sea, took possession of the ship,
and sailed southward. They procured wives for themselves among the natives of Tahiti, then proceeded to
a lonely little rock in mid-Pacific, called Pitcairn's
Island, wrecked the vessel, stripped her of everything
that might be useful to a new colony, and established
themselves on shore.

Pitcairn's is so far removed from the track of com-
merce that it was many years before another vessel
touched there. It had always been considered an
uninhabited island; so when a ship did at last drop
its anchor there, in 1808, the captain was greatly surprised to find the place peopled. Although the mutineers had fought among themselves, and gradually killed
each other off until only two or three of the original
stock remained, these tragedies had not occurred before
a number of children had been born; so in 1808 the
island had a population of twenty-seven persons. John

Adams, the chief mutineer, still survived, and was to live many years yet, as governor and patriarch of the flock. From being mutineer and homicide, he had turned Christian and teacher, and his nation of twenty-seven persons was now the purest and devoutest in Christendom. Adams had long ago hoisted the British flag and constituted his island an appanage of the British crown.

To-day the population numbers ninety persons, — sixteen men, nineteen women, twenty-five boys, and thirty girls, — all descendants of the mutineers, all bearing the family names of those mutineers, and all speaking English, and English only. The island stands high up out of the sea, and has precipitous walls. It is about three quarters of a mile long, and in places is as much as half a mile wide. Such arable land as it affords is held by the several families, according to a division made many years ago. There is some live stock, — goats, pigs, chickens, and cats; but no dogs, and no large animals. There is one church building, — used also as a capitol, a school-house, and a public library. The title of the governor has been, for a generation or two, "Magistrate and Chief Ruler, in subordination to her Majesty the Queen of Great Britain." It was his province to *make* the laws, as well as execute them. His office was elective; everybody over seventeen years old had a vote, — no matter about the sex.

The sole occupations of the people were farming and fishing; their sole recreation, religious services. There has never been a shop in the island, nor any money. The habits and dress of the people have always been primitive, and their laws simple to puerility. They have lived in a deep Sabbath tranquillity, far from the world and its ambitions and vexations, and neither knowing nor caring what was going on in the mighty empires that lie beyond their limitless ocean solitudes. Once in three or four years a ship touched there, moved them with aged news of bloody battles, devastating epidemics, fallen thrones, and ruined dynasties, then traded them some soap and flannel for some yams and bread-fruit, and sailed away, leaving them to retire into their peaceful dreams and pious dissipations once more.

On the 8th of last September, Admiral de Horsey, commander-in-chief of the British fleet in the Pacific, visited Pitcairn's Island, and speaks as follows in his official report to the admiralty : —

"They have beans, carrots, turnips, cabbages, and a little maize ; pineapples, fig-trees, custard apples, and oranges ; lemons and cocoa-nuts. Clothing is obtained alone from passing ships, in barter for refreshments. There are no springs on the island, but as it rains generally once a month they have plenty of water, although at times, in former years, they have suffered from drought. No alcoholic liquors, except for medicinal purposes, are used, and a drunkard is unknown. . . . .

"The necessary articles required by the islanders are best shown by those we furnished in barter for refreshments : namely, flannel, serge, drill, half-boots, combs, tobacco, and soap. They also stand much in need of maps and slates for their school, and tools of any kind are most acceptable. I caused them to be supplied from the public stores with a union-jack for display on the arrival of ships, and a pit saw, of which they were greatly in need. This, I trust, will meet the approval of their lordships. If the munificent people of England were only aware of the wants of this most deserving little colony, they would not long go unsupplied. . . . .

" Divine service is held every Sunday at 10.30 A. M. and at 3 P. M., in the house built and used by John Adams for that purpose until he died in 1829. It is conducted strictly in accordance with the liturgy of the Church of England, by Mr. Simon Young, their selected pastor, who is much respected. A Bible class is held every Wednesday, when all who conveniently can, attend. There is also a general meeting for prayer on the first Friday in every month. Family prayers are said in every house the first thing in the morning and the last thing in the evening, and no food is partaken of without asking God's blessing before and afterwards. Of these islanders' religious attributes no one can speak without deep respect. A people whose greatest pleasure and privilege is to commune in prayer with their God, and to join in hymns of praise, and who are, moreover, cheerful, diligent, and probably freer from vice than any other community, need no priest among them."

Now I come to a sentence in the admiral's report which he dropped carelessly from his pen, no doubt, and never gave the matter a second thought. He little imagined what a freight of tragic prophecy it bore ! This is the sentence : —

" One stranger, an American, has settled on the
island, — *a doubtful acquisition.*"

A doubtful acquisition indeed ! Captain Ormsby, in
the American ship " Hornet," touched at Pitcairn's
nearly four months after the admiral's visit, and from
the facts which he gathered there we now know all
about that American. Let us put these facts together,
in historical form. The American's name was Butterworth Stavely. As soon as he had become well ac-
qainted with all the people, — and this took but a few
days, of course, — he began to ingratiate himself with
them by all the arts he could command. He became
exceedingly popular, and much looked up to ; for one
of the first things he did was to forsake his worldly
way of life, and throw all his energies into religion.
He was always reading his Bible, or praying, or singing hymns, or asking blessings. In prayer, no one had
such "liberty" as he, no one could pray so long or so
well.

At last, when he considered the time to be ripe, he
began secretly to sow the seeds of discontent among
the people. It was his deliberate purpose, from the
beginning, to subvert the government, but of course
he kept that to himself for a time. He used different
arts with different individuals. He awakened dissatisfaction in one quarter by calling attention to the
shortness of the Sunday services ; he argued that there
should be three three-hour services on Sunday instead
of only two. Many had secretly held this opinion before ; they now privately banded themselves into a
party to work for it. He showed certain of the women
13

that they were not allowed sufficient voice in the prayer-meetings; thus another party was formed. No weapon was beneath his notice; he even descended to the children, and awoke discontent in their breasts because — as *he* discovered for them — they had not enough Sunday-school. This created a third party.

Now, as the chief of these parties, he found himself the strongest power in the community. So he proceeded to his next move, — a no less important one than the impeachment of the chief magistrate, James Russell Nickoy; a man of character and ability, and possessed of great wealth, he being the owner of a house with a parlor to it, three acres and a half of yam land, and the only boat in Pitcairn's, a whale-boat; and, most unfortunately, a pretext for this impeachment offered itself at just the right time. One of the earliest and most precious laws of the island was the law against trespass. It was held in great reverence, and was regarded as the palladium of the people's liberties. About thirty years ago an important case came before the courts under this law, in this wise: a chicken belonging to Elizabeth Young (aged, at that time, fifty-eight, a daughter of John Mills, one of the mutineers of the "Bounty") trespassed upon the grounds of Thursday October Christian (aged twenty-nine, a grandson of Fletcher Christian, one of the mutineers). Christian killed the chicken. According to the law, Christian could keep the chicken; or, if he preferred, he could restore its remains to the owner, and receive damages in "produce" to an amount equivalent to the waste and injury wrought by the trespasser. The court records set forth that "the said Christian aforesaid did deliver the aforesaid remains to the said Elizabeth Young, and did demand one bushel of yams in satisfaction of the damage done." But Elizabeth Young considered the demand exorbitant; the parties could not agree; therefore Christian brought suit in the courts. He lost his case in the justice's court; at least, he was awarded only a half-peck of yams, which he considered insufficient, and in the nature of a defeat. He appealed. The case lingered several years in an ascending grade of courts, and always resulted in decrees sustaining the original verdict; and finally the thing got into the supreme court, and there it stuck for twenty years. But last summer, even the supreme court managed to arrive at a decision at last. Once more the orginal verdict was sustained. Christian then said he was satisfied; but Stavely was present, and whispered to him and to his lawyer, suggesting, "as a mere form," that the original law be exhibited, in order to make sure that it still existed. It seemed an odd idea, but an ingenious one. So the demand was made. A messenger was sent to the magistrate's house; he presently returned with the tidings that it had disappeared from among the state archives.

The court now pronounced its late decision void, since it had been made under a law which had no actual existence.

Great excitement ensued, immediately. The news swept abroad over the whole island that the palladium of the public liberties was lost, — may be treasonably destroyed. Within thirty minutes almost the entire nation were in the court-room, — that is to say, the church. The impeachment of the chief magistrate followed, upon Stavely's motion. The accused met his misfortune with the dignity which became his great office. He did not plead, or even argue : he offered the simple defence that he had not meddled with the missing law ; that he had kept the state archives in the same candle-box that had been used as their depository from the beginning ; and that he was innocent of the removal or destruction of the lost document.

But nothing could save him ; he was found guilty of misprision of treason, and degraded from his office, and all his property was confiscated.

The lamest part of the whole shameful matter was the *reason* suggested by his enemies for his destruction of the law, to wit : that he did it to favor Christian, because Christian was his cousin ! Whereas Stavely was the only individual in the entire nation who was *not* his cousin. The reader must remember that all of these people are the descendants of half a dozen men ; that the first children intermarried together and bore grandchildren to the mutineers ; that these grandchildren intermarried ; after them, great and great-great-grandchildren intermarried : so that to-day everybody is blood kin to everybody. Moreover, the relationships are wonderfully, even astoundingly, mixed up and complicated. A stranger, for instance, says to an islander, —

" You speak of that young woman as your cousin ; a while ago you called her your aunt."

" Well, she *is* my aunt, and my cousin too. And

also my step-sister, my niece, my fourth cousin, my thirty-third cousin, my forty-second cousin, my great-aunt, my grandmother, my widowed sister-in-law, — and next week she will be my wife."

So the charge of nepotism against the chief magistrate was weak. But no matter ; weak or strong, it suited Stavely. Stavely was immediately elected to the vacant magistracy ; and, oozing reform from every pore, he went vigorously to work. In no long time religious services raged everywhere and unceasingly. By command, the second prayer of the Sunday morning service, which had customarily endured some thirty-five or forty minutes, and had pleaded for the world, first by continent and then by national and tribal detail, was extended to an hour and a half, and made to include supplications in behalf of the possible peoples in the several planets. Everybody was pleased with this ; everybody said, "Now *this* is something *like.*" By command, the usual three-hour sermons were doubled in length. The nation came in a body to testify their gratitude to the new magistrate. The old law forbidding cooking on the Sabbath was extended to the prohibition of eating, also. By command, Sunday-school was privileged to spread over into the week. The joy of all classes was complete. In one short month the new magistrate had become the people's idol !

The time was ripe for this man's next move. He began, cautiously at first, to poison the public mind against England. He took the chief citizens aside, one by one, and conversed with them on this topic. Presently he grew bolder, and spoke out. He said the

nation owed it to itself, to its honor, to its great tra-
ditions, to rise in its might and throw off " this galling
English yoke."

But the simple islanders answered, —

" We had not noticed that it galled. How does it
gall ? England sends a ship once in three or four years
to give us soap and clothing, and things which we
sorely need and gratefully receive; but she never
troubles us ; she lets us go our own way."

" She lets you go your own way ! So slaves have
felt and spoken in all the ages ! This speech shows
how fallen you are, how base, how brutalized, you have
become, under this grinding tyranny ! What ! has all
manly pride forsaken you ? Is liberty nothing ? Are
you content to be a mere appendage to a foreign and
hateful sovereignty, when you might rise up and take
your rightful place in the august family of nations,
great, free, enlightened, independent, the minion of no
sceptred master, but the arbiter of your own destiny,
and a voice and a power in decreeing the destinies of
your sister-sovereignties of the world ? "

Speeches like this produced an effect by and by. Citizens began to feel the English yoke; they did not know
exactly how or whereabouts they felt it, but they were
perfectly certain they did feel it. They got to grumbling
a good deal, and chafing under their chains, and longing for relief and release. They presently fell to hating
the English flag, that sign and symbol of their nation's
degradation ; they ceased to glance up at it as they
passed the capitol, but averted their eyes and grated
their teeth ; and one morning, when it was found

trampled into the mud at the foot of the staff, they left it there, and no man put his hand to it to hoist it again. A certain thing which was sure to happen sooner or later happened now. Some of the chief citizens went to the magistrate by night, and said, —

"We can endure this hated tyranny no longer. How can we cast it off?"

"By a *coup d'état.*"

"How?"

"A coup d'état. It is like this: everything is got ready, and at the appointed moment I, as the official head of the nation, publicly and solemnly proclaim its independence, and absolve it from allegiance to any and all other powers whatsoever."

"That sounds simple and easy. We can do that right away. Then what will be the next thing to do?"

"Seize all the defences and public properties of all kinds, establish martial law, put the army and navy on a war footing, and proclaim the empire!"

This fine programme dazzled these innocents. They said, —

"This is grand, — this is splendid; but will not England resist?"

"Let her. This rock is a Gibraltar."

"True. But about the empire? Do we *need* an empire, and an emperor?"

"What you *need*, my friends, is unification. Look at Germany; look at Italy. They are unified. Unification is the thing. It makes living dear. That constitutes progress. We must have a standing army, and a navy. Taxes follow, as a matter of course. All these things summed up make grandeur. With unification and grandeur, what more can you want? Very well, — only the empire can confer these boons."

So on the 8th day of December Pitcairn's Island was proclaimed a free and independent nation; and on the same day the solemn coronation of Butterworth I., emperor of Pitcairn's Island, took place, amid great rejoicings and festivities. The entire nation, with the exception of fourteen persons, mainly little children, marched past the throne in single file, with banners and music, the procession being upwards of ninety feet long; and some said it was as much as three quarters of a minute passing a given point. Nothing like it had ever been seen in the history of the island before. Public enthusiasm was measureless.

Now straightway imperial reforms began. Orders of nobility were instituted. A minister of the navy was appointed, and the whale-boat put in commission. A minister of war was created, and ordered to proceed at once with the formation of a standing army. A first lord of the treasury was named, and commanded to get up a taxation scheme, and also open negotiations for treaties, offensive, defensive, and commercial, with foreign powers. Some generals and admirals were appointed; also some chamberlains, some equerries in waiting, and some lords of the bed-chamber.

At this point all the material was used up. The Grand Duke of Galilee, minister of war, complained that all the sixteen grown men in the empire had been given great offices, and consequently would not consent to serve in the ranks; wherefore his standing army was at a stand-still. The Marquis of Ararat, minister of the navy, made a similar complaint. He said he was willing to steer the whale-boat himself, but he *must* have somebody to man her.

The emperor did the best he could in the circumstances : he took all the boys above the age of ten years away from their mothers, and pressed them into the army, thus constructing a corps of seventeen privates, officered by one lieutenant-general and two major-generals. This pleased the minister of war, but procured the enmity of all the mothers in the land ; for they said their precious ones must now find bloody graves in the fields of war, and he would be answerable for it. Some of the more heart-broken and inappeasable among them lay constantly in wait for the emperor and threw yams at him, unmindful of the body-guard.

On account of the extreme scarcity of material, it was found necessary to require the Duke of Bethany, postmaster-general, to pull stroke-oar in the navy, and thus sit in the rear of a noble of lower degree, namely, Viscount Canaan, lord-justice of the common pleas. This turned the Duke of Bethany into a tolerably open malcontent and a secret conspirator, — a thing which the emperor foresaw, but could not help.

Things went from bad to worse. The emperor raised Nancy Peters to the peerage on one day, and married her the next, notwithstanding, for reasons of state, the cabinet had strenuously advised him to marry Emmeline, eldest daughter of the Archbishop

of Bethlehem. This caused trouble in a powerful
quarter, — the church. The new empress secured the
support and friendship of two thirds of the thirty-six
grown women in the nation by absorbing them into
her court as maids of honor ; but this made deadly
enemies of the remaining twelve. The families of the
maids of honor soon began to rebel, because there was
now nobody at home to keep house. The twelve
snubbed women refused to enter the imperial kitchen
as servants ; so the empress had to require the Countess of Jericho and other great court dames to fetch
water, sweep the palace, and perform other menial
and equally distasteful services. This made bad blood
in that department.

Everybody fell to complaining that the taxes levied
for the support of the army, the navy, and the rest
of the imperial establishment were intolerably burden-
some, and were reducing the nation to beggary. The
emperor's reply — "Look at Germany ; look at Italy.
Are you better than they ? and have n't you unification ?" — did not satisfy them. They said, "People
can't *eat* unification, and we are starving. Agriculture
has ceased. Everybody is in the army, everybody is in
the navy, everybody is in the public service, standing
around in a uniform, with nothing whatever to do,
nothing to eat, and nobody to till the fields — "

"Look at Germany ; look at Italy. It is the same
there. Such is unification, and there 's no other way
to get it, — no other way to keep it after you 've got
it," said the poor emperor always.

But the grumblers only replied, "We can't *stand* the
taxes, — we can't *stand* them."

Now right on top of this the cabinet reported a national debt amounting to upwards of forty-five dollars, — half a dollar to every individual in the nation. And they proposed to fund something. They had heard that this was always done in such emergencies. They proposed duties on exports; also on imports. And they wanted to issue bonds; also paper money, redeemable in yams and cabbages in fifty years. They said the pay of the army and of the navy and of the whole governmental machine was far in arrears, and unless something was done, and done immediately, national bankruptcy must ensue, and possibly insurrection and revolution. The emperor at once resolved upon a high-handed measure, and one of a nature never before heard of in Pitcairn's Island. He went in state to the church on Sunday morning, with the army at his back, and commanded the minister of the treasury to take up a collection.

That was the feather that broke the camel's back. First one citizen, and then another, rose and refused to submit to this unheard-of outrage, — and each refusal was followed by the immediate confiscation of the malcontent's property. This vigor soon stopped the refusals, and the collection proceeded amid a sullen and ominous silence. As the emperor withdrew with the troops, he said, " I will teach you who is master here." Several persons shouted, "Down with unification ! " They were at once arrested and torn from the arms of their weeping friends by the soldiery.

But in the mean time, as any prophet might have foreseen, a Social Democrat had been developed. As the emperor stepped into the gilded imperial wheel-barrow at the church door, the social democrat stabbed at him fifteen or sixteen times with a harpoon, but fortunately with such a peculiarly social democratic unprecision of aim as to do no damage.

That very night the convulsion came. The nation rose as one man, — though forty-nine of the revolutionists were of the other sex. The infantry threw down their pitchforks; the artillery cast aside their cocoa-nuts; the navy revolted; the emperor was seized, and bound hand and foot in his palace. He was very much depressed. He said, —

"I freed you from a grinding tyranny; I lifted you up out of your degradation, and made you a nation among nations; I gave you a strong, compact, central-ized government; and, more than all, I gave you the blessing of blessings, — unification. I have done all this, and my reward is hatred, insult, and these bonds. Take me; do with me as ye will. I here resign my crown and all my dignities, and gladly do I release myself from their too heavy burden. For your sake I took them up; for your sake I lay them down. The imperial jewel is no more; now bruise and defile as ye will the useless setting."

By a unanimous voice the people condemned the ex-emperor and the social democrat to perpetual ban-ishment from church services, or to perpetual labor as galley-slaves in the whale-boat, — whichever they might prefer. The next day the nation assembled again, and rehoisted the British flag, reinstated the British tyranny, reduced the nobility to the condition of commoners again, and then straightway turned their diligent attention to the weeding of the ruined and neglected yam patches, and the rehabilitation of the old useful industries and the old healing and solacing pieties. The ex-emperor restored the lost trespass law, and explained that he had stolen it, — not to injure any one, but to further his political projects. Therefore the nation gave the late chief magistrate his office again, and also his alienated property.

Upon reflection, the ex-emperor and the social democrat chose perpetual banishment from religious services, in preference to perpetual labor as galley-slaves "*with* perpetual religious services," as they phrased it ; wherefore the people believed that the poor fellows' troubles had unseated their reason, and so they judged it best to confine them for the present. Which they did.

Such is the history of Pitcairn's "doubtful acquisition."

MRS. McWILLIAMS AND THE LIGHTNING.

WELL, sir, — continued Mr. McWilliams, for this was not the beginning of his talk, — the fear of lightning is one of the most distressing infirmities a human being can be afflicted with. It is mostly confined to women; but now and then you find it in a little dog, and sometimes in a man. It is a particularly distressing infirmity, for the reason that it takes the sand out of a person to an extent which no other fear can, and it can't be *reasoned* with, and neither can it be shamed out of a person. A woman who could face the very devil himself — or a mouse — loses her grip and goes all to pieces in front of a flash of lightning. Her fright is something pitiful to see.

Well, as I was telling you, I woke up, with that smothered and unlocatable cry of "Mortimer! Mortimer!" wailing in my ears; and as soon as I could scrape my faculties together I reached over in the dark and then said, —

"Evangeline, is that you calling? What is the matter? Where are you?"

"Shut up in the boot-closet. You ought to be ashamed to lie there and sleep so, and such an awful storm going on."

" Why, how *can* one be ashamed when he is asleep ? It is unreasonable ; a man *can't* be ashamed when he is asleep, Evangeline."

"You never try, Mortimer, — you know very well you never try."

I caught the sound of muffled sobs.

That sound smote dead the sharp speech that was on my lips, and I changed it to —

" I 'm sorry, dear, — I 'm truly sorry. I never meant to act so. Come back and — "

" MORTIMER ! "

" Heavens ! what is the matter, my love ? "

" Do you mean to say you are in that bed yet ? "

" Why, of course."

"Come out of it instantly. I should think you would take some *little* care of your life, for *my* sake and the children's, if you will not for your own."

" But my love — "

" Don't talk to me, Mortimer. You *know* there is no place so dangerous as a bed, in such a thunder-storm as this, — all the books say that ; yet there you would lie, and deliberately throw away your life, — for goodness knows what, unless for the sake of arguing and arguing, and — "

" But, confound it, Evangeline, I 'm *not* in the bed, *now*. I 'm — "

[Sentence interrupted by a sudden glare of lightning, followed by a terrified little scream from Mrs. McWilliams and a tremendous blast of thunder.]

" There ! You see the result. Oh, Mortimer, how *can* you be so profligate as to swear at such a time as this ? "

"I *did n't* swear. And that *was n't* a result of it, any way. It would have come, just the same, if I had n't said a word; and you know very well, Evangeline, — at least you ought to know, — that when the atmosphere is charged with electricity — "

"Oh, yes, now argue it, and argue it, and argue it! — I don't see how you can act so, when you *know* there is not a lightning-rod on the place, and your poor wife and children are absolutely at the mercy of Providence. What *are* you doing? — lighting a match at such a time as this! Are you stark mad?"

"Hang it, woman, where 's the harm? The place is as dark as the inside of an infidel, and — "

"Put it out! put it out instantly! Are you determined to sacrifice us all? You *know* there is nothing attracts lightning like a light. [*Fzt! — crash! boom — boloom-boom-boom!*] Oh, just hear it! Now you see what you 've done!"

"No, I *don't* see what I 've done. A match may attract lightning, for all I know, but it don't *cause* lightning, — I 'll go odds on that. And it did n't attract it worth a cent this time; for if that shot was levelled at my match, it was blessed poor marksmanship, — about an average of none out of a possible million, I should say. Why, at Dollymount, such marksmanship as that — "

"For shame, Mortimer! Here we are standing right in the very presence of death, and yet in so solemn a moment you are capable of using such language as that. If you have no desire to — Mortimer!"

"Well?"

"Did you say your prayers to-night?"

"I — I — meant to, but I got to trying to cipher out how much twelve times thirteen is, and —"

[*Fzt !* — boom - berroom - boom *!* bumble - umble bang-
SMASH !]

"Oh, we are lost, beyond all help! How *could* you neglect such a thing at such a time as this?"

"But it *was n't* 'such a time as this.' There was n't a cloud in the sky. How could *I* know there was going to be all this rumpus and pow-wow about a little slip like that? And I don't think it 's just fair for you to make so much out of it, any way, seeing it happens so seldom; I have n't missed before since I brought on that earthquake, four years ago."

"MORTIMER! How you talk! Have you forgotten the yellow fever?"

"My dear, you are always throwing up the yellow fever to me, and I think it is perfectly unreasonable. You can't even send a telegraphic message as far as Memphis without relays, so how is a little devotional slip of mine going to carry so far? I 'll *stand* the earthquake, because it was in the neighborhood; but I 'll be hanged if I 'm going to be responsible for every blamed —"

[*Fzt !* — BOOM *beroom*-boom ! boom ! — BANG !]

"Oh, dear, dear, dear! I *know* it struck something, Mortimer. We never shall see the light of another day; and if it will do you any good to remember, when we are gone, that your dreadful language — *Mortimer !*"

"Well! What now?"

"Your voice sounds as if — Mortimer, are you actually standing in front of that open fireplace?"

"That is the very crime I am committing."

"Get away from it, this moment. You do seem determined to bring destruction on us all. Don't you *know* that there is no better conductor for lightning than an open chimney? *Now* where have you got to?"

"I'm here by the window."

"Oh, for pity's sake, have you lost your mind? Clear out from there, this moment. The very children in arms know it is fatal to stand near a window in a thunder-storm. Dear, dear, I know I shall never see the light of another day. Mortimer?"

"Yes?"

"What is that rustling?"

"It's me."

"What are you doing?"

"Trying to find the upper end of my pantaloons."

"Quick! throw those things away! I do believe you would deliberately put on those clothes at such a time as this; yet you know perfectly well that *all* authorities agree that woollen stuffs attract lightning. Oh, dear, dear, it isn't sufficient that one's life must be in peril from natural causes, but you must do everything you can possibly think of to augment the danger. Oh, *don't* sing! What *can* you be thinking of?"

"Now where's the harm in it?"

"Mortimer, if I have told you once, I have told you a hundred times, that singing causes vibrations in the atmosphere which interrupt the flow of the electric fluid, and — What on *earth* are you opening that door for ? "

" Goodness gracious, woman, is there any harm in *that ?* "

" *Harm ?* There 's *death* in it. Anybody that has given this subject any attention knows that to create a draught is to invite the lightning. You have n't half shut it ; shut it *tight,* — and do hurry, or we are all destroyed. Oh, it is an awful thing to be shut up with a lunatic at such a time as this. Mortimer, what *are* you doing ? "

" Nothing. Just turning on the water. This room is smothering hot and close. I want to bathe my face and hands."

" You have certainly parted with the remnant of your mind ! Where lightning strikes any other sub- stance once, it strikes water fifty times. Do turn it off. Oh, dear, I am sure that nothing in this world can save us. It does seem to me that — Mortimer, what was that ? "

" It was a da— it was a picture. Knocked it down."

" Then you are close to the wall ! I never heard of such imprudence ! Don't you *know* that there 's no better conductor for lightning than a wall ? Come away from there ! And you came as near as anything to swearing, too. Oh, how can you be so desperately wicked, and your family in such peril ? Mortimer, did you order a feather bed, as I asked you to do ? "

" No. Forgot it."

"Forgot it! It may cost you your life. If you had a feather bed, now, and could spread it in the middle of the room and lie on it, you would be perfectly safe. Come in here, — come quick, before you have a chance to commit any more frantic indiscretions."

I tried, but the little closet would not hold us both with the door shut, unless we could be content to smother. I gasped awhile, then forced my way out. My wife called out, —

"Mortimer, something *must* be done for your preservation. Give me that German book that is on the end of the mantel-piece, and a candle; but don't light it; give me a match; I will light it in here. That book has some directions in it."

I got the book, — at cost of a vase and some other brittle things; and the madam shut herself up with her candle. I had a moment's peace; then she called out, —

"Mortimer, what was that?"

"Nothing but the cat."

"The cat! Oh, destruction! Catch her, and shut her up in the wash-stand. Do be quick, love; cats are *full* of electricity. I just know my hair will turn white with this night's awful perils."

I heard the muffled sobbings again. But for that, I should not have moved hand or foot in such a wild enterprise in the dark.

However, I went at my task, — over chairs, and against all sorts of obstructions, all of them hard ones, too, and most of them with sharp edges, — and at last

I got kitty cooped up in the commode, at an expense of over four hundred dollars in broken furniture and shins. Then these muffled words came from the closet : —

"It says the safest thing is to stand on a chair in the middle of the room, Mortimer; and the legs of the chair must be insulated, with non-conductors. That is, you must set the legs of the chair in glass tumblers. [*Fzt ! — boom — bang ! — smash !*] Oh, hear that ! Do hurry, Mortimer, before you are struck."

I managed to find and secure the tumblers. I got the last four, — broke all the rest. I insulated the chair legs, and called for further instructions.

"Mortimer, it says, 'Während eines Gewitters ent-ferne man Metalle, wie z. B., Ringe, Uhren, Schlüssel, etc., von sich und halte sich auch nicht an solchen Stellen auf, wo viele Metalle bei einander liegen, oder mit andern Körpern verbunden sind, wie an Herden, Oefen, Eisengittern u. dgl.' What does that mean, Mortimer ? Does it mean that you must keep metals *about* you, or keep them *away* from you ?"

"Well, I hardly know. It appears to be a little mixed. All German advice is more or less mixed. However, I think that that sentence is mostly in the dative case, with a little genitive and accusative sifted in, here and there, for luck ; so I reckon it means that you must keep some metals *about* you."

"Yes, that must be it. It stands to reason that it is. They are in the nature of lightning-rods, you know. Put on your fireman's helmet, Mortimer ; that is mostly metal."

I got it and put it on, — a very heavy and clumsy and uncomfortable thing on a hot night in a close room. Even my night-dress seemed to be more cloth-ing than I strictly needed.

"Mortimer, I think your middle ought to be pro-tected. Won't you buckle on your militia sabre, please ?"

I complied.

"Now, Mortimer, you ought to have some way to protect your feet. Do please put on your spurs."

I did it, — in silence, — and kept my temper as well as I could.

"Mortimer, it says, 'Das Gewitter läuten ist sehr gefährlich, weil die Glocke selbst, sowie der durch das Läuten veranlasste Luftzug und die Höhe des Thurmes den Blitz anziehen könnten.' Mortimer, does that mean that it is dangerous not to ring the church bells during a thunder-storm ?"

"Yes, it seems to mean that, — if that is the past participle of the nominative case singular, and I reckon it is. Yes, I think it means that on account of the height of the church tower and the absence of *Luftzug* it would be very dangerous (*sehr gefährlich*) not to ring the bells in time of a storm; and moreover, don't you see, the very wording — "

"Never mind that, Mortimer; don't waste the pre-cious time in talk. Get the large dinner-bell; it is right there in the hall. Quick, Mortimer dear; we are almost safe. Oh, dear, I do believe we are going to be saved, at last ! "

Our little summer establishment stands on top of a

high range of hills, overlooking a valley. Several farm-houses are in our neighborhood, — the nearest some three or four hundred yards away.

When I, mounted on the chair, had been clanging that dreadful bell a matter of seven or eight minutes, our shutters were suddenly torn open from without, and a brilliant bull's-eye lantern was thrust in at the window, followed by a hoarse inquiry : —

" What in the nation is the matter here ? "

The window was full of men's heads, and the heads were full of eyes that stared wildly at my night-dress and my warlike accoutrements.

I dropped the bell, skipped down from the chair in confusion, and said, —

" There is nothing the matter, friends, — only a little discomfort on account of the thunder-storm. I was trying to keep off the lightning."

" Thunder-storm ? Lightning ? Why, Mr. McWilliams, have you lost your mind ? It is a beautiful starlight night ; there has been no storm."

I looked out, and I was so astonished I could hardly speak for a while. Then I said, —

" I do not understand this. We distinctly saw the glow of the flashes through the curtains and shutters, and heard the thunder."

One after another of those people lay down on the ground to laugh, — and two of them died. One of the survivors remarked, —

" Pity you did n't think to open your blinds and look over to the top of the high hill yonder. What you heard was cannon ; what you saw was the flash.

You see, the telegraph brought some news, just at midnight : Garfield 's nominated, — and that 's what 's the matter ! "

Yes, Mr. Twain, as I was saying in the beginning (said Mr. McWilliams), the rules for preserving people against lightning are so excellent and so innumerable that the most incomprehensible thing in the world to me is how anybody ever manages to get struck.

So saying, he gathered up his satchel and umbrella, and departed ; for the train had reached his town.

ON THE DECAY OF THE ART OF LYING.

ESSAY, FOR DISCUSSION, READ AT A MEETING OF THE HIS-
TORICAL AND ANTIQUARIAN CLUB OF HARTFORD, AND
OFFERED FOR THE THIRTY-DOLLAR PRIZE. NOW FIRST
PUBLISHED.[1]

———◆———

OBSERVE, I do not mean to suggest that the
custom of lying has suffered any decay or interruption, — no, for the Lie, as a Virtue, a Principle, is
eternal; the Lie, as a recreation, a solace, a refuge in
time of need, the fourth Grace, the tenth Muse, man's
best and surest friend, is immortal, and cannot perish
from the earth while this Club remains. My complaint simply concerns the decay of the *art* of lying.
No high-minded man, no man of right feeling, can
contemplate the lumbering and slovenly lying of the
present day without grieving to see a noble art so
prostituted. In this veteran presence I naturally
enter upon this theme with diffidence; it is like an old
maid trying to teach nursery matters to the mothers
in Israel. It would not become me to criticise you,
gentlemen, who are nearly all my elders — and my

---

[1] Did not take the prize.

superiors, in this thing — and so, if I should here and there *seem* to do it, I trust it will in most cases be more in a spirit of admiration than of fault-finding; indeed if this finest of the fine arts had everywhere received the attention, encouragement, and conscientious practice and development which this Club has devoted to it, I should not need to utter this lament, or shed a single tear. I do not say this to flatter: I say it in a spirit of just and appreciative recognition. [It had been my intention, at this point, to mention names and give illustrative specimens, but indications observable about me admonished me to beware of particulars and confine myself to generalities.]

No fact is more firmly established than that lying is a necessity of our circumstances, — the deduction that it is then a Virtue goes without saying. No virtue can reach its highest usefulness without careful and diligent cultivation, — therefore, it goes without saying, that this one ought to be taught in the public schools — at the fireside — even in the newspapers. What chance has the ignorant, uncultivated liar against the educated expert? What chance have I against Mr. Per— against a lawyer? *Judicious* lying is what the world needs. I sometimes think it were even better and safer not to lie at all than to lie injudiciously. An awkward, unscientific lie is often as ineffectual as the truth.

Now let us see what the philosophers say. Note that venerable proverb: Children and fools *always* speak the truth. The deduction is plain, — adults and wise persons *never* speak it. Parkman, the historian, says, " The principle of truth may itself be carried into an absurdity." In another place in the same chapter he says, " The saying is old that truth should not be spoken at all times ; and those whom a sick conscience worries into habitual violation of the maxim are imbeciles and nuisances." It is strong language, but true. None of us could *live* with an habitual truth-teller ; but thank goodness none of us has to. An habitual truth-teller is simply an impossible creature ; he does not exist ; he never has existed. Of course there are people who *think* they never lie, but it is not so, — and this ignorance is one of the very things that shame our so-called civilization. Everybody lies — every day ; every hour ; awake ; asleep ; in his dreams ; in his joy ; in his mourning ; if he keeps his tongue still, his hands, his feet, his eyes, his attitude, will convey deception — and purposely. Even in sermons — but that is a platitude.

In a far country where I once lived the ladies used to go around paying calls, under the humane and kindly pretence of wanting to see each other ; and when they returned home, they would cry out with a glad voice, saying, " We made sixteen calls and found fourteen of them out," — not meaning that they found out anything against the fourteen, — no, that was only a colloquial phrase to signify that they were not at home, — and their manner of saying it expressed their lively satisfaction in that fact. Now their pretence of wanting to see the fourteen — and the other two whom they had been less lucky with — was that commonest and mildest form of lying which is sufficiently

described as a deflection from the truth. Is it justifiable? Most certainly. It is beautiful, it is noble;
for its object is, *not* to reap profit, but to convey a
pleasure to the sixteen. The iron-souled truth-monger
would plainly manifest, or even utter the fact that
he did n't want to see those people, — and he would be
an ass, and inflict a totally unnecessary pain. And
next, those ladies in that far country — but never
mind, they had a thousand pleasant ways of lying,
that grew out of gentle impulses, and were a credit to
their intelligence and an honor to their hearts. Let
the particulars go.

The men in that far country were liars, every one.
Their mere howdy-do was a lie, because *they* did n't care
how you did, except they were undertakers. To the
ordinary inquirer you lied in return; for you made no
conscientious diagnosis of your case, but answered at
random, and usually missed it considerably. You lied
to the undertaker, and said your health was failing —
a wholly commendable lie, since it cost you nothing
and pleased the other man. If a stranger called and
interrupted you, you said with your hearty tongue,
"I 'm glad to see you," and said with your heartier
soul, "I wish you were with the cannibals and it was
dinner time." When he went, you said regretfully,
"*Must* you go?" and followed it with a "Call again;"
but you did no harm, for you did not deceive anybody
nor inflict any hurt, whereas the truth would have
made you both unhappy.

I think that all this courteous lying is a sweet and
loving art, and should be cultivated. The highest

perfection of politeness is only a beautiful edifice, built, from the base to the dome, of graceful and gilded forms of charitable and unselfish lying.

What I bemoan is the growing prevalence of the brutal truth. Let us do what we can to eradicate it. An injurious truth has no merit over an injurious lie. Neither should ever be uttered. The man who speaks an injurious truth lest his soul be not saved if he do otherwise, should reflect that that sort of a soul is not strictly worth saving. The man who tells a lie to help a poor devil out of trouble, is one of whom the angels doubtless say, "Lo, here is an heroic soul who casts his own welfare into jeopardy to succor his neighbor's; let us exalt this magnanimous liar."

An injurious lie is an uncommendable thing; and so, also, and in the same degree, is an injurious truth, — a fact which is recognized by the law of libel.

Among other common lies, we have the *silent* lie, — the deception which one conveys by simply keeping still and concealing the truth. Many obstinate truth-mongers indulge in this dissipation, imagining that if they *speak* no lie, they lie not at all. In that far country where I once lived, there was a lovely spirit, a lady whose impulses were always high and pure, and whose character answered to them. One day I was there at dinner, and remarked, in a general way, that we are all liars. She was amazed, and said, "Not *all?*" It was before Pinafore's time, so I did not make the response which would naturally follow in our day, but frankly said, "Yes, *all* — we are all liars; there are no exceptions." She looked almost offended, and said,

"Why, do you include *me* ?"   "Certainly," I said, "I think you even rank as an expert." She said, "Sh— sh! the children!" So the subject was changed in deference to the children's presence, and we went on talking about other things.   But as soon as the young people were out of the way, the lady came warmly back to the matter and said, "I have made it the rule of my life to never tell a lie; and I have never departed from it in a single instance." I said, "I don't mean the least harm or disrespect, but really you have been lying like smoke ever since I've been sitting here.   It has caused me a good deal of pain, because I am not used to it." She required of me an instance — just a single instance.   So I said, —

"Well, here is the unfilled duplicate of the blank which the Oakland hospital people sent to you by the hand of the sick-nurse when she came here to nurse your little nephew through his dangerous illness.   This blank asks all manner of questions as to the conduct of that sick-nurse : 'Did she ever sleep on her watch? Did she ever forget to give the medicine?' and so forth and so on.   You are warned to be very careful and explicit in your answers, for the welfare of the service requires that the nurses be promptly fined or otherwise punished for derelictions.   You told me you were perfectly delighted with that nurse — that she had a thousand perfections and only one fault : you found you never could depend on her wrapping Johnny up half sufficiently while he waited in a chilly chair for her to rearrange the warm bed.   You filled up the duplicate of this paper, and sent it back to the hospital by the hand of the nurse. How did you answer this question, — 'Was the nurse at any time guilty of a negligence which was likely to result in the patient's taking cold?' Come — everything is decided by a bet here in California: ten dollars to ten cents you lied when you answered that question." She said, "I did n't; *I left it blank!*" "Just so — you have told a *silent* lie; you have left it to be inferred that you had no fault to find in that matter." She said, "Oh, was that a lie? And how *could* I mention her one single fault, and she so good? — it would have been cruel." I said, "One ought always to lie, when one can do good by it; your impulse was right, but your judgment was crude; this comes of unintelligent practice. Now observe the result of this inexpert deflection of yours. You know Mr. Jones's Willie is lying very low with scarlet fever; well, your recommendation was so enthusiastic that that girl is there nursing him, and the worn-out family have all been trustingly sound asleep for the last fourteen hours, leaving their darling with full confidence in those fatal hands, because you, like young George Washington, have a reputa— However, if you are not going to have anything to do, I will come around to-morrow and we'll attend the funeral together, for of course you'll naturally feel a peculiar interest in Willie's case, — as personal a one, in fact, as the undertaker."

But that was all lost. Before I was half-way through she was in a carriage and making thirty miles an hour toward the Jones mansion to save what was left of Willie and tell all she knew about the deadly nurse.

All of which was unnecessary, as Willie was n't sick; I had been lying myself. But that same day, all the same, she sent a line to the hospital which filled up the neglected blank, and stated the *facts*, too, in the squarest possible manner.

Now, you see, this lady's fault was *not* in lying, but only in lying injudiciously. She should have told the truth, *there*, and made it up to the nurse with a fraudulent compliment further along in the paper. She could have said, " In one respect this sick-nurse is perfection, — when she is on watch, she never snores." Almost any little pleasant lie would have taken the sting out of that troublesome but necessary expression of the truth.

Lying is universal — we *all* do it; we all *must* do it. Therefore, the wise thing is for us diligently to train ourselves to lie thoughtfully, judiciously; to lie with a good object, and not an evil one; to lie for others' advantage, and not our own; to lie healingly, charitably, humanely, not cruelly, hurtfully, maliciously; to lie gracefully and graciously, not awkwardly and clumsily; to lie firmly, frankly, squarely, with head erect, not haltingly, tortuously, with pusillanimous mien, as being ashamed of our high calling. Then shall we be rid of the rank and pestilent truth that is rotting the land; then shall we be great and good and beautiful, and worthy dwellers in a world where even benign Nature habitually lies, except when she promises execrable weather. Then — But I am but a new and feeble student in this gracious art; I cannot instruct *this* Club.

Joking aside, I think there is much need of wise examination into what sorts of lies are best and whole-somest to be indulged, seeing we *must* all lie and *do* all lie, and what sorts it may be best to avoid, — and this is a thing which I feel I can confidently put into the hands of this experienced Club, — a ripe body, who may be termed, in this regard, and without undue flattery, Old Masters.

15

THE CANVASSER'S TALE.

———◆———

POOR, sad-eyed stranger! There was that about his humble mien, his tired look, his decayed-gentility clothes, that almost reached the mustard-seed of charity that still remained, remote and lonely, in the empty vastness of my heart, notwithstanding I observed a portfolio under his arm, and said to myself, Behold, Providence hath delivered his servant into the hands of another canvasser.

Well, these people always get one interested. Before I well knew how it came about, this one was telling me his history, and I was all attention and sympathy. He told it something like this : —

My parents died, alas, when I was a little, sinless child. My uncle Ithuriel took me to his heart and reared me as his own. He was my only relative in the wide world ; but he was good and rich and generous. He reared me in the lap of luxury. I knew no want that money could satisfy.

In the fulness of time I was graduated, and went with two of my servants — my chamberlain and my valet — to travel in foreign countries. During four years I flitted upon careless wing amid the beauteous gardens of the distant strand, if you will permit this form of speech in one whose tongue was ever attuned to poesy; and indeed I so speak with confidence, as one unto his kind, for I perceive by your eyes that you too, sir, are gifted with the divine inflation. In those far lands I revelled in the ambrosial food that fructifies the soul, the mind, the heart. But of all things, that which most appealed to my inborn æsthetic taste was the prevailing custom there, among the rich, of making collections of elegant and costly rarities, dainty *objets de vertu*, and in an evil hour I tried to uplift my uncle Ithuriel to a plane of sympathy with this exquisite employment.

I wrote and told him of one gentleman's vast collection of shells; another's noble collection of meerschaum pipes; another's elevating and refining collection of undecipherable autographs; another's priceless collection of old china; another's enchanting collection of postage stamps, — and so forth and so on. Soon my letters yielded fruit. My uncle began to look about for something to make a collection of. You may know, perhaps, how fleetly a taste like this dilates. His soon became a raging fever, though I knew it not. He began to neglect his great pork business; presently he wholly retired and turned an elegant leisure into a rabid search for curious things. His wealth was vast, and he spared it not. First he tried cow-bells. He made a collection which filled five large *salons*, and comprehended all the different sorts of cow-bells that ever had been contrived, save one. That one — an antique, and the only specimen extant — was possessed by another collector. My uncle offered enormous sums for it, but the gentleman would not sell. Doubtless you know what necessarily resulted. A true collector attaches no value to a collection that is not complete. His great heart breaks, he sells his hoard, he turns his mind to some field that seems unoccupied.

Thus did my uncle. He next tried brickbats. After piling up a vast and intensely interesting collection, the former difficulty supervened; his great heart broke again; he sold out his soul's idol to the retired brewer who possessed the missing brick. Then he tried flint hatchets and other implements of Primeval Man, but by and by discovered that the factory where they were made was supplying other collectors as well as himself. He tried Aztec inscriptions and stuffed whales — another failure, after incredible labor and expense. When his collection seemed at last perfect, a stuffed whale arrived from Greenland and an Aztec inscription from the Cundurango regions of Central America that made all former specimens insignificant. My uncle hastened to secure these noble gems. He got the stuffed whale, but another collector got the inscription. A real Cundurango, as possibly you know, is a possession of such supreme value that, when once a collector gets it, he will rather part with his family than with it. So my uncle sold out, and saw his darlings go forth, never more to return; and his coal-black hair turned white as snow in a single night.

Now he waited, and thought. He knew another disappointment might kill him. He was resolved that he would choose things next time that no other man was collecting. He carefully made up his mind, and once more entered the field — this time to make a collection of echoes.

"Of what?" said I.

Echoes, sir. His first purchase was an echo in Georgia that repeated four times ; his next was a six-repeater in Maryland; his next was a thirteen-repeater in Maine ; his next was a nine-repeater in Kansas ; his next was a twelve-repeater in Tennessee, which he got cheap, so to speak, because it was out of repair, a portion of the crag which reflected it having tumbled down. He believed he could repair it at a cost of a few thousand dollars, and, by increasing the elevation with masonry, treble the repeating capacity ; but the architect who undertook the job had never built an echo before, and so he utterly spoiled this one. Before he meddled with it, it used to talk back like a mother-in-law, but now it was only fit for the deaf and dumb asylum. Well, next he bought a lot of cheap little double-barrelled echoes, scattered around over various States and Territories ; he got them at twenty per cent off by taking the lot. Next he bought a perfect Gatling gun of an echo in Oregon, and it cost a fortune, I can tell you. You may know, sir, that in the echo market the scale of prices is cumulative, like the carat-scale in diamonds ; in fact, the same phraseology is used. A single-carat echo is worth but ten dollars over and above the value of the land it is on ; a two-carat or double-barrelled echo is worth thirty dollars ; a five-carat is worth nine hundred and fifty ; a ten-carat is worth thirteen thousand. My uncle's Oregon echo, which he called the Great Pitt Echo, was a twenty-two carat gem, and cost two hundred and sixteen thousand dollars — they threw the land in, for it was four hundred miles from a settlement.

Well, in the mean time my path was a path of roses. I was the accepted suitor of the only and lovely daughter of an English earl, and was beloved to distraction. In that dear presence I swam in seas of bliss. The family were content, for it was known that I was sole heir to an uncle held to be worth five millions of dollars. However, none of us knew that my uncle had become a collector, at least in anything more than a small way, for æsthetic amusement.

Now gathered the clouds above my unconscious head. That divine echo, since known throughout the world as the Great Koh-i-noor, or Mountain of Repetitions, was discovered. It was a sixty-five-carat gem. You could utter a word and it would talk back at you for fifteen minutes, when the day was otherwise quiet. But behold, another fact came to light at the same time : another echo-collector was in the field. The two rushed to make the peerless purchase. The property consisted of a couple of small hills with a shallow swale between, out yonder among the back settlements of New York State. Both men arrived on the ground at the same time, and neither knew the other was there. The echo was not all owned by one man ; a person by the name of Williamson Bolivar Jarvis owned the east hill, and a person by the name of Harbison J. Bledso owned the west hill ; the swale between was the dividing line. So while my uncle was buying

Jarvis's hill for three million two hundred and eighty-five thousand dollars, the other party was buying Bledso's hill for a shade over three million.

Now, do you perceive the natural result? Why, the noblest collection of echoes on earth was forever and ever incomplete, since it possessed but the one half of the king echo of the universe. Neither man was content with this divided ownership, yet neither would sell to the other. There were jawings, bickerings, heart-burnings. And at last, that other collector, with a malignity which only a collector can ever feel toward a man and a brother, proceeded to cut down his hill !

You see, as long as he could not have the echo, he was resolved that nobody should have it. He would remove his hill, and then there would be nothing to reflect my uncle's echo. My uncle remonstrated with him, but the man said, "I own one end of this echo; I choose to kill my end ; you must take care of your own end yourself."

Well, my uncle got an injunction put on him. The other man appealed and fought it in a higher court. They carried it on up, clear to the Supreme Court of the United States. It made no end of trouble there. Two of the judges believed that an echo was personal property, because it was impalpable to sight and touch, and yet was purchasable, salable, and consequently taxable ; two others believed that an echo was real estate, because it was manifestly attached to the land, and was not removable from place to place; other of the judges contended that an echo was not property at all.

It was finally decided that the echo was property; that the hills were property; that the two men were separate and independent owners of the two hills, but tenants in common in the echo; therefore defendant was at full liberty to cut down his hill, since it belonged solely to him, but must give bonds in three million dollars as indemnity for damages which might result to my uncle's half of the echo. This decision also debarred my uncle from using defendant's hill to reflect his part of the echo, without defendant's consent; he must use only his own hill; if his part of the echo would not go, under these circumstances, it was sad, of course, but the court could find no remedy. The court also debarred defendant from using my uncle's hill to reflect *his* end of the echo, without consent. You see the grand result! Neither man would give consent, and so that astonishing and most noble echo had to cease from its great powers; and since that day that magnificent property is tied up and unsalable.

A week before my wedding day, while I was still swimming in bliss and the nobility were gathering from far and near to honor our espousals, came news of my uncle's death, and also a copy of his will, making me his sole heir. He was gone; alas, my dear benefactor was no more. The thought surcharges my heart even at this remote day. I handed the will to the earl; I could not read it for the blinding tears. The earl read it; then he sternly said, "Sir, do you call this wealth? — but doubtless you do in your inflated country. Sir, you are left sole heir to a vast collection of echoes — if a thing can be called a collection that is scattered far and wide over the huge length and breadth of the American continent; sir, this is not all; you are head and ears in debt; there is not an echo in the lot but has a mortgage on it; sir, I am not a hard man, but I must look to my child's interest ; if you had but one echo which you could honestly call your own, if you had but one echo which was free from incumbrance, so that you could retire to it with my child, and by humble, painstaking industry, cultivate and improve it, and thus wrest from it a maintenance, I would not say you nay ; but I cannot marry my child to a beggar. Leave his side, my darling ; go, sir ; take your mortgage-ridden echoes and quit my sight forever."

My noble Celestine clung to me in tears, with loving arms, and swore she would willingly, nay, gladly marry me, though I had not an echo in the world. But it could not be. We were torn asunder, she to pine and die within the twelvemonth, I to toil life's long journey sad and lone, praying daily, hourly, for that release which shall join us together again in that dear realm where the wicked cease from troubling and the weary are at rest. Now, sir, if you will be so kind as to look at these maps and plans in my portfolio, I am sure I can sell you an echo for less money than any man in the trade. Now this one, which cost my uncle ten dollars, thirty years ago, and is one of the sweetest things in Texas, I will let you have for —

" Let me interrupt you," I said. " My friend, I have not had a moment's respite from canvassers this day.

I have bought a sewing-machine which I did not want; I have bought a map which is mistaken in all its details; I have bought a clock which will not go; I have bought a moth poison which the moths prefer to any other beverage; I have bought no end of useless inventions, and now I have had enough of this foolishness. I would not have one of your echoes if you were even to give it to me. I would not let it stay on the place. I always hate a man that tries to sell me echoes. You see this gun? Now take your collection and move on; let us not have bloodshed."

But he only smiled a sad, sweet smile, and got out some more diagrams. You know the result perfectly well, because you know that when you have once opened the door to a canvasser, the trouble is done and you have got to suffer defeat.

I compromised with this man at the end of an intolerable hour. I bought two double-barrelled echoes in good condition, and he threw in another, which he said was not salable because it only spoke German. He said, "She was a perfect polyglot once, but somehow her palate got down."

AN ENCOUNTER WITH AN INTER-
VIEWER.

———◆———

THE nervous, dapper, "peart" young man took the chair I offered him, and said he was con- nected with the "Daily Thunderstorm," and added, —

"Hoping it's no harm, I've come to interview you."

"Come to what?"

"*Interview* you."

"Ah! I see. Yes — yes. Um! Yes — yes."

I was not feeling bright that morning. Indeed, my powers seemed a bit under a cloud. However, I went to the bookcase, and when I had been looking six or seven minutes, I found I was obliged to refer to the young man. I said, —

"How do you spell it?"

"Spell what?"

"Interview."

"Oh my goodness! what do you want to spell it for?"

"I don't want to spell it; I want to see what it means."

"Well, this is astonishing, I must say. *I* can tell you what it means, if you — if you —"

"Oh, all right! That will answer, and much obliged to you, too."

"In, *in,* ter, *ter, inter*— "

"Then you spell it with an *I ?* "

"Why, certainly ! "

"Oh, that is what took me so long."

"Why, my *dear* sir, what did *you* propose to spell it with ? "

"Well, I — I — hardly know. I had the Unabridged, and I was ciphering around in the back end, hoping I might tree her among the pictures. But it's a very old edition."

"Why, my friend, they would n't have a *picture* of it in even the latest e— My dear sir, I beg your pardon, I mean no harm in the world, but you do not look as — as — intelligent as I had expected you would. No harm — I mean no harm at all."

"Oh, don't mention it ! It has often been said, and by people who would not flatter and who could have no inducement to flatter, that I am quite remarkable in that way. Yes — yes; they always speak of it with rapture."

"I can easily imagine it. But about this interview. You know it is the custom, now, to interview any man who has become notorious."

"Indeed, I had not heard of it before. It must be very interesting. What do you do it with ? "

"Ah, well — well — well — this is disheartening. It *ought* to be done with a club in some cases; but customarily it consists in the interviewer asking questions and the interviewed answering them. It is all

the rage now. Will you let me ask you certain questions calculated to bring out the salient points of your
public and private history ? "

" Oh, with pleasure, — with pleasure. I have a very
bad memory, but I hope you will not mind that. That
is to say, it is an irregular memory, — singularly irregular. Sometimes it goes in a gallop, and then again it
will be as much as a fortnight passing a given point.
This is a great grief to me."

" Oh, it is no matter, so you will try to do the
best you can."

" I will. I will put my whole mind on it."

" Thanks. Are you ready to begin ? "

" Ready."

Q. How old are you ?

A. Nineteen, in June.

Q. Indeed ! I would have taken you to be thirty-
five or six. Where were you born ?

A. In Missouri.

Q. When did you begin to write ?

A. In 1836.

Q. Why, how could that be, if you are only nineteen now ?

A. I don't know. It does seem curious, somehow.

Q. It does, indeed. Whom do you consider the
most remarkable man you ever met ?

A. Aaron Burr.

Q. But you never could have met Aaron Burr, if
you are only nineteen years —

A. Now, if you know more about me than I do,
what do you ask me for ?

Q. Well, it was only a suggestion ; nothing more. How did you happen to meet Burr ?

A. Well, I happened to be at his funeral one day, and he asked me to make less noise, and —

Q. But, good heavens ! if you were at his funeral, he must have been dead ; and if he was dead, how could he care whether you made a noise or not ?

A. I don't know. He was always a particular kind of a man that way.

Q. Still, I don't understand it at all. You say he spoke to you, and that he was dead.

A. I did n't say he was dead.

Q. But was n't he dead ?

A. Well, some said he was, some said he was n't.

Q. What did you think ?

A. Oh, it was none of my business ! It was n't any of my funeral.

Q. Did you — However, we can never get this matter straight. Let me ask about something else. What was the date of your birth ?

A. Monday, October 31st, 1693.

Q. What ! Impossible ! That would make you a hundred and eighty years old. How do you account for that?

A. I don't account for it at all.

Q. But you said at first you were only nineteen, and now you make yourself out to be one hundred and eighty. It is an awful discrepancy.

A. Why, have you noticed that ? (Shaking hands.) Many a time it has seemed to me like a discrepancy, but somehow I could n't make up my mind. How quick you notice a thing !

Q. Thank you for the compliment, as far as it goes. Had you, or have you, any brothers or sisters?

A. Eh! I — I — I think so — yes — but I don't remember.

Q. Well, that is the most extraordinary statement I ever heard!

A. Why, what makes you think that?

Q. How could I think otherwise? Why, look here! Who is this a picture of on the wall? Is n't that a brother of yours?

A. Oh! yes, yes, yes! Now you remind me of it; that *was* a brother of mine. That 's William — *Bill* we called him. Poor old Bill!

Q. Why? Is he dead, then?

A. Ah! well, I suppose so. We never could tell. There was a great mystery about it.

Q. That is sad, very sad. He disappeared, then?

A. Well, yes, in a sort of general way. We buried him.

Q. Buried him! *Buried* him, without knowing whether he was dead or not?

A. Oh, no! Not that. He was dead enough.

Q. Well, I confess that I can't understand this. If you buried him, and you knew he was dead —

A. No! no! We only thought he was.

Q. Oh, I see! He came to life again?

A. I bet he did n't.

Q. Well, I never heard anything like this. *Somebody* was dead. *Somebody* was buried. Now, where was the mystery?

A. Ah! that 's just it! That 's it exactly. You see,

we were twins, — defunct and I, — and we got mixed
in the bath-tub when we were only two weeks old, and
one of us was drowned. But we did n't know which.
Some think it was Bill. Some think it was me.

Q. Well, that *is* remarkable. What do *you* think?

A. Goodness knows ! I would give whole worlds
to know. This solemn, this awful mystery has cast a
gloom over my whole life. But I will tell you a secret
now, which I never have revealed to any creature before. One of us had a peculiar mark — a large mole
on the back of his left hand ; that was *me*. *That
child was the one that was drowned !*

Q. Very well, then, I don't see that there is any
mystery about it, after all.

A. You don't? Well, *I* do. Anyway, I don't see
how they could ever have been such a blundering lot
as to go and bury the wrong child. But, 'sh ! — don't
mention it where the family can hear of it. Heaven
knows they have heart-breaking troubles enough without adding this.

Q. Well, I believe I have got material enough for
the present, and I am very much obliged to you for
the pains you have taken. But I was a good deal
interested in that account of Aaron Burr's funeral.
Would you mind telling me what particular circumstance it was that made you think Burr was such a
remarkable man ?

A. Oh ! it was a mere trifle ! Not one man in fifty
would have noticed it at all. When the sermon was
over, and the procession all ready to start for the
cemetery, and the body all arranged nice in the hearse,

he said he wanted to take a last look at the scenery, and so he *got up and rode with the driver.*

Then the young man reverently withdrew. He was very pleasant company, and I was sorry to see him go.

16

PARIS NOTES.[1]

THE Parisian travels but little, he knows no language but his own, reads no literature but his own, and consequently he is pretty narrow and pretty self-sufficient. However, let us not be too sweeping; there are Frenchmen who know languages not their own: these are the waiters. Among the rest, they know English; that is, they know it on the European plan, — which is to say, they can speak it, but can't understand it. They easily make themselves understood, but it is next to impossible to word an English sentence in such a way as to enable them to comprehend it. They think they comprehend it; they pretend they do; but they don't. Here is a conversation which I had with one of these beings; I wrote it down at the time, in order to have it exactly correct.

I. These are fine oranges. Where are they grown?

He. More? Yes, I will bring them.

I. No, do not bring any more; I only want to know where they are from — where they are raised.

---

[1] Crowded out of "A Tramp Abroad" to make room for more vital statistics. — M. T.

He. Yes? (with imperturbable mien, and rising inflection.)

I. Yes. Can you tell me what country they are from?

He. Yes? (blandly, with rising inflection.)

I. (disheartened). They are very nice.

He. Good night. (Bows, and retires, quite satisfied with himself.)

That young man could have become a good English scholar by taking the right sort of pains, but he was French, and would n't do that. How different is the case with our people; they utilize every means that offers. There are some alleged French Protestants in Paris, and they built a nice little church on one of the great avenues that lead away from the Arch of Triumph, and proposed to listen to the correct thing, preached in the correct way, there, in their precious French tongue, and be happy. But their little game does not succeed. Our people are always there ahead of them, Sundays, and take up all the room. When the minister gets up to preach, he finds his house full of devout foreigners, each ready and waiting, with his little book in his hand, — a morocco-bound Testament, apparently. But only apparently; it is Mr. Bellows's admirable and exhaustive little French-English dictionary, which in look and binding and size is just like a Testament, — and those people are there to study French. The building has been nicknamed "The Church of the Gratis French Lesson."

These students probably acquire more language than general information, for I am told that a French ser-

mon is like a French speech, — it never names an historical event, but only the date of it; if you are not
up in dates, you get left. A French speech is something like this : —

"Comrades, citizens, brothers, noble parts of the
only sublime and perfect nation, let us not forget that
the 21st January cast off our chains; that the 10th
August relieved us of the shameful presence of foreign
spies; that the 5th September was its own justification
before Heaven and humanity; that the 18th Brumaire
contained the seeds of its own punishment; that the
14th July was the mighty voice of liberty proclaim-
ing the resurrection, the new day, and inviting the oppressed peoples of the earth to look upon the divine
face of France and live; and let us here record our
everlasting curse against the man of the 2d December,
and declare in thunder tones, the native tones of
France, that but for him there had been no 17th
March in history, no 12th October, no 19th January,
no 22d April, no 16th November, no 30th September,
no 2d July, no 14th February, no 29th June, no 15th
August, no 31st May, — that but for him, France, the
pure, the grand, the peerless, had had a serene and
vacant almanac to-day !"

I have heard of one French sermon which closed in
this odd yet eloquent way : —

"My hearers, we have sad cause to remember the
man of the 13th January. The results of the vast
crime of the 13th January have been in just proportion
to the magnitude of the act itself. But for it there
had been no 30th November, — sorrowful spectacle !

The grisly deed of the 16th June had not been done but for it, nor had the man of the 16th June known existence ; to it alone the 3d September was due, also the fatal 12th October. Shall we, then, be grateful for the 13th January, with its freight of death for you and me and all that breathe ? Yes, my friends, for it gave us also that which had never come but for it, and it alone, — the blessed 25th December."

It may be well enough to explain, though in the case of many of my readers this will hardly be necessary. The man of the 13th January is Adam ; the crime of that date was the eating of the apple ; the sorrowful spectacle of the 30th November was the expulsion from Eden ; the grisly deed of the 16th June was the murder of Abel ; the act of the 3d September was the beginning of the journey to the land of Nod ; the 12th day of October, the last mountain-tops disappeared under the flood. When you go to church in France, you want to take your almanac with you, — annotated.

LEGEND OF SAGENFELD, IN GERMANY.[1]

I.

MORE than a thousand years ago this small district was a kingdom, — a little bit of a kingdom, a sort of dainty little toy kingdom, as one might say. It was far removed from the jealousies, strifes, and turmoils of that old warlike day, and so its life was a simple life, its people a gentle and guileless race; it lay always in a deep dream of peace, a soft Sabbath tranquillity; there was no malice, there was no envy, there was no ambition, consequently there were no heart-burnings, there was no unhappiness in the land.

In the course of time the old king died and his little son Hubert came to the throne. The people's love for him grew daily; he was so good and so pure and so noble, that by and by this love became a passion, almost a worship. Now at his birth the soothsayers had diligently studied the stars and found something written in that shining book to this effect : —

---

[1] Left out of "A Tramp Abroad" because its authenticity seemed doubtful, and could not at that time be proved. — M. T.

In Hubert's fourteenth year a pregnant event will happen; the animal whose singing shall sound sweetest in Hubert's ear shall save Hubert's life. So long as the king and the nation shall honor this animal's race for this good deed, the ancient dynasty shall not fail of an heir, nor the nation know war or pestilence or poverty. But beware an erring choice !

All through the king's thirteenth year but one thing was talked of by the soothsayers, the statesmen, the little parliament, and the general people. That one thing was this : How is the last sentence of the prophecy to be understood ? What goes before seems to mean that the saving animal will choose *itself*, at the proper time ; but the closing sentence seems to mean that the *king* must choose beforehand, and say what singer among the animals pleases him best, and that if he choose wisely the chosen animal will save his life, his dynasty, his people, but that if he should make "an erring choice " — beware !

By the end of the year there were as many opinions about this matter as there had been in the beginning ; but a majority of the wise and the simple were agreed that the safest plan would be for the little king to make choice beforehand, and the earlier the better. So an edict was sent forth commanding all persons who owned singing creatures to bring them to the great hall of the palace in the morning of the first day of the new year. This command was obeyed. When everything was in readiness for the trial, the king made his solemn entry with the great officers of the crown, all clothed in their robes of state. The king mounted his golden throne and prepared to give judgment. But he presently said, —

"These creatures all sing at once; the noise is unendurable; no one can choose in such a turmoil. Take them all away, and bring back one at a time."

This was done. One sweet warbler after another charmed the young king's ear and was removed to make way for another candidate. The precious minutes slipped by; among so many bewitching songsters he found it hard to choose, and all the harder because the promised penalty for an error was so terrible that it unsettled his judgment and made him afraid to trust his own ears. He grew nervous and his face showed distress. His ministers saw this, for they never took their eyes from him a moment. Now they began to say in their hearts, —

"He has lost courage — the cool head is gone — he will err — he and his dynasty and his people are doomed!"

At the end of an hour the king sat silent awhile, and then said, —

"Bring back the linnet."

The linnet trilled forth her jubilant music. In the midst of it the king was about to uplift his sceptre in sign of choice, but checked himself and said, —

"But let us be sure. Bring back the thrush; let them sing together."

The thrush was brought, and the two birds poured out their marvels of song together. The king wavered, then his inclination began to settle and strengthen —

one could see it in his countenance. Hope budded
in the hearts of the old ministers, their pulses began
to beat quicker, the sceptre began to rise slowly,
when —

There was a hideous interruption ! It was a sound
like this — just at the door : —

"Waw . . . . . . *he !* — waw . . . . . . *he !* — waw-he !
waw-he ! — waw-he !"

Everybody was sorely startled — and enraged at
himself for showing it.

The next instant the dearest, sweetest, prettiest little
peasant maid of nine years came tripping in, her
brown eyes glowing with childish eagerness; but when
she saw that august company and those angry faces
she stopped and hung her head and put her poor
coarse apron to her eyes. Nobody gave her welcome,
none pitied her. Presently she looked up timidly
through her tears, and said, —

"My lord the king, I pray you pardon me, for I
meant no wrong. I have no father and no mother,
but I have a goat and a donkey, and they are all in all
to me. My goat gives me the sweetest milk, and
when my dear good donkey brays it seems to me there
is no music like to it. So when my lord the king's
jester said the sweetest singer among all the animals
should save the crown and nation, and moved me to
bring him here — "

All the court burst into a rude laugh, and the child
fled away crying, without trying to finish her speech.
The chief minister gave a private order that she and
her disastrous donkey be flogged beyond the precincts

of the palace and commanded to come within them no more.

Then the trial of the birds was resumed. The two birds sang their best, but the sceptre lay motionless in the king's hand. Hope died slowly out in the breasts of all. An hour went by; two hours; still no decision. The day waned to its close, and the waiting multitudes outside the palace grew crazed with anxiety and apprehension. The twilight came on, the shadows fell deeper and deeper. The king and his court could no longer see each other's faces. No one spoke — none called for lights. The great trial had been made; it had failed; each and all wished to hide their faces from the light and cover up their deep trouble in their own hearts.

Finally — hark! A rich, full strain of the divinest melody streamed forth from a remote part of the hall, — the nightingale's voice!

"Up!" shouted the king, "let all the bells make proclamation to the people, for the choice is made and we have not erred. King, dynasty, and nation are saved. From henceforth let the nightingale be honored throughout the land forever. And publish it among all the people that whosoever shall insult a nightingale, or injure it, shall suffer death. The king hath spoken."

All that little world was drunk with joy. The castle and the city blazed with bonfires all night long, the people danced and drank and sang, and the triumphant clamor of the bells never ceased.

From that day the nightingale was a sacred bird.

Its song was heard in every house; the poets wrote its praises; the painters painted it; its sculptured image adorned every arch and turret and fountain and public building. It was even taken into the king's councils; and no grave matter of state was decided until the soothsayers had laid the thing before the state night-ingale and translated to the ministry what it was that the bird had sung about it.

II.

THE young king was very fond of the chase. When the summer was come he rode forth with hawk and hound, one day, in a brilliant company of his nobles. He got separated from them, by and by, in a great forest, and took what he imagined a near cut, to find them again; but it was a mistake. He rode on and on, hopefully at first, but with sinking courage finally. Twilight came on, and still he was plunging through a lonely and unknown land. Then came a catastrophe. In the dim light he forced his horse through a tangled thicket overhanging a steep and rocky declivity. When horse and rider reached the bottom, the former had a broken neck and the latter a broken leg. The poor little king lay there suffering agonies of pain, and each hour seemed a long month to him. He kept his ear strained to hear any sound that might promise hope of rescue; but he heard no voice, no sound of horn or bay of hound.   So at last he gave up all hope, and said, "Let death come, for come it must."

Just then the deep, sweet song of a nightingale swept across the still wastes of the night.

"Saved!" the king said.   "Saved! It is the sacred bird, and the prophecy is come true.   The gods themselves protected me from error in the choice."

He could hardly contain his joy; he could not word his gratitude.   Every few moments, now, he thought he caught the sound of approaching succor.   But each time it was a disappointment; no succor came.   The dull hours drifted on.   Still no help came, — but still the sacred bird sang on.   He began to have misgivings about his choice, but he stifled them.   Toward dawn the bird ceased.   The morning came, and with it thirst and hunger; but no succor.   The day waxed and waned.   At last the king cursed the nightingale.

Immediately the song of the thrush came from out the wood.   The king said in his heart, "This was the true bird — my choice was false — succor will come now."

But it did not come.   Then he lay many hours insensible.   When he came to himself, a linnet was singing.   He listened — with apathy.   His faith was gone.   "These birds," he said, "can bring no help; I and my house and my people are doomed."   He turned him about to die; for he was grown very feeble from hunger and thirst and suffering, and felt that his end was near.   In truth, he wanted to die, and be released from pain.   For long hours he lay without thought or feeling or motion.   Then his senses returned.   The dawn of the third morning was breaking. Ah, the world seemed very beautiful to those worn eyes. Suddenly a great longing to live rose up in the lad's heart, and from his soul welled a deep and fervent prayer that Heaven would have mercy upon him and let him see his home and his friends once more. In that instant a soft, a faint, a far-off sound, but oh, how inexpressibly sweet to his waiting ear, came floating out of the distance, —

"Waw . . . . . . *he!* — waw . . . . . . *he!* — waw-he! — waw-he! — waw-he!"

"*That,* oh, *that* song is sweeter, a thousand times sweeter, than the voice of nightingale, thrush, or linnet, for it brings not mere hope, but *certainty* of succor; and now indeed am I saved! The sacred singer has chosen itself, as the oracle intended; the prophecy is fulfilled, and my life, my house, and my people are redeemed. The ass shall be sacred from this day!"

The divine music grew nearer and nearer, stronger and stronger, — and ever sweeter and sweeter to the perishing sufferer's ear. Down the declivity the docile little donkey wandered, cropping herbage and singing as he went; and when at last he saw the dead horse and the wounded king, he came and snuffed at them with simple and marvelling curiosity. The king petted him, and he knelt down as had been his wont when his little mistress desired to mount. With great labor and pain the lad drew himself upon the creature's back, and held himself there by aid of the generous ears. The ass went singing forth from the place and carried the king to the little peasant maid's hut. She gave him her pallet for a bed, refreshed him with goat's milk, and then flew to tell the great news to the first scouting party of searchers she might meet.

The king got well. His first act was to proclaim the sacredness and inviolability of the ass; his second was to add this particular ass to his cabinet and make him chief minister of the crown; his third was to have all the statues and effigies of nightingales throughout his kingdom destroyed, and replaced by statues and effigies of the sacred donkey; and his fourth was to announce that when the little peasant maid should reach her fifteenth year he would make her his queen, — and he kept his word.

Such is the legend. This explains why the mouldering image of the ass adorns all these old crumbling walls and arches; and it explains why, during many centuries, an ass was always the chief minister in that royal cabinet, just as is still the case in most cabinets to this day; and it also explains why, in that little kingdom, during many centuries, all great poems, all great speeches, all great books, all public solemnities, and all royal proclamations, always began with these stirring words, —

" Waw . . . . . . *he!* — waw . . . . . . *he!* — waw-he ! — waw-he ! — waw-he !"

SPEECH ON THE BABIES,

AT THE BANQUET, IN CHICAGO, GIVEN BY THE ARMY
OF THE TENNESSEE TO THEIR FIRST COMMANDER, GEN-
ERAL U. S. GRANT, NOVEMBER, 1879.

[The fifteenth regular toast was " The Babies. — As they comfort us in our sorrows, let us not forget them in our festivities."]

I LIKE that. We have not all had the good fortune
to be ladies. We have not all been generals, or
poets, or statesmen ; but when the toast works down
to the babies, we stand on common ground. It is a
shame that for a thousand years the world's banquets
have utterly ignored the baby, as if he did n't amount
to anything. If you will stop and think a minute, —
if you will go back fifty or one hundred years to your
early married life and recontemplate your first baby, —
you will remember that he amounted to a good deal,
and even something over. You soldiers all know that
when that little fellow arrived at family headquarters
you had to hand in your resignation. He took entire
command. You became his lackey, his mere body-
servant, and you had to stand around too. He was
not a commander who made allowances for time, dis-

tance, weather, or anything else. You had to execute
his order whether it was possible or not. And there
was only one form of marching in his manual of tac-
tics, and that was the double-quick. He treated you
with every sort of insolence and disrespect, and the
bravest of you did n't dare to say a word. You could
face the death-storm at Donelson and Vicksburg, and
give back blow for blow; but when he clawed your
whiskers, and pulled your hair, and twisted your nose,
you had to take it. When the thunders of war were
sounding in your ears you set your faces toward the
batteries, and advanced with steady tread; but when
he turned on the terrors of his war-whoop you advanced in the other direction, and mighty glad of the
chance too. When he called for soothing-syrup, did
you venture to throw out any side remarks about
certain services being unbecoming an officer and a
gentleman? No. You got up and *got* it. When he
ordered his pap bottle and it was not warm, did you
talk back? Not you. You went to work and *warmed*
it. You even descended so far in your menial office
as to take a suck at that warm, insipid stuff yourself,
to see if it was right, — three parts water to one of
milk, a touch of sugar to modify the colic, and a drop
of peppermint to kill those immortal hiccoughs. I can
taste that stuff yet. And how many things you
learned as you went along! Sentimental young folks
still take stock in that beautiful old saying that when
the baby smiles in his sleep, it is because the angels
are whispering to him. Very pretty, but too thin, —
simply wind on the stomach, my friends. If the baby

proposed to take a walk at his usual hour, two o'clock in the morning, did n't you rise up promptly and remark, with a mental addition which would not improve a Sunday-school book *much*, that that was the very thing you were about to propose yourself? Oh! you were under good discipline, and as you went fluttering up and down the room in your undress uniform, you not only prattled undignified baby-talk, but even tuned up your martial voices and tried to *sing!* — "Rock-a-by baby in the tree-top," for instance. What a spectacle for an Army of the Tennessee! And what an affliction for the neighbors, too; for it is not everybody within a mile around that likes military music at three in the morning. And when you had been keeping this sort of thing up two or three hours, and your little velvet-head intimated that nothing suited him like exercise and noise, what did you do? [*"Go on"!*] You simply *went* on until you dropped in the last ditch. The idea that a *baby* does n't *amount* to anything! Why, *one* baby is just a house and a front yard full by itself. *One* baby can furnish more business than you and your whole Interior Department can attend to. He is enterprising, irrepressible, brimful of lawless activities. Do what you please, you can't make him stay on the reservation. Sufficient unto the day is one baby. As long as you are in your right mind don't you ever pray for twins. Twins amount to a permanent riot. And there ain't any real difference between triplets and an insurrection.

Yes, it was high time for a toast-master to recognize the importance of the babies. Think what is in store

17

for the present crop! Fifty years from now we shall all be dead, I trust, and then this flag, if it still survive (and let us hope it may), will be floating over a Republic numbering 200,000,000 souls, according to the settled laws of our increase. Our present schooner of State will have grown into a political leviathan, — a Great Eastern. The cradled babies of to-day will be on deck. Let them be well trained, for we are going to leave a big contract on their hands. Among the three or four million cradles now rocking in the land are some which this nation would preserve for ages as sacred things, if we could know which ones they are. In one of these cradles the unconscious Farragut of the future is at this moment teething, — think of it! — and putting in a world of dead earnest, unarticulated, but perfectly justifiable profanity over it, too. In another the future renowned astronomer is blinking at the shining Milky Way with but a languid interest, — poor little chap! — and wondering what has become of that other one they call the wet-nurse. In another the future great historian is lying, — and doubtless will continue to lie until his earthly mission is ended. In another the future President is busying himself with no profounder problem of state than what the mischief has become of his hair so early; and in a mighty array of other cradles there are now some 60,000 future office-seekers, getting ready to furnish him occasion to grapple with that same old problem a second time. And in still one more cradle, somewhere under the flag, the future illustrious commander-in-chief of the American armies is so little burdened with his approaching grandeurs and responsibilities as to be giving his whole strategic mind at this moment to trying to find out some way to get his big toe into his mouth, — an achievement which, meaning no disrespect, the illustrious guest of this evening turned *his* entire attention to some fifty-six years ago ; and if the child is but a prophecy of the man, there are mighty few who will doubt that he *succeeded*.

SPEECH ON THE WEATHER,

AT THE NEW ENGLAND SOCIETY'S SEVENTY-FIRST
ANNUAL DINNER, NEW YORK CITY.

———◆———

The next toast was: "The Oldest Inhabitant — The Weather
of New England."

> Who can lose it and forget it?
> Who can have it and regret it?

> "Be interposer 'twixt us Twain."
>
> *Merchant of Venice.*

To this Samuel L. Clemens (Mark Twain) replied as follows : —

I REVERENTLY believe that the Maker who made
us all makes everything in New England but the
weather. I don't know who makes that, but I think it
must be raw apprentices in the weather clerk's factory
who experiment and learn how, in New England, for
board and clothes, and then are promoted to make
weather for countries that require a good article, and
will take their custom elsewhere if they don't get it.
There is a sumptuous variety about the New England
weather that compels the stranger's admiration — and
regret. The weather is always doing something there;
always attending strictly to business; always getting

up new designs and trying them on the people to see
how they will go. But it gets through more business
in spring than in any other season. In the spring
I have counted one hundred and thirty-six different
kinds of weather inside of four-and-twenty hours. It
was I that made the fame and fortune of that man
that had that marvellous collection of weather on exhibition at the Centennial, that so astounded the
foreigners. He was going to travel all over the world
and get specimens from all the climes. I said, "Don't
you do it; you come to New England on a favorable
spring day." I told him what we could do in the way
of style, variety, and quantity. Well, he came and he
made his collection in four days. As to variety, why,
he confessed that he got hundreds of kinds of weather
that he had never heard of before. And as to quantity
— well, after he had picked out and discarded all that
was blemished in any way, he not only had weather
enough, but weather to spare; weather to hire out;
weather to sell; to deposit; weather to invest; weather to give to the poor. The people of New England
are by nature patient and forbearing, but there are
some things which they will not stand. Every year
they kill a lot of poets for writing about "Beautiful
Spring." These are generally casual visitors, who bring
their notions of spring from somewhere else, and cannot, of course, know how the natives feel about spring.
And so the first thing they know the opportunity to
inquire how they feel has permanently gone by. Old
Probabilities has a mighty reputation for accurate
prophecy, and thoroughly well deserves it. You take

up the paper and observe how crisply and confidently
he checks off what to-day's weather is going to be on
the Pacific, down South, in the Middle States, in the
Wisconsin region. See him sail along in the joy and
pride of his power till he gets to New England, and
then see his tail drop. *He* does n't know what the
weather is going to be in New England. Well, he
mulls over it, and by and by he gets out something
about like this: Probable northeast to southwest
winds, varying to the southward and westward and
eastward, and points between, high and low barometer
swapping around from place to place; probable areas
of rain, snow, hail, and drought, succeeded or preceded
by earthquakes, with thunder and lightning. Then
he jots down this postscript from his wandering mind,
to cover accidents. "But it is possible that the programme may be wholly changed in the mean time."
Yes, one of the brightest gems in the New England
weather is the dazzling uncertainty of it. There is
only one thing certain about it : you are certain there
is going to be plenty of it — a perfect grand review;
but you never can tell which end of the procession is
going to move first. You fix up for the drought; you
leave your umbrella in the house and sally out, and two
to one you get drowned. You make up your mind that
the earthquake is due; you stand from under, and
take hold of something to steady yourself, and the first
thing you know you get struck by lightning. These
are great disappointments; but they can't be helped.
The lightning there is peculiar; it is so convincing, that
when it strikes a thing it does n't leave enough of that

thing behind for you to tell whether — Well, you 'd think it was something valuable, and a Congressman had been there. And the thunder. When the thunder begins to merely tune up and scrape and saw, and key up the instruments for the performance, strangers say, " Why, what awful thunder you have here ! " But when the baton is raised and the real concert begins, you 'll find that stranger down in the cellar with his head in the ash-barrel. Now as to the *size* of the weather in New England, — lengthways, I mean. It is utterly disproportioned to the size of that little country. Half the time, when it is packed as full as it can stick, you will see that New England weather sticking out beyond the edges and projecting around hundreds and hundreds of miles over the neighboring States. She can't hold a tenth part of her weather. You can see cracks all about where she has strained herself trying to do it. I could speak volumes about the inhuman perversity of the New England weather, but I will give but a single specimen. I like to hear rain on a tin roof. So I covered part of my roof with tin, with an eye to that luxury. Well, sir, do you think it ever rains on that tin ? No, sir : skips it every time. Mind, in this speech I have been trying merely to do honor to the New England weather, — no language could do it justice. But, after all, there is at least one or two things about that weather (or, if you please, effects produced by it) which we residents would not like to part with. If we had n't our bewitching autumn foliage, we should still have to credit the weather with one feature which compensates for all its bullying vagaries, — the ice-storm : when a leafless tree is clothed with ice from the bottom to the top, — ice that is as bright and clear as crystal; when every bough and twig is strung with ice-beads, frozen dew-drops, and the whole tree sparkles cold and white, like the Shah of Persia's diamond plume. Then the wind waves the branches and the sun comes out and turns all those myriads of beads and drops to prisms that glow and burn and flash with all manner of colored fires, which change and change again with inconceivable rapidity from blue to red, from red to green, and green to gold, — the tree becomes a spraying fountain, a very explosion of dazzling jewels; and it stands there the acme, the climax, the supremest possibility in art or nature, of bewildering, intoxicating, intolerable magnificence. One cannot make the words too strong.

CONCERNING THE AMERICAN LANGUAGE.[1]

THERE was an Englishman in our compartment, and he complimented me on — on what? But you would never guess. He complimented me on my English. He said Americans in general did not speak the English language as correctly as I did. I said I was obliged to him for his compliment, since I knew he meant it for one, but that I was not fairly entitled to it, for I did n't speak English at all, — I only spoke American.

He laughed, and said it was a distinction without a difference. I said no, the difference was not prodigious, but still it was considerable. We fell into a friendly dispute over the matter. I put my case as well as I could, and said, —

"The languages were identical several generations ago, but our changed conditions and the spread of our people far to the south and far to the west have made many alterations in our pronunciation, and have introduced new words among us and changed the

[1] Being part of a chapter which was crowded out of "A Tramp Abroad." — M. T.

meanings of many old ones. English people talk through their noses; we do not. We say *know*, English people say *näo;* we say *cow*, the Briton says *käow;* we — "

"Oh, come! that is pure Yankee; everybody knows that."

"Yes, it is pure Yankee; that is true. One cannot hear it in America outside of the little corner called New England, which is Yankee land. The English themselves planted it there, two hundred and fifty years ago, and there it remains; it has never spread. But England talks through her nose yet; the Londoner and the backwoods New-Englander pronounce 'know' and 'cow' alike, and then the Briton unconsciously satirizes himself by making fun of the Yankee's pronunciation."

We argued this point at some length; nobody won; but no matter, the fact remains, — Englishmen say *näo* and *käow* for "know" and "cow," and that is what the rustic inhabitant of a very small section of America does.

"You conferred your *a* upon New England, too, and there it remains; it has not travelled out of the narrow limits of those six little States in all these two hundred and fifty years. All England uses it, New England's small population — say four millions — use it, but we have forty-five millions who do not use it. You say 'glahs of wawtah,' so does New England; at least, New England says *glahs*. America at large flattens the *a*, and says 'glass of water.' These sounds are pleasanter than yours; you may think they are not right, — well, in English they are *not* right, but in 'American' they are. You say *flahsk*, and *bahsket*, and *jackahss*; we say 'flask,' 'basket,' 'jackass,' — sounding the *a* as it is in 'tallow,' 'fallow,' and so on. Up to as late as 1847 Mr. Webster's Dictionary had the impudence to still pronounce 'basket' *bahsket*, when he knew that outside of his little New England all America shortened the *a* and paid no attention to his English broadening of it. However, it called itself an English Dictionary, so it was proper enough that it should stick to English forms, perhaps. It still calls itself an English Dictionary to-day, but it has quietly ceased to pronounce 'basket' as if it were spelt *bahsket*. In the American language the *h* is respected; the *h* is not dropped or added improperly."

"The same is the case in England, — I mean among the educated classes, of course."

"Yes, that is true; but a nation's language is a very large matter. It is not simply a manner of speech obtaining among the educated handful; the manner obtaining among the vast uneducated multitude must be considered also. Your uneducated masses speak English, you will not deny that; our uneducated masses speak American, — it won't be fair for you to deny that, for you can see, yourself, that when your stable-boy says, 'It is n't the 'unting that 'urts the 'orse, but the 'ammer, 'ammer, 'ammer on the 'ard 'ighway,' and our stable-boy makes the same remark without suffocating a single *h*, these two people are manifestly talking two different languages. But if the signs are to be trusted, even your educated classes used to drop the *h*. They say *humble*, now, and *heroic*, and *historic*, etc., but I judge that they used to drop those *h*'s because your writers still keep up the fashion of putting *an* before those words, instead of *a*. This is what Mr. Darwin might call a 'rudimentary' sign that that *an* was justifiable once, and useful, — when your educated classes used to say *'umble*, and *'eroic*, and *'istorical*. Correct writers of the American language do not put *an* before those words."

The English gentleman had something to say upon this matter, but never mind what he said, — I'm not arguing his case. I have him at a disadvantage, now. I proceeded : —

"In England you encourage an orator by exclaiming 'H'yaah! h'yaah!' We pronounce it *heer* in some sections, 'h'*yer*' in others, and so on ; but our whites do not say 'h'yaah,' pronouncing the *a*'s like the *a* in *ah*. I have heard English ladies say 'don't you' — making two separate and distinct words of it ; your Mr. Bernand has satirized it. But we always say 'dontchu.' This is much better. Your ladies say, 'Oh, it's oful nice!'" Ours say, 'Oh, it's *aw*ful nice!' We say, '*Four* hundred,' you say '*For*' — as in the word *or*. Your clergymen speak of 'the Lawd,' ours of 'the Lord'; yours speak of 'the gawds of the heathen,' ours of 'the gods of the heathen.' When you are exhausted, you say you are 'knocked up.' We don't. When you say you will do a thing 'directly,' you mean 'immediately'; in the American language — generally speaking — the word signifies 'after a little.' When you say 'clever,' you mean 'capable'; with us the word used to mean 'accommodating,' but I don't know what it means now. Your word 'stout' means 'fleshy'; our word 'stout' usually means 'strong.' Your words 'gentleman' and 'lady' have a very restricted meaning; with us they include the bar-maid, butcher, burglar, harlot, and horse-thief. You say, 'I have n't *got* any stockings on,' 'I have n't *got* any memory,' 'I have n't *got* any money in my purse'; we usually say, 'I have n't any stockings on,' 'I have n't any memory,' 'I have n't any money in my purse.' You say 'out of window'; we always put in a *the*. If one asks 'How old is that man?' the Briton answers, 'He will be about forty;' in the American language, we should say, 'He *is* about forty.' However,. won't tire you, sir; but if I wanted to, I could pile up differences here until I not only convinced you that English and American are separate languages, but that when I speak my native tongue in its utmost purity an Englishman can't understand me at all."

"I don't wish to flatter you, but it is about all I can do to understand you *now*."

That was a very pretty compliment, and it put us on the pleasantest terms directly, — I use the word in the English sense.

[*Later* — 1882. Æsthetes in many of our schools are now beginning to teach the pupils to broaden the *a*, and to say "don't you," in the elegant foreign way.]

ROGERS.

THIS man Rogers happened upon me and introduced himself at the town of ——, in the
South of England, where I stayed awhile. His step-
father had married a distant relative of mine who was
afterwards hanged, and so he seemed to think a blood
relationship existed between us. He came in every
day and sat down and talked. Of all the bland, serene human curiosities I ever saw, I think he was the
chiefest. He desired to look at my new chimney-pot
hat. I was very willing, for I thought he would notice the name of the great Oxford Street hatter in it,
and respect me accordingly. But he turned it about
with a sort of grave compassion, pointed out two or
three blemishes, and said that I, being so recently
arrived, could not be expected to know where to sup-
ply myself. Said he would send me the address of *his*
hatter. Then he said, "Pardon me," and proceeded
to cut a neat circle of red tissue-paper; daintily
notched the edges of it; took the mucilage and pasted
it in my hat so as to cover the manufacturer's name.
He said, "No one will know now where you got it. I
will send you a hat-tip of my hatter, and you can

paste it over this tissue circle." It was the calmest, coolest thing, — I never admired a man so much in my life. Mind, he did this while his own hat sat offensively near our noses, on the table, — an ancient extinguisher of the " slouch " pattern, limp and shapeless with age, discolored by vicissitudes of the weather, and banded by an equator of bear's grease that had stewed through.

Another time he examined my coat. I had no terrors, for over my tailor's door was the legend, " By Special Appointment Tailor to H. R. H. the Prince of Wales," etc. I did not know at the time that the most of the tailor shops had the same sign out, and that whereas it takes nine tailors to make an ordinary man, it takes a hundred and fifty to make a prince. He was full of compassion for my coat. Wrote down the address of his tailor for me. Did not tell me to mention my *nom de plume* and the tailor would put his best work on my garment, as complimentary people sometimes do, but said his tailor would hardly trouble himself for an unknown person (unknown person, when I thought I was so celebrated in England! — that was the cruelest cut), but cautioned me to mention *his* name, and it would be all right. Thinking to be facetious, I said, —

" But he might sit up all night and injure his health."

" Well, *let* him," said Rogers; " I 've done enough for him, for him to show some appreciation of it."

I might as well have tried to disconcert a mummy with my facetiousness. Said Rogers : " I get all my coats there, — they 're the only coats fit to be seen in."

I made one more attempt. I said, " I wish you had brought one with you — I would like to look at it."

" Bless your heart, have n't I got one on ? — *this* article is Morgan's make."

I examined it. The coat had been bought ready-made, of a Chatham Street Jew, without any question — about 1848. It probably cost four dollars when it was new. It was ripped, it was frayed, it was nap-less and greasy. I could not resist showing him where it was ripped. It so affected him that I was almost sorry I had done it. First he seemed plunged into a bottomless abyss of grief. Then he roused himself, made a feint with his hands as if waving off the pity of a nation, and said, — with what seemed to me a manufactured emotion, — " No matter ; no matter ; don't mind me ; do not bother about it. I can get another."

When he was thoroughly restored, so that he could examine the rip and command his feelings, he said, ah, *now* he understood it, — his servant must have done it while dressing him that morning.

His servant ! There was something awe-inspiring in effrontery like this.

Nearly every day he interested himself in some arti-cle of my clothing. One would hardly have expected this sort of infatuation in a man who always wore the same suit, and it a suit that seemed coeval with the Conquest.

It was an unworthy ambition, perhaps, but I *did* wish I could make this man admire *something* about me or something I did, — you would have felt the same way. I saw my opportunity : I was about to return to London, and had "listed" my soiled linen for the wash. It made quite an imposing mountain in the corner of the room, — fifty-four pieces. I hoped he would fancy it was the accumulation of a single week. I took up the wash-list, as if to see that it was all right, and then tossed it on the table, with pretended forgetfulness. Sure enough, he took it up and ran his eye along down to the grand total. Then he said, "You get off easy," and laid it down again.

His gloves were the saddest ruin, but he told me where I could get some like them. His shoes would hardly hold walnuts without leaking, but he liked to put his feet up on the mantel-piece and contemplate them. He wore a dim glass breastpin, which he called a "morphylitic diamond," — whatever that may mean, — and said only two of them had ever been found, — the Emperor of China had the other one.

Afterward, in London, it was a pleasure to me to see this fantastic vagabond come marching into the lobby of the hotel in his grand-ducal way, for he always had some new imaginary grandeur to develop — there was nothing stale about him but his clothes. If he addressed me when strangers were about, he always raised his voice a little and called me "Sir Richard," or "General," or "Your Lordship," — and when people began to stare and look deferential, he would fall to inquiring in a casual way why I disappointed the Duke of Argyll the night before ; and then remind me of our engagement at the Duke of Westminster's for the following day. I think that for the time being

18

these things were realities to him. He once came and invited me to go with him and spend the evening with the Earl of Warwick at his town house. I said I had received no formal invitation. He said that that was of no consequence, the Earl had no formalities for him or his friends. I asked if I might go just as I was. He said no, that would hardly do; evening dress was requisite at night in any gentleman's house. He said he would wait while I dressed, and then we would go to his apartments and I could take a bottle of champagne and a cigar while he dressed. I was very willing to see how this enterprise would turn out, so I dressed, and we started to his lodgings. He said if I didn't mind we would walk. So we tramped some four miles through the mud and fog, and finally found his "apartments:" they consisted of a single room over a barber's shop in a back street. Two chairs, a small table, an ancient valise, a wash-basin and pitcher (both on the floor in a corner), an unmade bed, a fragment of a looking-glass, and a flower-pot with a perishing little rose geranium in it, which he called a century plant, and said it had not bloomed now for upwards of two centuries — given to him by the late Lord Palmerston — been offered a prodigious sum for it) — these were the contents of the room. Also a brass candlestick and part of a candle. Rogers lit the candle, and told me to sit down and make myself at home. He said he hoped I was thirsty, because he would surprise my palate with an article of champagne that seldom got into a commoner's system; or would I prefer sherry, or port? Said he had port in bottles that were swathed in stratified cobwebs, every stratum representing a generation. And as for his cigars, — well, I should judge of them myself. Then he put his head out at the door and called, —

"Sackville!" No answer.

"Hi! — Sackville!" No answer.

"Now what the devil can have become of that butler? I *never* allow a servant to — Oh, confound that idiot, he's got the *keys*. Can't get into the other rooms without the keys."

(I was just wondering at his intrepidity in still keeping up the delusion of the champagne, and trying to imagine how he was going to get out of the difficulty.)

Now he stopped calling Sackville and began to call "Anglesy." But Anglesy did n't come. He said, "This is the *second* time that that equerry has been absent without leave. To-morrow I'll discharge him."

Now he began to whoop for "Thomas," but Thomas did n't answer. Then for "Theodore," but no Theodore replied.

"Well, I give it up," said Rogers. "The servants never expect me at this hour, and so they're all off on a lark. Might get along without the equerry and the page, but can't have any wine or cigars without the butler, and can't dress without my valet."

I offered to help him dress, but he would not hear of it; and besides, he said he would not feel comfortable unless dressed by a practised hand. However, he finally concluded that he was such old friends with the Earl that it would not make any difference how he was dressed. So we took a cab, he gave the driver some directions, and we started. By and by we stopped before a large house and got out. I never had seen this man with a collar on. He now stepped under a lamp and got a venerable paper collar out of his coat pocket, along with a hoary cravat, and put them on. He ascended the stoop, and entered. Presently he reappeared, descended rapidly, and said,—

"Come — quick !"

We hurried away, and turned the corner.

"Now we 're safe," he said, and took off his collar and cravat and returned them to his pocket.

"Made a mighty narrow escape," said he.

"How ?" said I.

"B' George, the Countess was there !"

"Well, what of that ? — don't she know you ?"

"Know me ? Absolutely worships me. I just did happen to catch a glimpse of her before she saw me — and out I shot. Have n't seen her for two months — to rush in on her without any warning might have been fatal. She could *not* have stood it. I did n't know *she* was in town — thought she was at the castle. Let me lean on you — just a moment — there ; now I am better — thank you ; thank you ever so much. Lord bless me, what an escape !"

So I never got to call on the Earl after all. But I marked his house for future reference. It proved to be an ordinary family hotel, with about a thousand plebeians roosting in it.

In most things Rogers was by no means a fool. In some things it was plain enough that he was a fool, but he certainly did not know it. He was in the "deadest" earnest in these matters. He died at sea, last summer, as the "Earl of Ramsgate."

THE LOVES OF ALONZO FITZ CLARENCE AND ROSANNAH ETHELTON.

IT was well along in the forenoon of a bitter winter's day. The town of Eastport, in the State of Maine, lay buried under a deep snow that was newly fallen. The customary bustle in the streets was wanting. One could look long distances down them and see nothing but a dead-white emptiness, with silence to match. Of course I do not mean that you could *see* the silence, —no, you could only hear it. The sidewalks were merely long, deep ditches, with steep snow walls on either side. Here and there you might hear the faint, far scrape of a wooden shovel, and if you were quick enough you might catch a glimpse of a distant black figure stooping and disappearing in one of those ditches, and reappearing the next moment with a motion which you would know meant the heaving out of a shovelful of snow. But you needed to be quick, for that black figure would not linger, but would soon drop that shovel and scud for the house, thrashing itself with its arms to warm them. Yes, it was too venomously cold for snow-shovellers or anybody else to stay out long.

Presently the sky darkened; then the wind rose and began to blow in fitful, vigorous gusts, which sent clouds of powdery snow aloft, and straight ahead, and everywhere. Under the impulse of one of these gusts, great white drifts banked themselves like graves across the streets; a moment later, another gust shifted them around the other way, driving a fine spray of snow from their sharp crests, as the gale drives the spume flakes from wave-crests at sea; a third gust swept that place as clean as your hand, if it saw fit. This was fooling, this was play; but each and all of the gusts dumped some snow into the sidewalk ditches, for that was business.

Alonzo Fitz Clarence was sitting in his snug and elegant little parlor, in a lovely blue silk dressing-gown, with cuffs and facings of crimson satin, elaborately quilted. The remains of his breakfast were before him, and the dainty and costly little table service added a harmonious charm to the grace, beauty, and richness of the fixed appointments of the room. A cheery fire was blazing on the hearth.

A furious gust of wind shook the windows, and a great wave of snow washed against them with a drenching sound, so to speak. The handsome young bachelor murmured, —

"That means, no going out to-day. Well, I am content. But what to do for company? Mother is well enough, Aunt Susan is well enough; but these, like the poor, I have with me always. On so grim a day as this, one needs a new interest, a fresh element, to whet the dull edge of captivity. That was very

neatly said, but it does n't mean anything.   One does
n't *want* the edge of captivity sharpened up, you know,
but just the reverse."

He glanced at his pretty French mantel-clock.

"That clock's wrong again.   That clock hardly
ever knows what time it is; and when it does know,
it lies about it, — which amounts to the same thing.
Alfred!"

There was no answer.

"Alfred! . . . Good servant, but as uncertain as
the clock."

Alonzo touched an electrical bell-button in the wall.
He waited a moment, then touched it again; waited a
few moments more, and said, —

"Battery out of order, no doubt.   But now that I
have started, I *will* find out what time it is."   He
stepped to a speaking-tube in the wall, blew its whistle,
and called, "Mother!" and repeated it twice.

"Well, *that's* no use.   Mother's battery is out of
order, too.   Can't raise anybody down-stairs, — that is
plain."

He sat down at a rosewood desk, leaned his chin on
the left-hand edge of it, and spoke, as if to the floor:
"Aunt Susan!"

A low, pleasant voice answered, "Is that you,
Alonzo?"

"Yes.   I'm too lazy and comfortable to go down-
stairs; I am in extremity, and I can't seem to scare
up any help."

"Dear me, what is the matter?"

"Matter enough, I can tell you!"

"Oh, don't keep me in suspense, dear! What *is* it?"

"I want to know what time it is."

"You abominable boy, what a turn you did give me! Is that all?"

"All, — on my honor. Calm yourself. Tell me the time, and receive my blessing."

"Just five minutes after nine. No charge, — keep your blessing."

"Thanks. It would n't have impoverished me, aunty, nor so enriched you that you could live without other means." He got up, murmuring, "Just five minutes after nine," and faced his clock. "Ah," said he, "you are doing better than usual. You are only thirty-four minutes wrong. Let me see . . . let me see. . . . Thirty-three and twenty-one are fifty-four; four times fifty-four are two hundred and thirty-six. One off, leaves two hundred and thirty-five. That's right."

He turned the hands of his clock forward till they marked twenty-five minutes to one, and said, "Now see if you can't keep right for a while . . . else I'll raffle you!"

He sat down at the desk again, and said, "Aunt Susan!"

"Yes, dear."

"Had breakfast?"

"Yes indeed, an hour ago."

"Busy?"

"No, — except sewing. Why?"

"Got any company?"

"No, but I expect some at half past nine."

"I wish *I* did. I'm lonesome. I want to talk to somebody."

"Very well, talk to me."

"But this is very private."

"Don't be afraid, — talk right along; there's nobody here but me."

"I hardly know whether to venture or not, but — "

"But what? Oh, don't stop there! You *know* you can trust me, Alonzo, — you know you can."

"I feel it, aunt, but this is very serious. It affects me deeply, — me, and all the family, — even the whole community."

"Oh, Alonzo, tell me! I will never breathe a word of it. What is it?"

"Aunt, if I might dare — "

"Oh, please go on! I love you, and can feel for you. Tell me all. Confide in me. What *is* it?"

"The weather!"

"Plague take the weather! I don't see how you can have the heart to serve me so, Lon."

"There, there, aunty dear, I'm sorry; I am, on my honor. I won't do it again. Do you forgive me?"

"Yes, since you seem so sincere about it, though I know I ought n't to. You will fool me again as soon as I have forgotten this time."

"No, I won't, honor bright. But such weather, oh, such weather! You've *got* to keep your spirits up artificially. It is snowy, and blowy, and gusty, and bitter cold! How is the weather with you?"

"Warm and rainy and melancholy. The mourners

go about the streets with their umbrellas running streams from the end of every whalebone. There's an elevated double pavement of umbrellas stretching down the sides of the streets as far as I can see. I've got a fire for cheerfulness, and the windows open to keep cool. But it is vain, it is useless : nothing comes in but the balmy breath of December, with its burden of mocking odors from the flowers that possess the realm outside, and rejoice in their lawless profusion whilst the spirit of man is low, and flaunt their gaudy splendors in his face whilst his soul is clothed in sack-cloth and ashes and his heart breaketh."

Alonzo opened his lips to say, "You ought to print that, and get it framed," but checked himself, for he heard his aunt speaking to some one else. He went and stood at the window and looked out upon the wintry prospect. The storm was driving the snow before it more furiously than ever ; window shutters were slamming and banging; a forlorn dog, with bowed head and tail withdrawn from service, was pressing his quaking body against a windward wall for shelter and protection ; a young girl was ploughing knee-deep through the drifts, with her face turned from the blast, and the cape of her water-proof blowing straight rear-ward over her head. Alonzo shuddered, and said with a sigh, "Better the slop, and the sultry rain, and even the insolent flowers, than this !"

He turned from the window, moved a step, and stopped in a listening attitude. The faint, sweet notes of a familiar song caught his ear. He remained there, with his head unconsciously bent forward, drinking in the melody, stirring neither hand nor foot, hardly breathing. There was a blemish in the execution of the song, but to Alonzo it seemed an added charm instead of a defect. This blemish consisted of a marked flatting of the third, fourth, fifth, sixth, and seventh notes of the refrain or chorus of the piece. When the music ended, Alonzo drew a deep breath, and said, "Ah, I never have heard 'In the Sweet By and By' sung like that before!"

He stepped quickly to the desk, listened a moment, and said in a guarded, confidential voice, "Aunty, who is this divine singer?"

"She is the company I was expecting. Stays with me a month or two. I will introduce you. Miss —"

"For goodness' sake, wait a moment, Aunt Susan! You never stop to think what you are about!"

He flew to his bed-chamber, and returned in a moment perceptibly changed in his outward appearance, and remarking, snappishly, —

"Hang it, she would have introduced me to this angel in that sky-blue dressing-gown with red-hot lapels! Women never think, when they get a-going."

He hastened and stood by the desk, and said eagerly, "Now, Aunty, I am ready," and fell to smiling and bowing with all the persuasiveness and elegance that were in him.

"Very well. Miss Rosannah Ethelton, let me introduce to you my favorite nephew, Mr. Alonzo Fitz Clarence. There! You are both good people, and I like you; so I am going to trust you together while I attend to a few household affairs. Sit down, Rosannah ; sit down, Alonzo. Good-by ; I shan't be gone long."

Alonzo had been bowing and smiling all the while, and motioning imaginary young ladies to sit down in imaginary chairs, but now he took a seat himself, mentally saying, " Oh, this is luck ! Let the winds blow now, and the snow drive, and the heavens frown ! Little I care ! "

While these young people chat themselves into an acquaintanceship, let us take the liberty of inspecting the sweeter and fairer of the two. She sat alone, at her graceful ease, in a richly furnished apartment which was manifestly the private parlor of a refined and sensible lady, if signs and symbols may go for anything. For instance, by a low, comfortable chair stood a dainty, top-heavy work-stand, whose summit was a fancifully embroidered shallow basket, with vari-colored crewels, and other strings and odds and ends, protruding from under the gaping lid and hanging down in negligent profusion. On the floor lay bright shreds of Turkey red, Prussian blue, and kindred fabrics, bits of ribbon, a spool or two, a pair of scissors, and a roll or so of tinted silken stuffs. On a luxurious sofa, upholstered with some sort of soft Indian goods wrought in black and gold threads inter-webbed with other threads not so pronounced in color, lay a great square of coarse white stuff, upon whose surface a rich bouquet of flowers was growing, under the deft cultivation of the crochet needle. The household cat was asleep on this work of art. In a bay-window stood an easel with an unfinished picture on it,

and a palette and brushes on a chair beside it.   There
were books everywhere : Robertson's Sermons, Tenny-
son, Moody and Sankey, Hawthorne, "Rab and his
Friends," cook-books, prayer-books, pattern-books,—
and books about all kinds of odious and exasperating
pottery, of course.   There was a piano, with a deck-
load of music, and more in a tender.   There was a
great plenty of pictures on the walls, on the shelves
of the mantel-piece, and around generally ; where
coigns of vantage offered were statuettes, and quaint
and pretty gimcracks, and rare and costly specimens
of peculiarly devilish china.   The bay-window gave
upon a garden that was ablaze with foreign and domes-
tic flowers and flowering shrubs.

But the sweet young girl was the daintiest thing
those premises, within or without, could offer for con-
templation : delicately chiselled features, of Grecian
cast ; her complexion the pure snow of a japonica that
is receiving a faint reflected enrichment from some
scarlet neighbor of the garden ; great, soft blue eyes
fringed with long, curving lashes ; an expression made
up of the trustfulness of a child and the gentleness of
a fawn ; a beautiful head crowned with its own prodi-
gal gold ; a lithe and rounded figure, whose every attitude and movement were instinct with native grace.

Her dress and adornment were marked by that exquisite harmony that can come only of a fine natural
taste perfected by culture.   Her gown was of a simple
magenta tulle, cut bias, traversed by three rows of
light blue flounces, with the selvage edges turned up
with ashes-of-roses chenille ; overdress of dark bay

tarlatan, with scarlet satin lambrequins; corn-colored
polonaise, *en panier*, looped with mother-of-pearl but-
tons and silver cord, and hauled aft and made fast by
buff-velvet lashings; basque of lavender reps, picked
out with valenciennes; low neck, short sleeves; ma-
roon-velvet necktie edged with delicate pink silk; inside handkerchief of some simple three-ply ingrain
fabric of a soft saffron tint; coral bracelets and locket-
chain; coiffure of forget-me-nots and lilies of the valley massed around a noble calla.

This was all; yet even in this subdued attire she
was divinely beautiful. Then what must she have
been when adorned for the festival or the ball?

All this time she has been busily chatting with
Alonzo, unconscious of our inspection. The minutes
still sped, and still she talked. But by and by she
happened to look up, and saw the clock. A crimson
blush sent its rich flood through her cheeks, and she
exclaimed, —

"There, good-by, Mr. Fitz Clarence; I must go
now!"

She sprang from her chair with such haste that she
hardly heard the young man's answering good-by.
She stood radiant, graceful, beautiful, and gazed, wondering, upon the accusing clock. Presently her pout-
ing lips parted, and she said, —

"Five minutes after eleven! Nearly two hours,
and it did not seem twenty minutes! Oh, dear, what
will he think of me!"

At the self-same moment Alonzo was staring at *his*
clock. And presently he said, —

"Twenty-five minutes to three! Nearly two hours, and I did n't believe it was two minutes! Is it possible that this clock is humbugging again? Miss Ethelton! Just one moment, please. Are you there yet?"

"Yes, but be quick; I 'm going right away."

"Would you be so kind as to tell me what time it is?"

The girl blushed again, murmured to herself, "It 's right down cruel of him to ask me!" and then spoke up and answered with admirably counterfeited unconcern, "Five minutes after eleven."

"Oh, thank you! You have to go, now, have you?"

"Yes."

"I 'm sorry."

No reply.

"Miss Ethelton!"

"Well?"

"You — you 're there yet, *ain't* you?"

"Yes; but please hurry. What did you want to say?"

"Well, I — well, nothing in particular. It 's very lonesome here. It 's asking a great deal, I know, but would you mind talking with me again by and by, — that is, if it will not trouble you too much?"

"I don't know — but I 'll think about it. I 'll try."

"Oh, thanks! Miss Ethelton? . . . Ah me, she 's gone, and here are the black clouds and the whirling snow and the raging winds come again! But she said *good-by!* She did n't say good-morning, she said good-by! . . . The clock was right, after all. What a lightning-winged two hours it was!"

He sat down, and gazed dreamily into his fire for a while, then heaved a sigh and said, —

"How wonderful it is ! Two little hours ago I was a free man, and now my heart's in San Francisco ! "

About that time Rosannah Ethelton, propped in the window-seat of her bed-chamber, book in hand, was gazing vacantly out over the rainy seas that washed the Golden Gate, and whispering to herself, " How different he is from poor Burley, with his empty head and his single little antic talent of mimicry ! "

------◆------

II.

Four weeks later Mr. Sidney Algernon Burley was entertaining a gay luncheon company, in a sumptuous drawing-room on Telegraph Hill, with some capital imitations of the voices and gestures of certain popular actors and San Franciscan literary people and Bonanza grandees. He was elegantly upholstered, and was a handsome fellow, barring a trifling cast in his eye. He seemed very jovial, but nevertheless he kept his eye on the door with an expectant and uneasy watchfulness. By and by a nobby lackey appeared, and delivered a message to the mistress, who nodded her head understandingly. That seemed to settle the thing for Mr. Burley ; his vivacity decreased little by little, and a dejected look began to creep into one of his eyes and a sinister one into the other.

19

The rest of the company departed in due time, leaving him with the mistress, to whom he said, —

"There is no longer any question about it. She avoids me. She continually excuses herself. If I could see her, if I could speak to her only a moment, — but this suspense — "

" Perhaps her seeming avoidance is mere accident, Mr. Burley. Go to the small drawing-room up-stairs and amuse yourself a moment. I will despatch a household order that is on my mind, and then I will go to her room. Without doubt she will be persuaded to see you."

Mr. Burley went up-stairs, intending to go to the small drawing-room, but as he was passing " Aunt Susan's " private parlor, the door of which stood slightly ajar, he heard a joyous laugh which he recognized ; so without knock or announcement he stepped confidently in. But before he could make his presence known he heard words that harrowed up his soul and chilled his young blood. He heard a voice say, —

" Darling, it has come ! "

Then he heard Rosannah Ethelton, whose back was toward him, say, —

" So has yours, dearest ! "

He saw her bowed form bend lower ; he heard her kiss something, — not merely once, but again and again ! His soul raged within him. The heart-breaking conversation went on, —

" Rosannah, I knew you must be beautiful, but this is dazzling, this is blinding, this is intoxicating ! "

" Alonzo, it is such happiness to hear you say it.   I

know it is not true, but I am *so* grateful to have you think it is, nevertheless! I knew you must have a noble face, but the grace and majesty of the reality beggar the poor creation of my fancy."

Burley heard that rattling shower of kisses again.

"Thank you, my Rosannah! The photograph flatters me, but you must not allow yourself to think of that. Sweetheart?"

"Yes, Alonzo."

"I am so happy, Rosannah."

"Oh, Alonzo, none that have gone before me knew what love was, none that come after me will ever know what happiness is. I float in a gorgeous cloud-land, a boundless firmament of enchanted and bewildering ecstasy!"

"Oh, my Rosannah! — for you are mine, are you not?"

"Wholly, oh, wholly yours, Alonzo, now and forever! All the day long, and all through my nightly dreams, one song sings itself, and its sweet burden is, 'Alonzo Fitz Clarence, Alonzo Fitz Clarence, Eastport, State of Maine!'"

"Curse him, I've got his address, any way!" roared Burley, inwardly, and rushed from the place.

Just behind the unconscious Alonzo stood his mother, a picture of astonishment. She was so muffled from head to heel in furs that nothing of herself was visible but her eyes and nose. She was a good allegory of winter, for she was powdered all over with snow.

Behind the unconscious Rosannah stood "Aunt Susan," another picture of astonishment. She was a good allegory of summer, for she was lightly clad, and was vigorously cooling the perspiration on her face with a fan.

Both of these women had tears of joy in their eyes.

"So ho!" exclaimed Mrs. Fitz Clarence, "this explains why nobody has been able to drag you out of your room for six weeks, Alonzo!"

"So ho!" exclaimed Aunt Susan, "this explains why you have been a hermit for the past six weeks, Rosannah!"

The young couple were on their feet in an instant, abashed, and standing like detected dealers in stolen goods awaiting Judge Lynch's doom.

"Bless you, my son! I am happy in your happiness. Come to your mother's arms, Alonzo!"

"Bless you, Rosannah, for my dear nephew's sake! Come to my arms!"

Then was there a mingling of hearts and of tears of rejoicing on Telegraph Hill and in Eastport Square.

Servants were called by the elders, in both places. Unto one was given the order, "Pile this fire high with hickory wood, and bring me a roasting-hot lemonade."

Unto the other was given the order, "Put out this fire, and bring me two palm-leaf fans and a pitcher of ice-water."

Then the young people were dismissed, and the elders sat down to talk the sweet surprise over and make the wedding plans.

Some minutes before this Mr. Burley rushed from the mansion on Telegraph Hill without meeting or taking formal leave of anybody. He hissed through his teeth, in unconscious imitation of a popular favorite in melodrama, " Him shall she never wed ! I have sworn it ! Ere great Nature shall have doffed her winter's ermine to don the emerald gauds of spring, she shall be mine ! "

III.

Two weeks later. Every few hours, during some three or four days, a very prim and devout-looking Episcopal clergyman, with a cast in his eye, had visited Alonzo. According to his card, he was the Rev. Melton Hargrave, of Cincinnati. He said he had retired from the ministry on account of his health. If he had said on account of ill health, he would probably have erred, to judge by his wholesome looks and firm build. He was the inventor of an improvement in telephones, and hoped to make his bread by selling the privilege of using it. " At present," he continued, " a man may go and tap a telegraph wire which is conveying a song or a concert from one State to another, and he can attach his private telephone and steal a hearing of that music as it passes along. My invention will stop all that."

" Well," answered Alonzo, " if the owner of the music could not miss what was stolen, why should he care ? "

" He should n't care," said the Reverend.

"Well?" said Alonzo inquiringly.

"Suppose," replied the Reverend, "suppose that, instead of music that was passing along and being stolen, the burden of the wire was loving endearments of the most private and sacred nature?"

Alonzo shuddered from head to heel. "Sir, it is a priceless invention," said he; "I must have it at any cost."

But the invention was delayed somewhere on the road from Cincinnati, most unaccountably. The impatient Alonzo could hardly wait. The thought of Rosannah's sweet words being shared with him by some ribald thief was galling to him. The Reverend came frequently and lamented the delay, and told of measures he had taken to hurry things up. This was some little comfort to Alonzo.

One forenoon the Reverend ascended the stairs and knocked at Alonzo's door. There was no response. He entered, glanced eagerly around, closed the door softly, then ran to the telephone. The exquisitely soft and remote strains of the "Sweet By and By" came floating through the instrument. The singer was flatting, as usual, the five notes that follow the first two in the chorus, when the Reverend interrupted her with this word, in a voice which was an exact imitation of Alonzo's, with just the faintest flavor of impatience added, —

"Sweetheart?"

"Yes, Alonzo?"

"Please don't sing that any more this week, — try something modern."

The agile step that goes with a happy heart was heard on the stairs, and the Reverend, smiling diabolically, sought sudden refuge behind the heavy folds of the velvet window curtains. Alonzo entered and flew to the telephone. Said he, —

"Rosannah, dear, shall we sing something together?"

"Something *modern?*" asked she, with sarcastic bitterness.

"Yes, if you prefer."

"Sing it yourself, if you like!"

This snappishness amazed and wounded the young man. He said, —

"Rosannah, that was not like you."

"I suppose it becomes me as much as your very polite speech became you, Mr. Fitz Clarence."

"*Mister* Fitz Clarence! Rosannah, there was nothing impolite about my speech."

"Oh, indeed! Of course, then, I misunderstood you, and I most humbly beg your pardon, ha-ha-ha! No doubt you said, 'Don't sing it any more *to-day.*'"

"Sing *what* any more to-day?"

"The song you mentioned, of course. How very obtuse we are, all of a sudden!"

"I never mentioned any song."

"Oh, you *did n't!*"

"No, I *did n't!*"

"I am compelled to remark that you *did.*"

"And I am obliged to reiterate that I *did n't.*"

"A second rudeness! That is sufficient, sir. I will never forgive you. All is over between us."

Then came a muffled sound of crying. Alonzo hastened to say, —

"Oh, Rosannah, unsay those words! There is some dreadful mystery here, some hideous mistake. I am utterly earnest and sincere when I say I never said anything about any song. I would not hurt you for the whole world . . . Rosannah, dear? . . . Oh, speak to me, won't you?"

There was a pause; then Alonzo heard the girl's sobbings retreating, and knew she had gone from the telephone. He rose with a heavy sigh and hastened from the room, saying to himself, "I will ransack the charity missions and the haunts of the poor for my mother. She will persuade her that I never meant to wound her."

A minute later, the Reverend was crouching over the telephone like a cat that knoweth the ways of the prey. He had not very many minutes to wait. A soft, repentant voice, tremulous with tears, said, —

"Alonzo, dear, I have been wrong. You *could* not have said so cruel a thing. It must have been some one who imitated your voice in malice or in jest."

The Reverend coldly answered, in Alonzo's tones, —

"You have said all was over between us. So let it be. I spurn your proffered repentance, and despise it!"

Then he departed, radiant with fiendish triumph, to return no more with his imaginary telephonic invention forever.

Four hours afterward, Alonzo arrived with his mother from her favorite haunts of poverty and vice. They summoned the San Francisco household; but there was no reply. They waited, and continued to wait, upon the voiceless telephone.

At length, when it was sunset in San Francisco, and three hours and a half after dark in Eastport, an answer came to the oft-repeated cry of " Rosannah ! "

But, alas, it was Aunt Susan's voice that spake. She said, —

" I have been out all day ; just got in. I will go and find her."

The watchers waited two minutes — five minutes — — ten minutes. Then came these fatal words, in a frightened tone, —

" She is gone, and her baggage with her. To visit another friend, she told the servants. But I found this note on the table in her room. Listen : ' I am gone ; seek not to trace me out ; my heart is broken ; you will never see me more. Tell him I shall always think of him when I sing my poor " Sweet By and By," but never of the unkind words he said about it.' That is her note. Alonzo, Alonzo, what does it mean ? What has happened ? "

But Alonzo sat white and cold as the dead. His mother threw back the velvet curtains and opened a window. The cold air refreshed the sufferer, and he told his aunt his dismal story. Meantime his mother was inspecting a card which had disclosed itself upon the floor when she cast the curtains back. It read, " Mr. Sidney Algernon Burley, San Francisco."

" The miscreant ! " shouted Alonzo, and rushed forth to seek the false Reverend and destroy him ; for the card explained everything, since in the course of the lovers' mutual confessions they had told each other all about all the sweethearts they had ever had, and thrown no end of mud at their failings and foibles, — for lovers always do that. It has a fascination that ranks next after billing and cooing.

IV.

During the next two months many things happened. It had early transpired that Rosannah, poor suffering orphan, had neither returned to her grandmother in Portland, Oregon, nor sent any word to her save a duplicate of the woful note she had left in the mansion on Telegraph Hill. Whosoever was sheltering her — if she was still alive — had been persuaded not to betray her whereabouts, without doubt ; for all efforts to find trace of her had failed.

Did Alonzo give her up? Not he. He said to himself, " She will sing that sweet song when she is sad ; I shall find her." So he took his carpet sack and a portable telephone, and shook the snow of his native city from his arctics, and went forth into the world. He wandered far and wide and in many States. Time and again, strangers were astounded to see a wasted, pale, and woe-worn man laboriously climb a telegraph pole in wintry and lonely places, perch sadly there an hour, with his ear at a little box, then come sighing down, and wander wearily away. Sometimes they shot at him, as peasants do at aeronauts, thinking him mad and dangerous. Thus his clothes were much shredded by bullets and his person grievously lacerated. But he bore it all patiently.

In the beginning of his pilgrimage he used often to say, " Ah, if I could but hear the ' Sweet By and By ' ! " But toward the end of it he used to shed tears of anguish and say, " Ah, if I could but hear something else ! "

Thus a month and three weeks drifted by, and at last some humane people seized him and confined him in a private mad-house in New York. He made no moan, for his strength was all gone, and with it all heart and all hope. The superintendent, in pity, gave up his own comfortable parlor and bed-chamber to him and nursed him with affectionate devotion.

At the end of a week the patient was able to leave his bed for the first time. He was lying, comfortably pillowed, on a sofa, listening to the plaintive Miserere of the bleak March winds, and the muffled sound of tramping feet in the street below, — for it was about six in the evening, and New York was going home from work. He had a bright fire and the added cheer of a couple of student lamps. So it was warm and snug within, though bleak and raw without ; it was light and bright within, though outside it was as dark and dreary as if the world had been lit with Hartford gas. Alonzo smiled feebly to think how his loving vagaries had made him a maniac in the eyes of the world, and was proceeding to pursue his line of thought further, when a faint, sweet strain, the very ghost of sound, so remote and attenuated it seemed, struck upon his ear. His pulses stood still ; he listened with parted lips and bated breath. The song flowed on, — he waiting, listening, rising slowly and unconsciously from his recumbent position. At last he exclaimed, —

"It is! it is she! Oh, the divine flatted notes!"

He dragged himself eagerly to the corner whence the sounds proceeded, tore aside a curtain, and discovered a telephone. He bent over, and as the last note died away he burst forth with the exclamation, —

"Oh, thank Heaven, found at last! Speak to me, Rosannah, dearest! The cruel mystery has been unravelled; it was the villain Burley who mimicked my voice and wounded you with insolent speech!"

There was a breathless pause, a waiting age to Alonzo; then a faint sound came, framing itself into language, —

"Oh, say those precious words again, Alonzo!"

"They are the truth, the veritable truth, my Rosannah, and you shall have the proof, ample and abundant proof!"

"Oh, Alonzo, stay by me! Leave me not for a moment! Let me feel that you are near me! Tell me we shall never be parted more! Oh, this happy hour, this blessed hour, this memorable hour!"

"We will make record of it, my Rosannah; every year, as this dear hour chimes from the clock, we will celebrate it with thanksgivings, all the years of our life."

"We will, we will, Alonzo!"

"Four minutes after six, in the evening, my Rosannah, shall henceforth — "

"Twenty-three minutes after twelve, afternoon, shall — "

"Why, Rosannah, darling, where are you?"

"In Honolulu, Sandwich Islands. And where are

you? Stay by me; do not leave me for a moment. I cannot bear it. Are you at home?"

"No, dear, I am in New York, — a patient in the doctor's hands."

An agonizing shriek came buzzing to Alonzo's ear, like the sharp buzzing of a hurt gnat; it lost power in travelling five thousand miles. Alonzo hastened to say, —

"Calm yourself, my child. It is nothing. Already I am getting well under the sweet healing of your presence. Rosannah?"

"Yes, Alonzo? Oh, how you terrified me! Say on."

"Name the happy day, Rosannah!"

There was a little pause. Then a diffident small voice replied, " I blush — but it is with pleasure, it is with happiness. Would — would you like to have it soon?"

"This very night, Rosannah! Oh, let us risk no more delays. Let it be now! — this very night, this very moment!"

"Oh, you impatient creature! I have nobody here but my good old uncle, a missionary for a generation, and now retired from service, — nobody but him and his wife. I would so dearly like it if your mother and your aunt Susan — "

"*Our* mother and *our* aunt Susan, my Rosannah."

"Yes, *our* mother and *our* aunt Susan, — I am content to word it so if it pleases you; I would so like to have them present."

"So would I. Suppose you telegraph Aunt Susan. How long would it take her to come?"

"The steamer leaves San Francisco day after to-morrow. The passage is eight days. She would be here the 31st of March."

"Then name the 1st of April: do, Rosannah, dear."

"Mercy, it would make us April fools, Alonzo!"

"So we be the happiest ones that that day's sun looks down upon in the whole broad expanse of the globe, why need we care? Call it the 1st of April, dear."

"Then the 1st of April it shall be, with all my heart!"

"Oh, happiness! Name the hour, too, Rosannah."

"I like the morning, it is so blithe. Will eight in the morning do, Alonzo?"

"The loveliest hour in the day, — since it will make you mine."

There was a feeble but frantic sound for some little time, as if wool-lipped, disembodied spirits were exchanging kisses; then Rosannah said, "Excuse me just a moment, dear; I have an appointment, and am called to meet it."

The young girl sought a large parlor and took her place at a window which looked out upon a beautiful scene. To the left one could view the charming Nu-uana Valley, fringed with its ruddy flush of tropical flowers and its plumed and graceful cocoa palms; its rising foot-hills clothed in the shining green of lemon, citron, and orange groves; its storied precipice beyond, where the first Kamehameha drove his defeated foes over to their destruction, — a spot that had forgotten its grim history, no doubt, for now it was smiling, as almost always at noonday, under the glowing arches of a succession of rainbows. In front of the window one could see the quaint town, and here and there a picturesque group of dusky natives, enjoying the blistering weather; and far to the right lay the restless ocean, tossing its white mane in the sunshine.

Rosannah stood there, in her filmy white raiment, fanning her flushed and heated face, waiting. A Kanaka boy, clothed in a damaged blue neck-tie and part of a silk hat, thrust his head in at the door, and announced, "'Frisco *haole !*"

"Show him in," said the girl, straightening herself up and assuming a meaning dignity. Mr. Sidney Algernon Burley entered, clad from head to heel in dazzling snow, — that is to say, in the lightest and whitest of Irish linen, He moved eagerly forward, but the girl made a gesture and gave him a look which checked him suddenly. She said coldly, "I am here, as I promised. I believed your assertions, I yielded to your importunities, and said I would name the day. I name the 1st of April, — eight in the morning. Now go !"

"Oh, my dearest, if the gratitude of a life-time —"

"Not a word. Spare me all sight of you, all communication with you, until that hour. No, — no supplications; I will have it so."

When he was gone, she sank exhausted in a chair, for the long siege of troubles she had undergone had wasted her strength. Presently she said, "What a narrow escape ! If the hour appointed had been an hour earlier — Oh, horror, what an escape I have made! And to think I had come to imagine I was loving this beguiling, this truthless, this treacherous monster! Oh, he shall repent his villany!"

Let us now draw this history to a close, for little more needs to be told. On the 2d of the ensuing April, the Honolulu "Advertiser" contained this notice:—

MARRIED. — In this city, by telephone, yesterday morning, at eight o'clock, by Rev. Nathan Hays, assisted by Rev. Nathaniel Davis, of New York, Mr. Alonzo Fitz Clarence, of Eastport, Maine, U. S., and Miss Rosannah Ethelton, of Portland, Oregon, U. S. Mrs. Susan Howland, of San Francisco, a friend of the bride, was present, she being the guest of the Rev. Mr. Hays and wife, uncle and aunt of the bride. Mr. Sidney Algernon Burley, of San Francisco, was also present, but did not remain till the conclusion of the marriage service. Captain Hawthorne's beautiful yacht, tastefully decorated, was in waiting, and the happy bride and her friends immediately departed on a bridal trip to Lahaina and Haleakala.

The New York papers of the same date contained this notice:—

MARRIED. — In this city, yesterday, by telephone, at half past two in the morning, by Rev. Nathaniel Davis, assisted by Rev. Nathan Hays, of Honolulu, Mr. Alonzo Fitz Clarence, of Eastport, Maine, and Miss Rosannah Ethelton, of Portland, Oregon. The parents and several friends of the bridegroom were present, and enjoyed a sumptuous breakfast and much festivity until nearly sunrise, and then departed on a bridal trip to the Aquarium, the bridegroom's state of health not admitting of a more extended journey.

Toward the close of that memorable day, Mr. and Mrs. Alonzo Fitz Clarence were buried in sweet converse concerning the pleasures of their several bridal tours, when suddenly the young wife exclaimed : " Oh, Lonny, I forgot! I did what I said I would."

" Did you, dear?"

"Indeed I did. I made *him* the April fool! And I told him so, too! Ah, it was a charming surprise! There he stood, sweltering in a black dress suit, with the mercury leaking out of the top of the thermometer, waiting to be married. You should have seen the look he gave when I whispered it in his ear! Ah, his wickedness cost me many a heartache and many a tear, but the score was all squared up, then. So the vengeful feeling went right out of my heart, and I begged him to stay, and said I forgave him everything. But he would n't. He said he would live to be avenged; said he would make our lives a curse to us. But he can't, *can* he, dear?"

" Never in this world, my Rosannah!"

Aunt Susan, the Oregonian grandmother, and the young couple and their Eastport parents, are all happy at this writing, and likely to remain so. Aunt Susan brought the bride from the Islands, accompanied her across our continent, and had the happiness of witnessing the rapturous meeting between an adoring husband and wife who had never seen each other until that moment.

A word about the wretched Burley, whose wicked machinations came so near wrecking the hearts and

20

lives of our poor young friends, will be sufficient. In a murderous attempt to seize a crippled and helpless artisan who he fancied had done him some small offence, he fell into a caldron of boiling oil and expired before he could be extinguished.